"This book beautifully and often hilariously and sometimes movingly reminded me what a powerfully strange place America is, and that any reductive shorthand method of pigeonholing this eccentric country and its eccentric inhabitants—such as "blue state" and "red state"—does all of us a disservice. Where are the storm-chasing lesbians in such a scheme, the skateboards and erudition and jokes cracked in the middle of the Great Plains? If Ken Kesey and Wallace Stegner and Nick Hornby had collaborated on a novel, it would be something like *Wichita*."—Kurt Andersen, *New York Times* bestselling author of *Turn of the Century* and *Heyday*

"The world of *Wichita* is rich, subtle and funny. Thad Ziolkowski has created some vital characters who subvert our expectations in the most delightful and human ways. With *Wichita* we are not in "Kansas" anymore, we are in Kansas, in life, and what is life but a tornado to be watched or carried up by, or else an ancient hippy ex-boyfriend camping uninvited in your yard? This is a truly striking novel."—Sam Lipsyte, *New York Times* bestselling author of *The Ask*

"*Wichita* is a wise, funny and haunting story of our time. Illuminated by Ziolkowski's particular wit and brilliance, the book gives us a sense of family as a conspiracy of improvised myths. Fasten your seatbelts: Abby, Lewis and Seth are going to take you into the eye of the storm."—Susanna Moore, *New York Times* bestselling author of *In the Cut* and *The Big Girls*

WICHITA

Thad Ziolkowski

WICHITA

Europa
editions

Europa Editions
214 West 29th Street
New York, N.Y. 10001
www.europaeditions.com
info@europaeditions.com

Library of Congress Cataloging in Publication Data is available
ISBN 978-1-60945-070-0

Ziolkowski, Thad
Wichita

Book design by Emanuele Ragnisco
www.mekkanografici.com

Cover illustration by Marina Sagona

Prepress by Grafica Punto Print – Rome

Printed in the USA

For Adam Ziolkowski

1

N   ot far from the airport they come to the farm where a tornado struck the day before. Fields stretch away on both sides of the highway. It has a way of fleeing into its own interior, all this wide-open Kansan space, retaining a vast, dwarfing privacy, in the face of which Lewis is feeling a familiar weightlessness and drift. He tries to concentrate on what his mother is saying, in her newly acquired language, about "Fujita scale," "meso-cyclone," "shear."

She's started, or is about to start, a storm-chasing business—Angry Goddess? Grateful Gaia? Something like that. It was hard to gauge from afar how seriously to take the scheme. Abby has announced more than one life-transfiguring venture that never got off the ground or failed to hold her interest if it did. But there's a new SLR digital camera on the armrest by his elbow and a laptop loaded with meteorological software (ThreatNet) in the backseat. Which is all it takes apparently, that and a website.

A red pickup, jacked high on oversized tires, slows to rubberneck too, and without a glance in the rearview Abby follows it across the slow lane like a wingman, then comes more or less to a halt beside the guardrail. Cursing under his breath, Lewis twists around in his seat to be sure they're not about to get rear-ended.

The coast is clear but back along the horizon behind them a low, ominous wall of cloud has sprung up, its bruised underbelly lit up by a wash of lightning as he watches. Facing forward again, he decides to keep this development to himself, lest she get a look at this squall line and decide to chase it too.

He finds the hazards button on the unfamiliar dash and pushes it in and Abby leans over the steering wheel to see past him. He spots a slight sag in her jawline and feels petty for noticing it. She's essentially as beautiful as ever, if anything more glamorously so than he remembers, with expensive-looking highlights and an outfit of some chic, diaphanous material, spotlessly white Grecian sandals. Anyway, she was the one to first call attention to it, the incipient sag, back when she was seeing a plastic surgeon, Rennie. They broke up before she got the free "work" done.

On the tailgate of the red pickup, which fills the view ahead like a small movie screen, is a bumper sticker of an attack helicopter with the caption, "Who's Your Baghdaddy?"

"Wow, look at that, Lewis," Abby says, lifting her chin in the direction of the farm. Turning, he encounters a dim reflection of himself in the passenger window: the full beard, grown out slightly ahead of the New York fashion curve, seems to have lost its quotation marks in transit: he looks like a laid-off lumberjack. He rolls the window down and hot dry air, with an acrid chemical trace, pours into the SUV.

Other than a downed stand of trees, the trunks held intact by skin-like strips of bark, there's not much to see. Then Abby eases the car forward and a mangled metal shed comes into view.

She has the new SLR out of its case. "That's where the meth lab was," she whispers excitedly, as if they're near skittish safari wildlife. Lewis notices dull silver gas tanks lying scattered on the ground, curled rubber tubing. A length of yellow police tape has been looped around the area, one end of which snaps in the wind like a striking snake.

"Don't you find it totally allegorical," she whispers as she fires off frames on the SLR, meanwhile inching the SUV for-

ward, "how it uncovered a *meth lab*, this symbol of our addic-
tions?"

"Wow, yeah," Lewis says, unsure of what she's really driving at but hoping to get her to move on.

A man on an ATV, unbuttoned plaid shirt flapping from his
thin pale torso, rides up to the split-rail fence and gawks at the
wreckage. "Wonder what he's up to," Abby says, taking his
picture.

"Hoping there's some meth to snort some off the ground,"
Lewis says, glancing nervously behind them again. The red
pickup has driven off. He rolls up his window conclusively.

Abby checks the images on the SLR, gives a satisfied nod
and pulls away. He can sense her setting this local destruction
alongside 9/11, Hurricane Katrina, the melting polar ice-
caps—the rapidly mounting evidence that the end of the rule
of the "dominators" is nigh. The date Lewis heard referred to
most often growing up was 2012, the "end time" on the Mayan
Calendar. What will happen in 2012? Time as we know it will
come to an end, human consciousness will be upgraded and
renewed. It's a new-age version of the Rapture, it struck him at
some point. Not that he would say so to Abby. The prospect of
a big, redemptive change is too important to her, if not in 2012
then at some point, somehow. As for Lewis, the idea tires him,
as if rising to the occasion would take more faith and energy
than he could summon.

Abby makes a sweep with her arm to include the fields running to the horizon, a half-built ex-urban housing development that has appeared in the distance. "This whole region
may be uninhabitable before long."

"I guess I better get healed up before it's too late then,"
Lewis says in a play for some overdue attention. That was how
Abby half-facetiously pitched his coming to Kansas, "the heal-
ing powers of the Great Plains," when Lewis was dumped last
month by Victoria, his graduate-student girlfriend of three

years. Abby was the first person he called, and he told her between sobs, which he regrets now—calling Mommy first, blubbering like a baby.

She darts a look to gauge his state and, apparently deciding he's fine, gives his arm a light, encouraging pat. She's having trouble seeing what all there is to mourn about. Abby was bored and a little mystified by his relationship with Victoria, try as she might to conceal it. It struck her, he sensed, as prematurely middle-aged and turned in on itself, the yearly rituals of Victoria's family that Lewis so quickly became absorbed by, like the opening up of their summer house on the Connecticut shore. And how, of all the amazing women in New York, the rockers and artists and fashion designers, did Lewis settle on this rather prim, rather dour Emily Dickinson scholar? Abby would have preferred he date around, lead a more varied and interesting love life—one more like her own. Lewis had thoughts like this too sometimes. His reward for nobly ignoring them? Being dropped for a Rhodes Scholar named Andrew Feeling.

Abby gets off at an exit to turn around. "We should also probably fill up here," she murmurs and pulls into a service station as a warning bell begins pinging frantically. The engine seems to actually shut down but the car coasts up to a pump, where she parks at a wacky angle and casually passes Lewis a credit card.

Watching in the sideview mirror as he stands filling the tank—he had to draw out the gas line to its limit then crank the pump hard right—she pats the flank of the SUV and says, "You haven't said anything about my new ride."

Having assumed it was borrowed, Lewis looks the huge SUV over with new eyes: a midnight-blue Cadillac Escalade, a notch or so below a Hummer. "Not exactly fuel-efficient, is it?"

Four high-school kids in a canary-yellow jeep with a black roll bar—two guys, two girls—have pulled up to the next pump and sit eavesdropping as if they can sense something odd or noteworthy is about to be said.

Abby lets her head drop forward in mock despair. *"Please* don't say my 'carbon footprint' is too big, Lewis.*"*

"Your carbon footprint's too big," Lewis says and the high-schoolers grin as Abby covers her ears with her hands.

"Though it probably is, right?" Lewis says, watching the numbers for the cost of the gas scrolling madly.

"Oh, Lewis, please. There's no solution at the level of the problem. You just can't *get* there from here. Do you really believe, does *anyone* truly believe, that if we tiptoe around and reduce our collective carbon footprint it's going to *solve this mess?"* She lets out an incredulous laugh and shakes her head, a wing of her fine blond hair flickering beyond the window. The high-schoolers turn to see what Lewis's response is but Lewis has no response. Lewis has always found carbon counting hopeless too.

"You can reduce your carbon footprint to *zero* and it won't address the root of the issue, since it's *not material.* Which is actually a lot more hopeful a position than the materialism of the eco-movement, since what I'm saying is that it can all turn *on a dime."* She pauses. "The way the Berlin Wall came down. Remember the Berlin Wall?"

"No, I don't," Lewis says.

"Exactly!" Abby says.

He hangs up the pump and climbs back into his seat with his fingers smelling of gasoline. As with 2012, he understands perfectly well but can't quite see or intuit the true spirit of the sort of change she means. The high-schoolers, who still haven't made a move to pump gas, watch them pull out.

"What did you do, sell a bunch of Hydro Sticks?" Lewis asks. Dr. Hayashi's Original Hydrogen-Rich Water Stick is the latest multi-level marketing product she's invested in. Aside from a brief stint as a realtor, Abby's never held down a job and he's never fully understood (or wanted to look closely at) how she pays the bills, though it's really no mystery: boyfriends, the ones who move in at any rate, carry her financially. And in the rare, brief stretches when there's not a man in the picture, she's been known to hit up her sweet rock of a father, who owns an auto parts store in Austin.

Before Hayashi's Water Stick, there was "Ageless," a dietary supplement, a Tahitian panacea called "noni." And before that, the portable L'il Vixen stripper poles ("spice up the marriage"), which Abby memorably unveiled when Victoria came to Wichita for a visit during Christmas break two years ago, mildly scandalizing Victoria, who did her best not to show it, though she had plenty to say to Lewis in private about how "problematic" she found it. Abby is right about Victoria: she's a sort of feminist prude. But that was a facet of a larger, more (to Lewis, anyway) appealing conservatism: the tight-knitness of her family and their traditions; even her glowingly white skin kept out of the sun by large hats, her level, assured gaze out of a Sargent portrait—Lady Agnew. He remembers the moment, early on, when he saw an email in which her brother addressed her as V. and she explained that family and old friends called her V. She then shyly, almost ceremonially invited Lewis to called her V. That was the side of her Abby never saw, wasn't in effect invited to see.

Something else he keeps circling back to, an afternoon in December, also early on. Darkness fallen in Victoria's apartment on Claremont Avenue, city lights blinking faintly through the muslin curtains. They were meeting her parents and brother at a restaurant later. They made love on her narrow bed, fell asleep and woke at the same moment, looked into each other's eyes. That was all: they were wed.

Abby is getting back on the highway going the right way to get home, which will put the squall line out ahead of them. Lewis is relieved to see that it's meanwhile shape-shifted upward into a mild mountain of purplish cloud, reaching out from which are broad flat blades of sunlight. He gets an unexpected glimpse of his rival high school's stadium. It was out in open prairie back when Lewis played football but is now being surrounded by a development of cheap-looking houses—slurbs.

"Birthday Party?" he asks now and she frowns with her eyes closed and lets out a brief, aggrieved sigh, as she used to at his father's absent-mindedness. "Look in my purse."

He slides the soft leather bag from the plump armrest into his lap. Inside, giving off a maternal fragrance of mint chewing gum and perfume, is a morass of sunglasses, cosmetic cases, prescription bottles, business cards, reading glasses, a zip drive, a small conical pendulum of the sort he's seen her hold by a thread over melons in Whole Foods, testing for ripeness. "Purse open," he reports, "utter chaos surveyed."

"You don't see an envelope in there?" she asks with a touch of panic, glancing over. "Check the inside pocket."

"This?" It's in metallic rainbow colors, "Lewis" written across it with a Sharpie in her hard-slanting, extroverted hand.

"Is that your name?" she asks sweetly: it's Christmas morning, he's eight years old. He lifts the flap and peers inside—a thick stack of one-hundred dollar bills from what he can make out, so new they cling together in a block and he has trouble riffling them with his thumb.

"Happy graduation, Lewis!" she says. Adding in a low, matter-of-fact voice, "That's five thousand."

He sits frowning down at it. He's never held so much cash before. Or a check for that much either. His father's graduation gift was a battered Latin dictionary that had belonged to his own father with a Latin inscription that took Lewis an hour and the use of the dictionary itself to translate. "Gosh," he says finally.

"Don't sound so burdened!" she snaps. "You don't *owe* me

anything. It's a *gift*! You won't have to get a crumby *job* now!"
she points out.

"Right, right," Lewis says hastily. "No, it's great." He's been
looking forward to throwing himself into something like waiting tables to keep his mind off Victoria. Well, he'll still need to
work; he hasn't won the lottery. Turning to her with a smile, he
says, "I'm just sort of stunned."

That answer pleases her. "And the thing is," she says, jig-
gling her eyebrows, "there's more where that came from."

"Yeah, not to look this horse in the mouth or anything, but
where *did* it come from, Abby?" *She's in a counterfeiting ring*
flickers through his mind. It's Abby's sort of crime: nonviolent
and isn't it all a big lie to begin with, money?

"The Birthday Party," she says in a patient, pleased tone, "is
just women getting together and sharing wealth outside the
dominator economy."

"'Sharing wealth,'" he echoes. "What's that mean?" It doesn't
sound like a euphemism for counterfeiting at least.

"Six women meet at a nice restaurant," she says. It sounds
like the beginning of a joke. "*Five* of the women give a gift—
of five thousand dollars each, in cash—to the *sixth*. And when
I say *give*," she adds sternly, as if he's being initiated himself, "I
mean completely and totally *surrender it up*, with no expectations of a return of *any kind*. That's crucial."

He read about this in a sociology course. "Isn't that just a
kind of pyramid scheme?"

"Oh, please!" She shifts in her seat with annoyance. "What
is that, 'pyramid scheme?' That's just some Dominator slur. It's
so interesting how powerful language can be, isn't it? *They* do
business; everyone *else* is involved in 'schemes.' *Social Security*," she says, with a triumphant glance his way, "now *there's*
a pyramid scheme. Along with *most* of what goes down on
Wall Street."

She drives for a stretch in agitated silence. "Do you know

how the Federal Reserve 'injects capital' to prop up some failing bank?" she asks, turning to him. "They just print up some
new money and a figure appears in the credit column of
Citibank! Now why can't I get together with a few girlfriends
and do the basically the same thing?"

Hey, why can't she? Aside from the fact that it must be illegal. But he doesn't want to take the stick-in-the-mud position,
which he finds himself doing all too often with his mother.
Then he wonders whether he's not already some sort of acces-
sory after the fact and could go to jail. Then he wonders how
far five thousand could take him, how long he could live in,
say, Bali, on that minus airfare. Quite a while.

"Hey, sounds great," he says.

"It *is* great," Abby says, smiling at him to show she's not
angry or annoyed.

But he can't quite leave it at that. "What happens when you
can't find new recruits?"

"First of all, we don't 'recruit' *anyone*, ever—"

"OK, so they come to you somehow. But isn't that the way
it always falls apart—with people out of their five grand?"

She's about to reply but shakes her head instead, waves the
subject away. "You'll see," she says, flashing a mysterious
smile. "We have a technique I'll share with you when you're
ready . . ."

Lewis thanks her again and stuffs the envelope into the
front pocket of his jeans.

2

A long Kellogg Ave., things are as they ever were, if a degree or two shabbier with the ongoing shift of belief outward to the ex-urbs—fluttering pennants of car dealerships; the sooty white sepulcher of Towne East mall, its enormous parking lot where after an ice storm Lewis and his friends would spin cars in circles: wholesome small-town delights of the sort his consummate New Yorker friend Eli likes to elicit stories of then listen to with an air of wonderment tinged with condescension.

The traffic has slowed—a cloud of pale dust floats above road work being done at the intersection ahead. A motorcycle pulls a U, its absurdly loud, indignant snarl filling the car, and Abby waits until she can make herself heard then asks, "So how did you leave things with Virgil?"

"Oaf!" Lewis says quietly, shrugging—a Gallic mannerism picked up from Sylvie, Virgil's French wife—former wife. Expecting more, Abby looks over at him. His general practice, when reporting about one parent to the other, is to keep things hazy and uncritical, which is much easier in Virgil's case, since his inquiries about Abby are few and rote to the point of insult. But about Virgil's campaign to get Lewis to proceed straight on into a PhD program, Lewis has blabbed quite a bit to Abby, hence her whetted appetite for more of the story, if only a retelling: the application forms for major fellowships—Marshall, Mellon, Rhodes—left in the pool of tensor-lamp light on his desk, Post-it notes with arrows drawn in Virgil's spidery hand indicating the deadlines. Later, calls from a "baffled and disappointed" Grandma Gerty, from a "surprised and frankly dismayed" Uncle Bruno, who was "bemused by this failure to capitalize on a promising beginning"; even an email from the eminent Grandpa Cyrus himself, with the costly interruption to his train of thought entailed thereby, expressing "real concern as to the longer-range consequences of a gap of this sort in a career aspiring to be of the first rank." How even when the deadlines were finally past, encounters on campus with certain of Virgil's colleagues who assured Lewis they would see to it that his application would still be considered, *it was not too late*, the most guilt-inducing of which were with Richard Pearson, the Assistant Professor for whom Lewis had been working as a research assistant on Richard's first book, about the multiple variants of the early poems of John Clare. Lewis knew by then that he couldn't bear another summer in the library, another autumn at seminar tables, maybe a career in the academy at all. His skin felt pickled by institutional air and the whole enterprise seemed somehow false, or if not false then more like diplomacy or sophistry than truth-seeking. Victoria was baffled and disappointed too: what did Lewis propose to do, *work*?

Abby seems to think his silence means that Virgil and the Chopiks have accepted Lewis's decision but if anything they view his return to Wichita and Abby as act of ingratitude and self-exile.

"Well, *good for him*," Abby says as if complimenting a slow child, which is what she considers Virgil to be, emotionally speaking. Then, almost as if to be sure they're talking about the same person, she asks what he's working on.

"The Virgilians," Lewis says. He's told her about the project several times. She just wants it led out into the pasture one more time in order to take a few shots. "That's the title. It's a sort of compendium of writings about Virgil."

"Virgil on Virgil!" Abby says, cheering up.

"The first seventeen hundred years," Lewis adds lamely. The full title is *The Virgilians: the First Seventeen Hundred Years*. Lewis was given two short passages to translate, bizarre medieval legends concerning Virgil's abilities as a sorcerer. They took him an embarrassingly long time to get through but get through them he did, and now his initials will appear at the bottom of the section (LC) and then again in a "List of Contributors," with the following biographical note: "LC = Lewis Chopik, who graduated summa cum laude with a degree in English Literature from Columbia University."

Pursing her lips, Abby frowns and says, "I just *can't wait* to know why he stopped at seventeen hundred years." Then she has an idea: "Can't you see Virgil bucking to be reincarnated so that he can publish the *second* seventeen hundred years?" She looks over, expecting him to join in the fun. It's not as though he never does. But there's an undercurrent of vehemence in her tone that's causing him to be wary. He's been back to visit her so little, on account of the Chopiks and part-time academic work, that she has cause for resentment toward Virgil on that score. But she's not a score-keeper when it comes to visits and other conventional markers of filial devotion; she lives too much in the moment. If she's stewing, it's about how Virgil mishandled Seth, Lewis's younger brother, who went to New York in April to audition for a part in a Gus Van Sant film then got busted while doing "research" with coke dealers. Whereupon Virgil let him sit in jail longer than was strictly necessary, thinking to teach him a lesson. It was not Seth's first time in jail. Lewis would think she'd be more sympathetic to Virgil in that situation. Apparently not. Assuming that's what's bugging her. Assuming anything is.

"I'm sorry but *someone* has to laugh, Lewis." She lets out a mirthless chuckle as if to lead the way. "They're pretty damn funny, the whole clan. *Sequestering* themselves." She rocks forward in amusement. "You'd think they were on the verge of *curing cancer.*" She throws her arm across the seat as if to prevent Lewis from going through the windshield, startling him. "'Keep it down, you might disturb the genius! This might be the day, the moment, when he forms! The final link! In the chain! Of the *argument!*'"

"Hey, no need to tell *me*," Lewis says. His earliest memory is of being scolded by Grandma Gerty for ringing the funny doorbell in Cambridge during Grandpa Cyrus's "thinking time." The morphing of gentle Grandma into guard dog shocked him deeply, gouged a glyph on the cave wall of his psyche.

"And one day they open the office door . . . " Abby is saying, taking her hands off the wheel to mime the solemn presentation of a tome. "And lo and behold, it's this book or article that is the *definition* of academic!" She looks at Lewis with eyes wide, mouth open. "Don't you think that's just a total *hoot?*"

Lewis lets out a concessionary laugh. She's right: they can be unpleasantly self-serious and self-involved—Virgil too, if he feels his time is being encroached upon. Then again, they've made names for themselves. Abby's not immune to the appeal of that cachet, if mainly as a piquant, unlikely chapter of her story. Lewis hears her allude to it regularly enough, the academics she's connected to by her first marriage: "Virgil, the boys' father, is a professor at Columbia, a Medievalist; his brother and his brother's wife are at NYU, both in comparative religion, and *they* have twins who are in the PhD program at Yale, studying Chinese. Cyrus, the paterfamilias, was at Harvard—German lit. He's emeritus now. It's the family business."

Abby's cellphone rings and she fishes it from her purse, telling someone—her boyfriend, Donald, from the sound of it—that they'll be home in about ten minutes. "If any of the ladies arrive early just give them some white wine."

"Ladies arriving?" Lewis asks with a sinking feeling. He's not in the mood for socializing, especially after traveling all day, but then he seldom is. Abby, by contrast, thrives on meeting new people, hearing their stories and problems, and never quite gives up on trying to convert Lewis to her convivial ways.

"I'm having some friends from the Racquet Club over to show them the Hydro Stick." She glances at her watch. "We're actually cutting it a little close."

With slightly sad civic pride she's pointing out new stores and restaurants tucked in among the chains in a strip mall. Here's Escargot, a recently opened French restaurant, excellent reviews, which apparently makes her think of Sylvie. "I wonder how Sylvie handles it," she says—meaning, Lewis guesses, life with Virgil, life with the Chopiks. Abby has always liked Sylvie, not least for the improvements she made in how Virgil dresses. Pre-Sylvie, there was a bow-tie phase, which overlapped with a fedora-and-trench-coat phase: Medievalist as private investigator.

Lewis was going to wait to break the news but this seems as good a moment as any. "Sylvie's *not* handling it," he announces. "Sylvie's going back to Paris." She abandoned her dissertation on Bataille and got a job at French MTV.

"They're *splitting up*?" A horn blows nearby and Abby swerves back across the divider line with an absent-minded adjustment. "God, what happened?"

"They were trying to get pregnant," he says. "For, like, years." Hearing himself, Lewis is struck by how long he kept that to himself. "I don't know all the gory details," he adds to head her off. He actually does know details. "I mean, I know they tried fertility treatments, which didn't work. Nothing worked."

To which Abby, in a low, unexpectedly sympathetic voice, says simply, "Wow. That's rough." She looks over at him. "I have to say, I expected them to make it, didn't you?"

"I did, yeah," he says. But then he thought the same about himself and V. and wishes he hadn't brought it up.

"Sylvie is all of what, thirty-four?" Abby asks, thinking aloud. "Maybe Virgil's motility ain't what it used to be." Lewis winces and closes his eyes and Abby hums the opening bars of "The Old Gray Mare."

"Did they consider adoption?" she asks now.

"Virgil's not into it." That didn't come out right.

Abby scoffs. "No, of course not. The child might not grow up to be a professor."

Lewis decides not to take offense. Though he's amazed at moments like this that she was ever married to his father. Her stock reply is that Virgil was a genetic catch. They met in the dining hall at UT Austin, where Abby was a sophomore, Virgil a post-doc fellow. When she got pregnant with Lewis, they got married and she dropped out and—to the undying horror of the Chopiks—never completed her degree.

"Sylvie says she doesn't want to adopt at this point either," Lewis adds now.

In reply to which Abby smiles knowingly. "She's not being given much choice, is she?" She's nosing the Escalade into Forest Hills, the leafy subdivision where they've been in the same house since moving here from Austin, when her "lifetime companion" Cary was headhunted by Boeing.

"I guess not," Lewis admits. When they broke up a year later, Cary moved to Seattle but Abby stayed on here—along with Lewis and Seth, "her boys."

There are more pickup trucks in the driveways than he remembers ever seeing at once, shiny Fords and Dodges, red or black. Bass boats under tarpaulins, trailers with plywood siding. The tone is no-nonsense, stowed and lashed down, like military housing. There are no other cars on the streets, no one out walking. But fireflies throb in the twilit yards.

It hits him as they approach their street: they've driven

home from the airport without talking about Seth, the latest meds, whether there's been any recent "ideation." In an email she sent Lewis two weeks ago, Abby announced that she had landed Seth a summer job at a kind of art school/spa for the wealthy on a former ranch near Vail. Mornings, he models for life drawing classes; afternoons, he does lawn and pool maintenance. The nude modeling Lewis can picture. That actually suits Seth to a T. It's the laboring in the summer heat for an hourly wage that resists coming into focus. Has Seth ever even had a job? Yes, as a dishwasher, and he quit halfway through the first shift. He's tried competitive skateboarding, he's tried modeling for catalogues. He's tried singing in a band, he's tried acting. He looked into applying to art schools, bringing a portfolio of drawings to New York. None of it has come to anything. Lewis holds out a squalid little hope that Seth will become a rock or film star but will settle for his survival at this point. Meanwhile, he's really glad he's out of town.

But suddenly Abby is braking and here Seth is, waving his arms in the middle of the street as if flagging down a car on a country road. His blue jeans ride low over white boxers and covering his collarbone is a swath of new-tattoo bandage, which glows faintly in the dusk. Tats everywhere, including part of his face, so that his lithe, fat-free body is nearly black with ink. He has a short-cropped, hacked-at looking haircut, which, if it's meant to diminish a handsomeness that verges on pretty, just gives it something to triumph over. He looks like a squatter punk parachuted into Kansas from the Haight or the East Village.

"He showed up a couple of days ago," Abby says helplessly. "He wanted to surprise you." She must have worried Lewis wouldn't come if he knew. Lewis sighs and rakes a hand through his hair, playing the part, but in fact he feels a sort of all-bets-are-off happiness at the sight of his brother.

Seth has his arms braced on the grill as if he brought the car to a halt with super-human strength. He springs onto the hood and makes a "forward, ho!" chop with one arm, a gesture Lewis saw a tank driver make on CNN during the invasion of Iraq.

3

There was apparently too little lawn maintenance," Abby explains, turning cautiously into the driveway beneath the low-hanging limbs of an elm badly in need of trimming, "too much sleeping with the ladies in the life-drawing classes." The tone is a familiar blend: anxious, exasperated, resigned, ruefully admiring. Seth is pretending to lash the car along like a jockey. "He was basically told to get out of Dodge."

Seth hops down from his hood-ornament perch while the car is still moving then circles back to the hatch, which he bangs on until Abby releases the lock. Getting out, she and Lewis exchange wry, here-we-go looks as Seth takes up Lewis's small suitcase and slings the book bag over one shoulder, hops on a skateboard and rides into the garage and up a wheelchair ramp. He slams his shoulder against the door to the kitchen, somehow seizing the knob with his free hand, and when he opens it, three small mutts squeeze past, the remnant of a pack of strays Abby adopted after Lewis left home to live with Virgil and finish high school in New York. The dogs greet her with wild, keening ecstasy, writhing on the gritty garage floor and exposing their gums and sharp little teeth.

Now Seth trots down the wheelchair ramp to stand with his arms crossed, half bellhop, half B-boy. Moths and clear-winged flies batter the bare bulb above his head and in the flickering light he looks like a mosaic of some forgotten pagan deity.

"Thank you, honey," Abby tells him on her way inside.

Pausing to lay a soothing hand on his arm, she gazes up into his eyes with such naked maternal love that Lewis feels queasy and intrusive bearing witness to it.

"Brother!" Lewis calls and Abby moves mistily along.

"Brother!" Seth replies with frowning mock gravity, stepping forward with hand outthrust in a little send-up of stern masculine bond-renewal. Lewis can see the facial tattoo clearly now. From a distance it looks like tight dark beard growth on his jaw and cheek but reveals itself up close to be microscriptural pictograms and vaguely runic letters invented by Seth and the tattoo artist. Nonsense, in other words. He loves to be asked what it means and improvise absurdist proverbs. What it actually means is he'll probably never have an acting career.

Lewis can also see the scar and dent on Seth's brow from the time he was bashed by a brick in Golden Gate Park. He was living on the streets following a breakup with Candy, an older punk woman who had a nine-year-old daughter and a job as a stripper. They met at a hardcore show and got married at City Hall a week or two later then maxed out Candy's credit cards in a coke binge that ended with her declaring bankruptcy and losing custody of the daughter. Eventually the marriage was annulled, to the enormous relief of Virgil, who had been keeping top secret the existence of one "Candy Chopik."

Lewis likes to think he's blasé about the scar, but seeing it afresh is like glimpsing a crack through which evil seeped into their world, the attempted murder of his brother by a group of fellow street punks, who lured him into the bushes with the offer of a joint then left him for dead. Why? Some vague bad blood between them, some vying for status. The doctor warned Seth that if he didn't stay in the hospital and recover properly, he risked having seizures, even dying.

Now, instead of shaking hands, Seth throws his ropey, muscular arms around Lewis, nearly knocking him over, as much by the surprise as the impact. Seth has always been a limp, reluctant hugger, leaving the impression that he deems the practice hippie-sentimental. Once as little boys they spent a week apart and when Lewis came home, Seth cried, "Lewis!" and ran into his arms. That's how far back Lewis has to go for a similar moment.

Seth stands peering into his eyes as for a sign of some sort. Then, standing aside, he makes a courtly flourish with one hand and, when Lewis has gone forward a few steps, leaps onto his back.

"Ugh!" Lewis says, staggering. But he's pleased too, and, sensing a test of strength beneath the goofiness, hooks his hands under Seth's legs and begins slogging toward the open door to the kitchen.

Seth says, "Damn, son, you're *thin*!" He pats Lewis's ribs as if checking for weapons. "That bitch really stuck a *knife* in you."

"Thanks for reminding me," Lewis mutters, torn between wanting to object to Seth's "bitch" and liking it.

"That's OK, a *wound* is a *blessing*: it lets the light in," Seth whispers urgently as Lewis slogs along. "But did she really say, 'Change is good'?"

Abby has evidently been passing along details. Lewis grunts his assent. They were Victoria's parting words.

"*Change* isn't *good*—change is *Satan incarnate*," Seth says. "I hope you set the bitch straight on *that*. Because that is some dark-side shit if I ever heard it."

Abby, who has been watching their progress fondly, is now unsticking an envelope taped to the wall beside the door to the kitchen. Seth clears his throat and in a stuffy, maudlin voice recites, "'I'm just *so grateful* to have you in my life—'"

Abby lets her head fall forward then her shoulders shake in silent laughter. "'As a *friend*,'" Seth goes on, "'as a *lover*, as a PARTNER!'"

Seth lets out a triumphant bark of a laugh and Abby tosses

the unopened envelope on the cluttered workbench and goes inside. "Signed 'D'!" Seth calls after her.

"D" is for "Donald." Lewis met him briefly in the spring, when he and Abby stopped in New York on the way back from a trip to Virginia, where Donald's children from a former marriage live with their mother in a Christian Fundamentalist compound. Lewis just hopes he hasn't moved in. There's been no word of that from Abby, but then there was no word from her about Seth either.

Lewis carries Seth up the wheelchair ramp and across the threshold of the kitchen, where he sets him down. Bright new copper pots hang from a wire mesh frame on the ceiling and there's a big gleaming espresso machine, a wood block slotted with fancy knives—a general air of prosperity and renovation. Lewis wonders whether it's connected to the Birthday Party money then touches the slab of bills in his pocket to be sure it's still there—yes. Thinking too of Seth's hug and piggy-backing, the possibility of a pickpocketing from proudly street-schooled Seth, if only as a prank.

Abby is busily laying out hors-d'oeuvres on trays for the Hydro Stick cocktail party. She declines Lewis's offer of help as if slightly startled by the idea, while behind her Seth, two beers held aloft, beckons frowningly: leave the little woman to her work and come party.

Lewis follows him into the adjoining breakfast nook, where, resting light as a puppet in her wheelchair pulled up to the table, is teenaged Stacy. She suffers from a mystery degenerative condition but is pretty in a pale, pixieish way that reminds Lewis of the illustrations of Loki in *D'Aulaire's Book of Norse Gods and Goddesses*. With a thin arm, she hails Lewis, who waves back feeling the usual initial stab of pity for her and guilt at his own health and able body.

Sitting next to her is Cody, Seth's homeschool classmate and sometime bandmate who moved to Wichita to live with an aunt when he was kicked out of a FLDS "plyg" community in Texas. His credulous, stoned brown eyes lighting up at the sight of Lewis, he hops up to give him a pounds embrace, his wife-beater T tucked into a pair of jeans so truncated that the entirety of his narrow ass bulges beneath the taut cotton like a head concealed in a perp walk.

Across from them is Harry, Seth's shrink, though at this point more a psychopharmacological family friend than anything else—compassionately upswept caterpillar eyebrows and what's left of his hair tied in a ponytail. Lewis is always surprised to find him still here, this New Agey Jewish psychiatrist in Christian Right Kansas.

Finally there's a mystery guest, a homeless-looking man with gray Willie Nelson pigtails that are, on closer inspection, matted into dreadlocks. He has a fine scar looping behind one ear and wears a trucker hat that says "Emerald City, Seattle WA." Seth introduces him as Butch and Butch gives an imperious nod. It's a type Seth has an affinity for, and not just because he's lived on the streets himself. The affinity came first, from somewhere else—a past life, Abby believes (and/or a simultaneous life being lived out in a separate but related dimension). On visits to see Virgil in New York when he was a little boy, Seth would plop down next to someone with a cardboard sign and festering facial sores and chat about who-knows-what until drawn away by the hand. He doubtless knows Butch from the Inter-Faith Ministries Homeless Shelter, where he volunteers occasionally, Abby and Harry having decided that helping others—serving food, changing sheets—will help Seth focus less obsessively and self-destructively on himself. Has it worked? Abby and Harry think so, absolutely. That there's no control-group Seth who *didn't* volunteer at the Inter-Faith shelter and thus no way of knowing is something Lewis sees no good reason to point out.

He's not in the mood, after traveling all day, to try to make conversation with this crew but sits down at the table lest he be judged stuck-up. Abby's households have always been havens for oddballs and outcasts of various sorts and Lewis just needs to reacclimate to this woolier, inclusive world.

A silence falls and Seth breaks it by announcing daffily, with an air of imitating someone specific, "I can't decide whether to get an *iPhone* or not." He wrinkles his nose and looks from face to face. "It's all I can *think* about! I'm just ob*sessed*! Butch, think I should get an *iPhone?*"

Butch sips his beer and stares stonily into the middle distance and as if he hasn't heard.

Smiling fondly, Harry raises his unopened can of Foster's and says, "Lewis, congratulations! You did it!"

"Did what?" Cody asks.

"Graduated from college, stoner," Seth says, rolling his eyes. "What do you think he's been up to for the past five years?"

Frowning, Cody hesitates then says tentatively, "I thought college was *four* years."

"Ah, yes, well, *Cody*, that's true," Seth says, glancing at Lewis as if embarrassed for him, regretful to have this awkward matter arise. "And normally, people *do* graduate in four years. But Lewis took a little *longer* and we're not going to *judge* that because everyone has their own *rate*."

"From *Columbia*," Harry tells Butch, playing the proud parent, which Lewis is grateful for. "Summa cum laude."

"Some cum loudly?" Seth asks, frowning innocently. Cody snickers into one hand and Stacy blushes and fiddles with a switch on the arm of her wheelchair. "No, really," Seth protests with a befuddled look. "They give *awards* for that?"

"*Anyway*," Harry says to Lewis, sighing and shaking his head at puerile Seth.

"By God, they give awards for *that*," Seth says, looking around the table, "I better *clear some space on my trophy shelf!*" Then falls out laughing, backwards in his chair with both arms flung out, then falling forward to bang his forehead on the table.

"God, that doesn't hurt at all!" he pauses to announce with alarm. "I can't *feel* that!" He resumes banging his forehead. "Am I banging my forehead against the table, Cody?"

"Sure are, dude," Cody says.

"Why can't I *feel* anything?" He bangs on. "Harry, we need to discuss my *meds.*"

"Ivy League," Butch says appraisingly, turning toward Lewis. He has a deep, raspy voice.

Lewis shrugs. "Lots of ivy," he says.

Seth leans toward Butch. "Now it's also true that Lewis came limping home to live with his mommy at age twenty-three with no job and no prospects *whatsoever,*" he says, scratching the facial tattoo and shaking his head sadly. "No one's trying to deny that. But it's also true and has to be said that Lewis has rejected the dry and delusional life of the mind for true wide-open realms of freedom and experience. Brav-*o!* Am I right? Brav-*o!*"

All of which Butch waits out with a sort of steely patience. "You're set for life," he says to Lewis.

"That's the first I heard of it," Lewis says lightly, looking around at the others. Butch seems to be mistaking Lewis for George Bush—a quip Lewis swallows, unsure of the man's stability.

"Nah," Butch says, waving a hand, loath to be so lightly contradicted, "you're in *the club.*"

"Now maybe if he'd gone to *Harvard*—" Seth says, which gets a laugh from everyone except Butch, who continues to hold Lewis in the tractor beam of his gaze.

Lewis takes a sip of beer and looks away. He could explain that a BA, from the Ivy League or not, doesn't amount to all that much anymore. That one needs a "terminal degree" of some kind, in business or law or whatever. That Lewis, because he was on track to become a professor, has walked away from the Ivy League and its prestige prematurely. But he suspects that anything he says will just find its proper place in Butch's Talk Radio conspiracy theory. He settles for catching Seth's eye to quickly scowl his annoyance, with Seth cocking his head in canine puzzlement.

Stacy leans toward Cody and makes a remark about something. Her speech is garbled by her condition and most of what she says is incomprehensible to Lewis. But he has the sense that she's tactfully changing the subject. It seems to work: psycho Butch is now peering dully at Cody, who's prodding what looks like a bite or welt on his thin forearm.

"Nah, I'm pretty much used to it," Cody says. He's an assistant to a beekeeper, he explains. Last Lewis heard Cody was learning to install security cameras. What Cody imagined when he took this new job was peaceful stoned days spent sliding trays of honey out of those cool white boxes. But Cody's boss is getting most of his work from banks that have foreclosed on homes, which, after standing empty, sometimes become infested by bees. And these bees get pretty damn pissed-off when you evict 'em. Hence all the stings.

Then, as if remembering, Cody looks up and announces, "Yo, I'm gonna hop a freight up to work the sugar beet harvest in August!"

"South Dakotee?" Butch asks.

"Yep," Cody says, nodding eagerly. "Or Minnesota."

"Minneso*tee*," Seth says.

"People still ride freight trains?" Lewis asks. He actually knows they do; he's heard Seth talk about it. He's read about it. The question just popped out.

"Hell, yeah!" Cody says, turning to him. "Dude, you should come with me! You can make ten g's in, like, a matter of *weeks!*"

Lewis imagines a lush summer landscape clattering past the

open doorway of a boxcar. Maybe he will hop a freight train with Cody, work the sugar-beet harvest. But his attention is drawn back to Butch, who is staring at Lewis in disgusted amazement.

"Citizen," Butch mutters, shaking his head with contempt.

"Pardon me?" Lewis says.

"Now, fellas!" Seth says and leans across the table with his arms spread as if to keep Lewis and Butch separated.

"Pardon you?" Butch says. He makes a regal gesture of dismissal with a puffy, reddish hand. "OK, you're pardoned!"

"Fellas!" Seth says again, unable to keep the excitement out of his voice. "Let's keep this civilized!"

"So Cody," Harry begins, looking a little pale.

"I said you're a *citizen*," Butch tells Lewis, with the slight shrug of someone stating a value-neutral fact.

"So what are you?" Lewis asks and hears Cody suck in a breath.

"Not that," says Butch, raising his chin. "I'm not at liberty to *say* what *I* am."

"Oh, I see," Lewis says. "Top secret." But regrets it as Butch's face flushes darkly.

"I just can't *decide*," Seth says. "I mean, I *love* the way it feels in my hand—it's *so sexy*—but they say the *line* drops a lot. What do you think, Butch? iPhone?"

Butch sits staring murderously at Lewis. Now Abby appears with a tray of hors d'oeuvres. "Anyone like to try one of these mushroom things?" she asks. She holds the tray over the table and the current between Lewis and Butch is broken. "They're really good."

Harry takes a mushroom puff. "Thanks, Abby."

"Butch, have a damn shroom, already!" Seth says, pushing the tray toward Butch.

Butch shakes his head, the matted gray ponytails swinging. "I'm gonna head out," he says, rising from his chair suddenly enough to make Lewis flinch, he hopes not too obviously.

Looking buffeted by the violence in the air, sensitive Stacy pushes a switch on the arm of her wheelchair and reverses away from the table to clear a path for Butch's exit.

"I'll give you a lift, Butch," Harry offers cheerfully. Lewis gets up from his chair to let Seth and Harry out, conscious of rising to his full height and peering down at Butch, who looks more stooped and brittle than menacing now that he's on his feet. Avoiding Lewis's eyes, he walks deliberately out of the kitchen wearing a haughty expression, followed by Harry and Seth, who shakes his head at Lewis as if to say, "I can't bring you anywhere!"

"Thanks, Mrs. Seth!" Butch calls from the garage, his froggy voice echoing.

"Any time, Butch!" Abby calls back. She closes the door and turns with a wide-eyed, perplexed expression. "What was *that* all about?" But the front door bell rings and she goes to answer it before anyone can reply.

"Do you know that guy?" Lewis asks Cody. Cody shakes his head decisively, defensively, as if Lewis might hold him to account. "*I* don't know him! He must be a traveler-hobo dude." He opens the door and peers out into the garage as if worried there might be more from Butch then closes it and returns to Lewis's side. "They don't consider themselves US citizens," he whispers. "Have their own code and shit."

Seth comes in from the garage as Abby returns from the living room, where women's laughter and festive voices can now be heard.

"So what was that all about with Butch?" Abby asks, looking at Seth then Lewis as she hoists a tray of hors d'oeuvres.

"Butch called Lewis a 'citizen' and Lewis, like, *lost it!*" Seth says in faux dismay. "I think he's ashamed to be *American* or something, Mom!"

Abby goes out with the tray without dignifying this with a reply; Seth lets out a triumphant cackle and thumps Lewis dismissively on the chest and Lewis seizes his hand, catching him off guard, and bends it downward at the wrist in a drop-the-weapon move he learned from Seth himself. Bigger and stronger, Lewis has always enjoyed a casually dominant physical relation to Seth, though Seth played football and the rest too, before spurning it all in favor of skateboarding. But while Lewis has been essentially ignoring his body for the past five or six years, doing the minimum to keep it healthy and functioning, Seth has devoted himself to mixed martial arts: his torso is cut and hard, his neck and upper shoulders thickened as if for head-butting or withstanding a battering. He's also picked up a new attitude, whether on the streets and in jail or just in the course of training, a dangerous glint in his eye.

So Lewis is taking care to inflict no more than a playful, light pain, just enough to hold Seth in check for a moment, repay him in part for the presence of Butch and that riff about the extra year it took Lewis to graduate, which stung more than Lewis let himself feel when he sat listening to it with a tolerant smile. In his junior year he decided that if he were actually going to read all the pages of Kant and Hegel and Žižek being assigned, he would have to take a lighter load. Virgil and Gerty, even Victoria, tried to dissuade him but he went ahead with it: he would show them how to be authentic; a truly serious student read every single word assigned. Well, no, he didn't; it wasn't possible, for one thing. And even with the lighter load, Lewis read about the same percentage as always. Adding the extra year, it seems to him now, simply lengthened his stay and made him vulnerable to being called slow, irresolute. It was another stick on the fire burning down Victoria's belief in him. As for being twenty-three, he just turned. He's surprised Seth knew or noticed; he can't remember the last time Seth acknowledged his or anybody else's birthday. But Seth notices and notes more than he lets on.

Set has managed to flex impressively backwards and sideways far enough to reach inside an open cutlery drawer with his free hand. He's grinning, Lewis is relieved to see; everything is still in jest. He's no doubt detecting having succeeded in annoying Lewis enough to cut through Lewis's galling aloofness: this is already a victory.

Stacy, Lewis sees, has nestled her wheelchair into the far rear of the breakfast nook and is reading a paperback as if adept at tuning out such chaos. The frilly pink leather knapsack hanging from the handlebars of the wheelchair always has books in it—*The Chronicles of Narnia*, Tolkien, Harry Potter. She reads them over and over. Cody stands beaming his approval at the tussle from close by but ready to flee if it surges his way.

Lewis increases the pressure on Seth's wrist then abruptly lets go and pulls Cody over to use as a shield against the butter-knife attack Seth is mounting. The dogs are barking shrilly around their legs. Cody screams.

And in comes Donald bearing grocery bags in each hand and stops in his tracks. He's a large, lumbering guy in his fifties, mop of dark straight hair speckled with gray, thick glasses, thick moustache like a gay clone from the seventies. In New York he would be considered fat, in Wichita he's "big." He's wearing pale khakis and a white T-shirt and a pair of enormous cross-trainers that have enough rubber to shoe a village in the tropics.

"Put that knife away, please," he tells Seth, blinking nervously. Lewis has no idea what's already gone down between these two: Donald may have good cause to be nervous. Lewis has meanwhile been moving crabwise away to dissociate himself from the scene.

"Of course!" Seth says and pretends to stab Cody in the gut and Cody obliges by folding forward and screaming again.

"Seth, *put it away*," Donald says through clenched teeth.

Seth pouts and flips the knife back in the drawer with a clatter. "It's a *butter* knife, Don buddy, not a *shank*."

Donald sighs forbearingly and sets the grocery bags on the counter.

"Lewis!" he says now, coming forward to shake his hand as if singling out a fellow rational adult among the tattooed savages. And unwittingly echoing Seth's burlesque of the same gesture in the driveway. "Welcome."

"Thanks," Lewis murmurs, though "welcome" from Donald's lips is worrisome, not to mention a little presumptuous. While Donald unpacks the groceries (more supplies for Abby's cocktail party, Lewis notes, not day-to-day basics that would suggest permanent residency) he and Lewis make small talk about Donald's visit to New York while Seth grumbles to Cody about how Donald must have some undiagnosed *vision* problem if the man can't distinguish a *butter* knife from a *shank*.

Abby comes in for more finger food and wine, gives Donald a distracted, oblivious kiss, and goes back out. Hands on hips now, Donald surveys the kitchen and sets about tidying up with a stoic mien, shaking the dregs from a Foster's can into the sink and dropping the can into a blue recycle bin with a clank.

"Donald, *buddy*," Seth says languidly, watching from a chair at the breakfast nook table now, the soles of his bare feet up and exposed in a way that makes Lewis think of how the posture is deemed an insult in certain Middle Eastern cultures, "you don't have to do that!" Meanwhile winking at Lewis to say: it's actually really nice to have a man servant, you'll see. He pushes with a finger a beer-filmed glass an inch or two closer to the edge of the table to make it easier for Donald to pick up.

"It's so hard to *know* what happened in past lives," Seth says to Lewis quasi-speculatively, "isn't it? Why certain people have certain relations to others in *this* life. You have your teachers and your students, then you have the folks who come in after class to empty the trash and whatnot. Why?"

While Cody gives straightforward consideration to this chestnut, Lewis frowns at Seth over Donald's shoulder, annoyed to be made a party to mockery of a man he barely knows. Though Donald may be too dim or unaware to be getting Seth's drift.

"The whole question of *hierarchy* is what I'm getting at," Seth says and too tired to head this off, Lewis is preparing to fly the coop when Abby reappears looking flushed and pleased. "They're *loving* the hydro-stick! *Tons* of enrollment!"

Seth is on his feet. "I need to get a *look* at these ladies."

"Put a shirt on first," Abby tells him and he rolls his eyes but snatches a sleeveless black T-shirt from the back of his chair and slips it on as he lopes off toward the living room.

"Get my note?" Donald asks, embracing Abby from behind, his enormous head slotted over her shoulder by the jaw, fleshy fingers interlaced at her waist. If there were a zoological sign for Abby's type it would be the Bear.

"Note," she echoes, preoccupied with arranging another tray of hors d'oeuvres. "Oh, yes! Thank you for that."

"I meant every word of it," Donald says. Really? Lewis thinks snarkily. Did he mean the "the's" and the "and's"? Now *that's* true love.

Seth is back from recon. "Yo, you should bust out those stripper poles!" he tells Abby. She must have kept the L'il Vixen "erotic supports" she invested in two years ago, without much success, or Lewis would have heard about it.

Donald pauses in his loading of the dishwasher. "Stripper poles?" He's amused, titillated.

"Trust me," Seth says knowingly, "them ladies are lubed up and ready to *roll*!"

"You think?" Abby says.

"And what *I* will do, *Donald*," Seth says, pulling out his cellphone, "as a way to contribute to the 'household economy,' is place a call to a couple of *professionals* I happen to have in my personal network of *professional contacts*. Said professionals who will be happy to give Mom's friends *a demonstration*."

Abby stares at Seth abstractly, considering the idea.

"Operators are standing by!" Seth says in a singsong voice, waggling his cell.

"Go for it," she says. Seth grins and, opening the sliding glass door with his elbow, slips outside while scrolling through numbers on his cell.

While Abby and Donald pour more wine for the Racquet Club ladies, Lewis watches Seth talking on his cell, gesture expansively with his free hand in which he's holding an unlit cigarette. Does he have a disease like malaria that goes dormant then flares up under certain conditions? Or is this another pathology with a shelf life of a decade or two? The meds prescribed by Harry—lithium mostly—do even out Seth's moods, which is apparently as good a proof of bipolar disorder as there is: lithium works. Not that anyone understands how or why. That's when Seth takes his lithium. Sometimes he refuses, or lies about it.

Lewis inclines toward an old-fashioned, moralistic position on Seth and Seth's troubles with the police and the world and himself, chalking it up to a combination of drug abuse, hubris and unhumbled high intelligence. There was a moment when Seth went to live on an organic farm community in Missouri— forever, he assured everyone at the time. It was run by a former monk and had the structure of a monastery, with each hour of the day assigned a task. And Seth thrived there, in that well-ordered world. Until he no longer did, until he got bored and left. But Lewis thinks he would have been better off if the place had been surrounded by high, unscalable walls.

Later, he spent a month in the mental-health center of the Topeka State Hospital. This following his and Cody's arrest for stealing US flags from neighborhood lawns and porches: "flag-sorcism," he called it. It was either Topeka or jail. He became friends with Superfly, an older black man with a gray Afro. "We run this joint!" Seth told Lewis and Abby, introducing Superfly. The other inmates shuffled around or stared into space; one or two shouted occasionally for no apparent reason. But if keeping Seth alive is the goal, even a psych ward seems a better bet than a world of beer and bongs and strippers.

4

They arrive before long, striding into the kitchen through the garage without knocking, Tori and Kaylee, both in their mid-twenties: breast implants, big loose T-shirts, black boots. Biker-chick chic, though they may be actual biker chicks. Kaylee has thin dyed-blond hair and slightly bulging, slightly accusatory hazel eyes. Tori looks enough like Seth's Candy to give Lewis a brief start. If Abby likes the bear, Seth's tastes run toward the raptor: large, predatory eyes, beaky nose, slash of a mouth, cleavage suggestive of blissful asphyxiation.

Cody and Seth have hauled boxes of the L'il Vixen poles up from the basement and assembled a sample in the middle of the living room. Lewis watches from the doorway to the dining room with Stacy and Cody, where they can see some of the Racquet Club women: frosted hair and game expressions, tanned legs, leather sandals, pedicures. Lewis doesn't recognize any of them. He'd rather not meet any of the mothers of his high-school teammates or classmates, should any be here tonight, since in addition to the sheer awkwardness of it, he doesn't want word of his return to get out. It's more embarrassing to be here post graduation than he expected it would be.

Abby's winding up a little speech: " . . . reclaim certain aspects of the female sexuality that have been made, under patriarchy and the 'dark feminine,' the province of porn and strip clubs." She pauses for effect. "In other words," she says, "it can just be hot!"

The Racquet Club women applaud, shout lustily. Abby steps out of Lewis's line of sight and Seth dims the lights with the rheostat switch. He then cues up a remix of Prince's "Nicky" on Tori's iPod, which has been connected to the stereo. Wearing sparkly mini-bikinis and stiletto heels, Tori and Kaylee take turns on the pole as the ladies stare open-mouthed and enthralled, the bolder and more soused of them slipping folded dollar bills into the G-strings, reaching out to stroke a passing thigh.

Lewis wonders how Stacy's reacting but can't see her face from where he's standing. Is it wrong, her being here, or is it wrong to think so? She's probably just curious in the same way as everyone else. As for Lewis, he's turned on despite himself, which Seth leeringly intuits from across the living room, where he stands with his arms folded like some punk Mephistopheles, Donald appearing behind him holding a sponge in one hand, figures in a cryptic allegory.

The Racquet Club women have gone and Tori and Kaylee are back in their street clothes. Cody left to see Stacy home, promising to return. There's been talk of going out somewhere but either because it's assumed Lewis will come along or because they're being casually rude, Lewis hasn't been invited explicitly. Trying to decide which it is has made him feel too tired to go in any case. Donald is cleaning up around them in the living room, carrying out the wine glasses and half-eaten hors d'oeuvres on trays. For all the tipsy enthusiasm, stripper-pole sign-ups were modest. But Abby is content. It's Tori and Kaylee, maybe taking it as a criticism of their performance, who seem miffed that sales weren't better.

As if hoping to lift the mood, Abby says, "I get the sense, watching you, that dancing is something you feel empowered by."

Kaylee all but laughs in her face and when Seth joins in

Lewis cuts him a look. "Empowered?" Kaylee says, slapping her knee. "Oh my God."

Looking a little hurt, Abby says, "I always imagined that it put you in control—"

"Have you ever even *been* to a club?" Kaylee asks her.

Abby shakes her head. "But I'd love to—"

"No you wouldn't," Kaylee says. Lewis is tempted to jump in and put this girl in her place but Abby brought this on herself.

"It just makes you hate men," Tori says, playing the good cop.

Picking disconsolately at a scale on one of the L'il Vixen's faux-alligator carrying cases, Kaylee says, "What we do mostly is peeps anyways."

"Peeps?" Abby asks. "What's that?"

"Yeah," Kaylee says with an unpleasant snicker, rising from her chair on thick thighs to high-five Tori, "I don't think your country-club ladies are ready for the peeps."

Abby turns to Seth. "They basically dance around in a little plexiglas *veal pen*, doing stuff to themselves with sex toys while dudes slag off and shove money through a slot."

Seth claps his hands as if he's had a brainstorm: "L'il Vixen Veal Pens!"

"Don't worry," Tori assures everyone, "we shake 'em down."

"Portable," Seth says, "collapsible, comes with free bottle of all-purpose cleaner." He makes a spritzing motion, mimes wiping something disgusting from a surface.

"Them tricks leave flat broke!" Kaylee concurs, leaning over to slap Seth's arm.

Lewis stands up. "Well, it's time for this 'trick' to go to bed," he says, eliciting a sour glance from Kaylee though Tori gives him a begrudging smirk.

Abby holds up her arms in a V and he bends to kiss her on the cheek.

He's in the hallway outside the door to his room, book bag and suitcase in tow, when Seth catches up.

"Yo, Lew!" he says in a low voice, looking back over his shoulder to make sure they're alone. "So did Mom give you that graduation present or whatever?"

"Why?" he asks.

Taking this for a yes, Seth bites his lower lip. "OK, so check it: do you want to let half of that *ride*, Lew, and make like ten, fifteen thousand *more*?"

Lewis has the sinking feeling he gets in New York when he finds a street hustler has fallen into step beside him. "'Let it ride'? What are we, at a craps table?"

Seth glances over his shoulder. It's like he's auditioning for the Gus Van Sant film after all, the thought of which makes Lewis feel sorry for him: he missed that shot at glory. "No, listen: *she gave me the same amount*, Mom did! I should've said that up front: she gave me the same amount. So all the money comes through the Birthday Party thing, but that's just for women. She explained the Birthday Party, right?"

"More or less," Lewis says, elbowing open the door to his room.

"So check it," Seth says, "what I'm thinking is we each put up twenty-five hundred and give it to *Tori*, who then becomes part of the Birthday Party thing, and when she 'celebrates' and gets her twenty-five grand, we split it up! See what I'm saying now?"

"Let me sleep on it," Lewis says, half turning away then back. "But if Mom gave you the same amount, why don't you just front *that* to Tori and leave me out of it?"

"No, no, sleep on it," Seth says, pursing his lips and frowning and nodding rapidly with his eyes closed.

Lewis sets down his suitcase and flicks the tat bandage beneath Seth's sleeveless T-shirt. "Because you already *spent* half of it? On this new ink and *whatever else*?" Hinting that

Seth is coked up or how else explain his energy level. Aside from manic insanity, which Lewis would prefer not to seriously consider unless forced to.

"What?" Seth says, pulling in his chin. "Come on."

"Yeah, all right," Lewis says, turning away again.

"I will say this," Seth adds. "*Tori* would be *grateful*."

Lewis looks at him with a frown.

"I mean, I can tell you appreciate Tori's, uh, charms," Seth says coyly. "Well, Tori would be appreciative *in return* is all I'm saying."

Lewis speaks through the nearly shut door as to some dogged Jehovah's Witness. "What are you, her Mac?" He asks it in jest but it's not outside the realm of possibility that Seth is, in some form, actually Tori's pimp.

"Just think about it," Seth says and Lewis gives a thumbs-up through the crack in the door. As it's closing, Seth adds, "I just want to leave her something, you know?"

Lewis stands in his room absorbing this last remark then opens the door and catches up to Seth before he reaches the turn in the hall.

"Hey," he says sternly, taking him by the arm. "Don't do that."

"What?" Seth says, glancing frowningly down at Lewis's hand where he grips his elbow somewhat harder than he meant to. Maybe he tosses off these veiled threats so often that he doesn't realize he's doing it. He seems genuinely caught off guard. Or maybe he's just a better actor than Lewis gives him credit for.

"Don't play the 'I'm not long for this earth' card with me," Lewis tells him. "That's bullshit."

Seth opens his mouth to reply then hesitates, his expression shifting from wily to sober. "All right," he says, looking into Lewis's eyes. "I won't."

Lewis would like to press his advantage and exact something

more, an apology, an explicit promise, but worries it would backfire and decides to leave it at this, which is, after all, a victory. "Good, OK," he says, releasing his hold on Seth's elbow.

"Good, OK," Seth echoes a little pugnaciously. They stand looking at each other for a beat or two then turn away as if on a signal.

ewis carries his suitcase and book bag over to the bed and sits down. Abby uses the room for guests now; there's a little less of his presence left each time he comes back. It seems if anything bigger than he remembers it. Maybe because it's just been repainted.

On the night stand is a coffee-table book, *Storm Chase: A Photographer's Journey*. The cover shot shows a twisting mass of gray-black cloud, like a vast hostile spacecraft descending, or an apocalyptic sky being sucked down a drain. Off to the right, a wire of lightning meets the earth through smoky curtains of rain, while the sun sets in a strip of sky along the horizon, a narrow band of light about to be snuffed out by the darkness above. It's like one of those Hudson River School paintings where there are four or five distinct meteorological events occurring simultaneously.

On the back, a white car sits as if stalled or halted, rear lights aglow in the dusky light, while out ahead of it a towering tornado drills into the earth, gray-brown dust and debris flinging out from it like gore from a butcher's saw.

He turns the book over, looks again at the cover. It's hard to believe people try to get close to these killers, that his mother is among them, nutty as she is.

He puts the book back on the night stand and hangs up the few dress shirts he brought in the closet.

When he was seventeen and packing to leave, Seth appeared in the door. He wore a mohawk back then, stalked around Towne East Mall alone or with Cody: look at me; don't look at me.

"So you're really doing this?" he said. "Going to—what's it called, Anus Man?"

"Horace Mann."

"Whorish Men, right." Seth shook his head in disgusted wonder. "You're, like, being *tapped*."

Lewis made a sour, uncomprehending face. "I just want to give New York a try." He folded something. "What's that supposed to mean, 'tapped?'" But he knew.

"Like, from the white-trash minors," Seth said. "They think you might be worthy of the name." That was about the extent of it: in an essay he wrote for English class and emailed to Virgil, Virgil and Gerty had seen something.

To hide his face, Lewis went to the closet and pretended to look through it for something at the back. "Since when do you care what they think?" he asked finally.

"Hey, I *don't* care," Seth barked. "*I* don't!"

Lewis went on pretending to search for something.

"We'll be *fine*, Mom and me," Seth said. "No problem, no worries."

"I wasn't worried."

"No, yeah, I can fucking *tell*! Go for it, Lewis! You know, climb that ladder! You and Virgil: go, go, go! Have a great life."

There's still a whiff of paint in the air. He opens a window. The screen and part of the pane are smothered in ivy, tendrils gripping with tiny cups. He slips his fingers into the plastic grooves on the bottom of the frame, slides them inward, and pulls up and the window comes loose with a tearing noise, an acrid scent wafting up like a green recrimination.

He crouches there for a moment, listening to the wind in the trees. He's startled after a moment by a rustling noise, like that of a large animal moving through underbrush, which quickly fades. He sits listening but nothing follows. A sudden gust makes the blinds whirr ominously until he raises them further.

Flopping back on the bed, he drifts toward sleep, then, remembering the graduation cash, sits up and looks around for somewhere to stash it. Under the mattress is so obvious it might be brilliant; under the rug, taped to the underside of the desk chair?

The shelves of the bookcase are filled with overflow from Abby's library. He recognizes the orange dust jacket of Pema Chödrön's *When Things Fall Apart: Heart Advice for Difficult Times.* Lewis read and liked that one, the spell it cast: for a day or two he was a compassionate Tibetan Buddhist.

He hides the money behind the jacket flap of *When Things Fall Apart* and puts the book back on the shelf and stands reading the other titles. There's an awful lot on psychedelics here: *Salvia Divinorum: Shamanic Plant Medicine; The Apples of Apollo; Persephone's Quest: Entheogens and the Origins of Religion.* It goes on for shelves. The thought that Abby might be into a drug phase—"exploration," she would call it—causes a wavelet of worry to crest in him. She tried and liked Ecstasy, he knows that. But Ex is not a psychedelic. Maybe it's just an armchair thing; it's not like he's found a sack of magic mushrooms under the bed. But it also can't be ruled out that she's brewing up mail-order ayahuasca. When she was married to Virgil, she contented herself with reading. Post Virgil, if she took an interest in reincarnation, she hired a past-life regression therapist; if she fell under the spell of a new-age guru du jour, she booked a berth on that guru's cruise/seminar series. Now, if she takes a fancy to storm-chasing, she orders the software and starts a business. She does whatever the hell she wants and that's great, good for her. Still, the image of his mother sprawled on the living room couch eyes aflutter, with Donald or someone comparably clueless as trip-sitter, quietly freaks him out.

So does the idea that she might be keeping it from him. Unless leaving all these books in his room is her way of breaking the news. But indirection is not Abby's style: she tells Lewis if anything more than he wants to know, the sort of male body she finds attractive, for instance (like Donald's, big and fleshy), or how at the start of her relationship with Rennie the plastic surgeon, she was having sex "around the clock" (which Lewis, helplessly grossing himself out further, found himself thinking of as a sexual position: *around the clock*).

He pulls down the tome-like *PIHKAL: A Chemical Love Story* by Ann and Alexander Shulgin and fans through it. There are recipes for designer drugs in a kind of index, someone's cryptic marginal notes, chemist's symbols. Did she buy it used? He flips to the front, where there's a book plate: *Ex Libris* Bishop Furlow, a boyfriend. He must have left them here when he moved out. Calming down, Lewis checks in a sampling of the other drug books and finds the plate.

He was a lovely guy, Bishop, smart, goofily sweet, game for anything: not one of the conventional primitives Abby tends to bring home and attempt to mold. He teaches chemistry and "future studies" at Wichita State University. He was probably, in that way, too much like Virgil, something he compounded by smoking a lot of pot, asking Abby one too many times whether she'd seen his wallet or car keys.

The image on the bookplate is a medieval alchemical painting of a beaker set in the foreground of a landscape. Inside the beaker, at the bottom, a man and woman copulate, watched by four floating heads; in the neck of the beaker an angel, who seems to be sipping a cup of coffee, it's hard to make out, looks on; and sprouting from the mouth of the beaker, buds that look like wild onions. At the bottom the words "Solutio Perfecta."

To the right of the bookshelves are marks of his time here that haven't been effaced: nicks in the plaster from posters he put up using double-sided foam tape—reproductions of a Hopper cityscape and an Ellsworth Kelly abstraction he found at the Whitney Museum on a visit to New York at Christmas when he was fifteen. It was mainly to impress Virgil and Sylvie that he bought them. They looked on coolly, winter light bathing the severe little museum shop. Should they take him up, was he worth grooming? But that wasn't correct, he realized later: they were probably just thinking about what to do next. The long, culture-packed days of these once-a-year visits were less about counterbalancing the blank vulgarity of his middle-American life than a way to keep things nervously moving out of a fear that to stop would reveal they had nothing in common, nothing to say to each other.

At the time of the Whitney gift shop moment, Virgil had been married to Sylvie for a year, but it was Lewis's first time meeting her. She had short auburn hair, sleepy intelligent eyes, a slight overbite and crooked front teeth that pushed her top puffy lip upward. She stroked Lewis's shoulders, bulked up by training for football, and said he looked like he'd been lifting weights in prison. She was sexy enough to frighten him.

When he taped the posters to the wall he was aware of doing it for their eyes but gradually forgot about that and fell into contemplating the contrast between the realism of the Hopper and the pure abstraction of the Kelly, the strangeness of a world in which two such opposed ideas of art could coexist. Who on Virgil's side of the family worked in what academic fields was something he was then just becoming aware of and he fantasized of occupying a niche of his own in art history. The only problem with this plan was that he was colorblind—not severely, just to certain shades of red and green. He knew from reading around about the field that such "retinal" concerns were no longer preeminent, that the emphasis fell on theories of viewership and cultural critique, art in its social context. Still, he worried he would eventually be unmasked as an impostor. But it wasn't until the spring of his freshman year at Columbia that he fully gave up the art-historical ghost. That's when he saw, on the walls of Eli's fortress-like apartment, actual Hoppers—along with Hockneys, a Wharhol, some Matisse prints. He hadn't believed such wealth really existed, or guessed what form it took. When he flew back to Wichita for Christmas break he pulled down the Whitney posters in a fit of embarrassment. But the nicks remain to remind him.

He finishes unpacking his clothes quickly. There's not much but it's every stitch he owns, the rest having been put out on the street, along with anything else that didn't go into the single box Virgil gave him to store things in. Lewis chose mostly required and expensive tomes—Chaucer, Milton, Shakespeare, his French and Latin dictionaries, the barely opened *Deutsches Universal Worterbuch*—and the box was so heavy he had to push it across the apartment's parquet floor and out to the elevator. Virgil helped him lift it into the back of a station wagon cab and they left it in the dank wire unit of a storage place where Virgil was stashing some of his own stuff. Lewis went on to LaGuardia in the cab, turning to catch a glimpse of Virgil, standing under the enormous Self Storage sign, looking down at the pavement with an air of bafflement. Sylvie gone, now Lewis. Forced to move from the sprawling three bedroom with its view of the Hudson to a dark one bedroom on the second floor of a newer, charmless building.

Not forced, actually: he could have stayed on in the big apartment. But to get the lease to begin with, Virgil told University Housing that Sylvie was pregnant. She was thirty-one; she would be soon enough, they were confident. In the early days, when Lewis first moved in, they alluded to it from time to time, guiltily, triumphantly, the little real-estate fib. Meanwhile they had a sort of trial child, an Australian terrier named Couscous that Lewis chased from room to room out of sibling rivalry until Sylvie caught him in the act and dressed him down in such a way that remembering it will never not cause him to feel at least a little ashamed. As the years passed and she failed to get pregnant, the original white lie was no longer mentioned. Sometimes it seemed to have been forgotten; sometimes it took on the force of a curse whispering in the shadows.

Once a week, typically on Sunday and therefore tinged with melancholy, there was dinner at the apartment of Sylvie's mother and grandmother's a few blocks away, which they bought to be close to Sylvie following the death of her father, an American businessman. "We don't hold such big pieces of baguette," the mother told Lewis with a smile at table early on. "Maman!" Sylvie cried. "He's not on the farm anymore, chérie." "What farm, Maman?" "It's for his own benefit." "But *what farm, Maman!*" On his way to campus in the morning, Virgil left Couscous with the grandmother, who spent her days cooking and walking the dog in Riverside Park. Virgil or Sylvie went back for him in the evening, the grandmother emerging from the lobby wearing a trench coat and a thin plastic bonnet over her white hair against the rain, Pyrex dishes of *coq au vin* and *choufleurs frites* in a shopping bag in one hand, Couscous jerking on the leather leash. She spoke no English, which allowed Lewis to practice his French: *Le temps est mauvais. Couscous est malin.*

There was Sunday brunch once a month with Uncle Bruno, who took after Grandma Gerty—chubby-faced, dark-haired— and Bruno's wife, Lynn, who live in an NYU townhouse on Washington Square Park. "Smug Bruno" was Sylvie's epithet. "Sounds like a town in Croatia," Virgil would remark. "Cardinal Richelieu, Lewis?" Uncle Bruno put such sudden questions to Lewis while Lynn looked on with a tense smile, vigilant and high-strung, like a miniature collie. Lewis was a new, unexpected element. Who was he? They wanted to be sure he didn't somehow demote or diminish Izzy and Eckhart's place. "Do they still teach you about Cardinal Richelieu and all that good stuff?"

In the summer, there were the weeklong visits to the grandparents in Cambridge. They drove up in Virgil's champagne Prius, which he paid an exorbitant monthly fee to keep parked in a tiny lot, though aside from the trips to Cambridge he took it out only to the occasional conference. Though there was a period of a couple of years when he and Sylvie would go off on their own upstate for the weekend. She spent August in France, with Virgil usually joining her for the latter half.

And if all that could break apart like bread in water, what is it, what was it?

6

There's a loud fist hammering on the door and Seth opens it and pokes in his head to take in what Lewis is doing—standing at the bookshelf looking startled and annoyed.

Seth makes a disappointed face, as though he hoped to catch him in act of something compromising, and says, "Dude, come out with us. It's—" he glances at the clock on Lewis's nightstand—"nine-fucking-thirty."

"Out where?" Lewis is touched to be invited, if belatedly and possibly at Abby's insistence, but doesn't want to seem overeager. He's expecting Seth to name a bar or club or strip joint but he says: "Bowling!"

Lewis ends up in the backseat of Kaylee's Honda with his knees up, squeezed between Tori and Seth, who is humming "This Could Be the Last Time." The windows are rolled half way down and hip-hop gusts around the interior. Outside is the subdued glitter of passing subdivisions, light traffic: a weeknight in Wichita, with its signature watery blankness.

"I thought you'd be in Yurup—or France," Seth says to Lewis, playing the hick.

"France is *in* Europe!" Kaylee cries after a pause, glancing in the rearview with outrage. On the floor is a paperback called *Indecent: How To Make It and Fake It as a Girl for Hire.*

Seth turns to face Lewis. "You came back for me, didn't you?"

Lewis senses by a shift in her posture that Tori waits to see how Lewis will react. There's been a lot of less-than-necessary-seeming passing of a silver one-hit pipe and lighter and bag of weed that entails Tori's mashing her artificially enhanced boobs into Lewis, his first. He wishes he could say they didn't succeed in turning him on. He had a puff to be sociable and is regretting it. "I didn't know you were here," he says.

"Your Oversoul knew," Seth says.

"His *what?*" Tori said. She wears a lot of musk, not patchouli but something like it, and Lewis's clothes must be saturated in it.

"Don't mind Tori: she's from the Dark Side," Seth tells Lewis in a low voice. "There's a little more you need to learn *from the Master*," Seth says.

"The Master!" Tori hoots, turning aside to look out of the window.

"And you straight-up care about me. Admit it," Seth says, elbowing Lewis. "I want to hear you say it."

"Say it about *me*," Lewis says, taken aback again by Seth's uncharacteristic touchy-feelyness.

"I care about you, Lewis," Seth says evenly.

Tori shakes her head. "You guys talk like bitches."

"OK, stop the car!" Seth calls to Kaylee, who slows down to play along, looking in the rearview. "Let's put Tori out on the side of the road. She doesn't believe in brotherly love."

"Brotherly *bitches*," Tori says.

"She'll just have to suck some truck-driver dick to get home," Seth says as if it's a ho-hum routine they've been through many times. "No problem there."

"Bring it on, right, Kaylee?" Tori says, leaning forward toward Kaylee. "Big truck-driver dick, hmm—good!"

"There's a truck now!" Seth says. He lunges forward and steers the wheel to the left and the car veers sharply toward oncoming traffic, headlights flaring, horns blow wildly. Kaylee wrestles the wheel back into the lane, cuffing Seth in the face back-handed.

Holding his nose with both hands, he reels backwards into his seat.

There's a momentary shock then Cody peers wide-eyed over the top of his seat. "Yo, *what the fuck*, Seth?"

Crushing her breasts against Lewis, Tori whacks Seth in the head. Lewis would hit him too if Seth weren't already bleeding.

Pressing the hem of his T-shirt to his nose, Seth says, "Oh, they died in a head-on collision, boo-hoo!'"

"Fuckin' A, Seth!" Kaylee says in the rearview. "Fuckin' nut case!"

"Ah, you think it's so painful and tragic," Seth says through his upheld shirt hem, "but it's just a little bump and then you're sucked through into pure joy. I'm trying to HELP! I took the vows!"

Ignoring him, Tori pounds on Kaylee's seat and hollers, "Turn this shit up!" Everyone seems to have recovered miraculously quickly from nearly dying in a head-on collision but maybe it wasn't as close as it seemed or this is a more commonplace form of excitement than Lewis knows.

Tori and Kaylee are singing lustily along to a hip-hoppish song as if it's their anthem:

I've been knowing her for years!
I've been seeing her for years!
She got dark dark wavy hair!
With a voice like she just don't care!
She got a skirt with a halter top!
She got a daddy never gave her fuck!
She drinks a beer with a malted top!
She got knocked up in a pickup truck!

"I love you, Lewis," Seth says, turning back to him, prodding him in the arm. "Say that."

"I love you, Seth," Lewis says and it's true: why not say it? Seth leans closer, speaking in a low urgent voice, like a trainer to a boxer. Except he's the one who's bleeding. "You have a great opportunity here, you realize that, right? It's like when Candy and I split. Not to compare the two. I mean your thing with what's-her-name is, let's be real, a *joke* compared to the towering insane legendary passion and love of the Candy-Seth conflagration." He pauses to gauge Lewis's reaction to this insult.

"All's I'm saying is you need to, like, stretch the lips of the wound *wide*. There's a hole in the thick elephant hide of your ego now. Maybe, just *maybe*, a little light will pass through to you. People say, 'Keep it together, don't go to pieces over a bitch, excuse me, a girl, a woman, a wench, a skank, ho, whatever the quote unquote politically correct term is at this moment in time." Again he checks Lewis's reaction as if glancing at a monitor for readout. "But *I* say, do you know what *I* say? I say *let* yourself fall apart. It's your only fucking *hope*: collapse and total dilapidation. The same goes for Virgil, now that Sylvie has left his sorry ass. Gone back to Yurup! I know all their dirty little secrets. He needs to come to me for help cracking himself open but he can't deal with the fact that I'm his teacher. But he will! Oh yes. And here we are!"

Kaylee turns into the parking lot of the bowling alley, which is nearly full.

"Must be *league night*," Seth says as he climbs out. "Cool!"

Lewis walks with Cody. "North Rock's got the most lanes of *anywhere in the state*," he says, rolling his eyes but also clearly proud of the distinction. Inside at the long counter, Seth burlesques a bored big-spender show of paying for the lane, the last available, rental of everyone's shoes and higher-grade, glittery-colorful bowling balls, topping it off with an enormous cardboard tray of soft drinks and junk food from the snack bar. Licking his thumb, he peels the bills out of a money clip. His nose starts bleeding again and the clerk passes him a stack of napkins.

The league players in the lanes to either side cast curious, wary, lingering glances at Kaylee and Tori but above all at Seth, who reacts by twitching and muttering to himself like an escapee from a mental ward, letting out random bleats, staring at the bowling ball as if it's a meteor fallen at his feet through the ceiling. He's twisted a napkin and shoved it into one nostril to stanch the flow of blood and the napkin is slowly turning red. It's not merely goofy exhibitionism: something is going on with, in Seth; he may be on the verge of an "episode." Though Lewis no sooner settles into this alarmist conclusion than Seth puts a lighter, more purely pranksterish inflection on what then comes to seem like mere cutting up. And if the league bowlers weren't so bovine and "decent" and easy to outrage, Seth might find no resistance in them and cease acting out. Maybe. In any case it seems within Seth's control and therefore wrong to Lewis, his messing with their heads, unnecessary, aggressive, idle. He's remembering how exhausting and stressful it can be to be out in public with his brother, how it chafes against the grain of Lewis's preference for blending in, for anonymity.

His cell phone is thrumming in his pocket. Checking the screen, he recognizes Eli's number and feels inordinately grateful to be located in North Rock Lanes, reminded that there's a world beyond New York. Eli his friend of many firsts: door-man building (Eli's), after-hours club, game of squash, line of cocaine.

"Where the fuck *are* you?" Eli asks when Lewis answers. He has an enviably deep, relaxed voice, as of a bygone era of masculine entitlement. They were in the same freshman class at Columbia but Eli graduated on time and has already finished his first year at Harvard Law.

Lewis presses closed his free ear with his index finger to hear over the din. "Bowling!"

"He's *bowling!*" Eli tells someone delightedly.

Standing behind Tori now, Seth is showing her how to hold the ball then "slips" and they collapse onto the floor together. The ball drops thunderously onto the boards and rumbles into the gutter. Eli is speaking but Lewis can't hear what he's saying. Tori is face down but her back is arched, rump up, and each time Seth attempts to rise, pressing up off the floor with his arms on both sides of her, he quickly falls, landing a thrust with his pelvis into Tori's ass. "Oop! Damn, sorry, babe!"

"That's OK!" she says, giggling, casting pornographic looks over her shoulder.

"Here, Jeez, it's these damn slippery *shoes!*"

"And watching my brother simulate sex with his stripper girlfriend," Lewis says into the phone, having backed up to the snack bar area to put distance between himself and them, though Seth and Tori have now disentangled themselves and gotten up off the floor of the lane.

"Your *brother's* there? I thought your brother was in Colorado." The only child of a happily married neurologist and angelic—if heavily medicated—former-model mother, Eli is fascinated by the tumult of Lewis's family life.

"I did too," Lewis says. "Where are you?"

"We're in a cab—on 86th—heading over to dinner with limey friends of Mi's."

Shifting into a serious, paternal register, he asks how Lewis is holding up. Like Abby, Eli is if anything relieved to be rid of V., who disapproved of his hard-partying ways, specifically the coke, which Eli quipped was like disapproving of joie de vivre. But it was through Eli that Lewis met Victoria, back when Eli was dating Victoria's best friend, a grad student in English named Bethany. Now, two girlfriends later, Eli is seeing a British grad student in Art History named Hermione, "Mi."

"I'm really doing OK," Lewis says self-consciously, as if Hermione were eavesdropping, which she may as well be: what

Lewis tells Eli probably finds its way to V. through Hermione—the two, while not friends, are friendly. "Getting out of town was the right move," Lewis adds, thinking of this. He has pieced together from things dropped by Eli that in V's circle, the cold social reality is that her dumping of Lewis for Andrew the Rhodes Scholar has restored her credibility, which had been damaged by the protracted involvement with the relatively aimless, younger Lewis.

"Good deal!" Eli says, audibly relieved not to have to listen to more. "Well, just wanted to check in! Mi says 'hi.' Roll a strike for us! Talk soon!"

Lewis watches a ball bowled apparently by Cody gradually overtake a ball thrown either by Kaylee or Tori, while a third ball, ahead of these other two but in the same lane, crashes so softly into the pins that it's closer to a slow-motion replay than an event occurring in real time.

If the manager doesn't kick them out, it's going to be a long night.

But here comes the manager.

7

L ewis's eyes click open like a doll's for no discernible reason. He lies listening to the faint hum of the air-conditioning; a stringy murmur in a pipe inside a wall; wind in the trees outside; pouring through the trees, pausing; pouring through the trees again.

He sits up and stares at his long pale feet that seem to float below as though dangled from a dock then pulls on his jeans and goes into the den and turns on the flat-screen TV and channel surfs with the mute on: prison cellblock, wedding, open-heart surgery, delousing chimps, Amish barn raising, particle accelerator, star fruit, home birth, red sauce on simmer, corkscrewing seal, bar scene.

On the coffee table is a cork bulletin board, images torn from magazines, a clear plastic box of pushpins. Abby's been working on her "inspiration board," which hangs above the computer, a technique recommended in *The Secret*, last year's big book. She employs the technique in a modified fashion, he can't remember how. In the light of the TV, he shuffles through the piles, his hand moving aside an image of an espresso machine in the kitchen, underneath which is an image of an airliner with "Lewis" written in Abby's hand across the fuselage.

A figure sweeps by the doorway to the living room. Lewis sees it out of the corner of his eye and sits frozen, listening hard. His first thought is that it's Butch, who performed some ancient hobo trick on the lock to the back door (assuming Abby even bothers locking up) and has come back to take revenge on Lewis for "disrespecting" him. Seth is to blame, Seth the head wound through which evil enters.

Lewis stands listening in the doorway of the den then pads across the living room and stops on the threshold of the dining room and listens. The wind flings a handful of grit against the side of the house. There's a faint concussion; he feels it in the floor. Now it sounds like chairs are being rearranged in the kitchen, followed by a series of soft blows.

He picks up a heavy candlestick on the hutch and goes on to the doorway to the kitchen with the candlestick held tight in his hand. He peers around the corner of the doorjamb into the kitchen and sees Donald, wearing a voluminous T-shirt and boxers, his face lit by the light of the microwave.

Lewis switches on the overhead lights. "Donald!" he says with relief.

Donald blinks and bites his thick moustache but otherwise makes no reaction, staring into the microwave with mild consternation, as at an aquarium where a guppy floats belly-up. The smell of cineplex popcorn fills the air. Is he sleep-walking?

Then Lewis notices the silhouette in the breakfast nook and hops straight into the air with fright. It's Seth. Lewis puts his hand to his heart. "Fuck!"

Seth says, "Who says white men can't jump?"

Lewis turns on the breakfast nook light. Seth sits in a chair, shirtless, tat bandage, hands in the pockets of his jeans. "What the fuck are you doing in here?"

Seth lifts his chin at Donald. "Making sure this fool doesn't burn the house down."

"You scared the shit out of me," Lewis scolds, heart pounding hard. "You should have said something."

"You were gonna be scared either way."

Lewis decides this is probably true but it doesn't lessen his irritation.

"Hey, *Donald*," he says and prods Donald in the soft flesh

of his upper arm, to no effect. He seems to be reading a copy of the *Wichita Eagle* lying on the counter. Lewis can see part of the headline: *Autopsy Shows Kansas*.

"What're you doing up?" Lewis asks, turning back to Seth. Seth shrugs. Not sleeping can be a symptom of an oncoming episode. "Seriously, why aren't you sleeping?"

"Why aren't you?"

Donald is opening drawers in search of something.

Now the microwave beeps and shuts off and Donald opens the door and slides out a pan of Low-Cal Orville Redenbacher. With a fork he found, he plucks an opening in the swollen foil and begins to eat small handfuls of the popcorn while staring straight ahead.

Seth gets up and goes to the counter. "Hey, Donald, think I should get an *iPhone?*"

Donald goes on eating. Seth scoots the pan out of his reach. Frowning, Donald gropes for it with both hands as if playing chords on a keyboard.

"Seth," Lewis says feebly. "Come on."

"Donald!" Seth says. "iPhone or *not*, you know?" He wrinkles his nose. "I just can't seem to *decide*. What's your take? On the *iPhone*. Donald! Someone help me fucking *decide*! Donald! iPhone or no iPhone?"

Lewis is getting up to intervene, despite the fact that he's finding it pretty funny and obscurely well-deserved, when Donald turns and looks Seth in the eye.

"No," Donald says firmly. "Don't get one."

"Okay," Seth says, nodding thoughtfully. "Thank you."

"You're welcome."

With that, he takes Donald by the arm and leads him back through the house to Abby's room.

8

I n the morning, too groggy to deal with figuring out the new espresso machine, Lewis searches in the cabinets until he finds a familiar old Braun coffee maker. No one else seems to be up. Like evidence of something that might have been a dream, a blue sponge trails a smear of fake butter on the counter by his elbow.

When the coffee is brewed, he pours a cup and goes out through the sliding glass door of the breakfast nook and sits on the back stoop. The sky is a clear cornflower blue fading to a paler band toward the horizon, the sun already intense. At the bottom of a tumbler left outside by someone, sugar ants swarm over orange juice dregs.

The backyard has gone dramatically to the weeds, goldenrod, Queen Anne's lace, a tall, tobacco-like plant with floppy dark-green leaves. Ivy cascades over the patch where Abby made an attempt at a small Zen garden; over the mound where there was a compost heap during her Alice Waters/organic garden moment; over the collapsed remains of a plywood skate ramp built by Seth and Cody; up and over the fence into the yard of the neighbor, lawn-proud Baptist minister Oren, who can't be too pleased with that.

A vine with heart-shaped leaves winds up the rust-speckled legs of a white outdoor chair and over an electrical outlet with hinged caps. An orange extension cord is plugged into one of the outlets. It disappears at an angle into the underbrush like a snake.

Sipping his coffee, Lewis idly follows it around the corner

of house, dandelion spores twinkling in the air, a grasshopper launching into a side-slipping arc.

The cord vanishes under the side of a yellow and purple tent made of light silky material. A clothesline runs from the center pole of the tent to a drainpipe on the side of the house and fastened to it with large black paperclips are half a dozen Tibetan prayer flags, a beach towel, a pair of yellowing cream boxer shorts and two small aluminum signs. One says, SLOW NO WAKE ZONE; the other, Gone Phishing.

The weeds have been trampled into footpaths leading to the spigot and hose alongside the house and to a moped on a kickstand, an Army-surplus helmet hanging by its strap from the handlebar. There's a green hammock on a metal frame drawn up close to the house in the shade of the roof.

As Lewis gets closer, the tent quivers and he hears a voice. Wondering with quiet dread whether some homeless person or persons from Inter-Faith Ministries has set up camp here with Abby's consent, Lewis puts his cup of coffee on the ground and stands by the flap and says, "Hello in there!"

The tent shudders again and a tousled white-haired head with white beard emerges in profile from the entrance flap and looks squintingly around—Bishop. He has a sun/windburn and a mosquito bite on his cheek. He withdraws into the tent like a tortoise and Lewis hears him say, in a slightly panicky tone, "How'd you calculate that?"

Now he crawls out of the opening and gets creakily to his feet, still without noticing Lewis, who's standing about four feet away. How old is Bishop, sixty? Quietly, so as not to startle him, Lewis says, "Hi."

Bishop remains impervious, head bowed. He's wearing jogging shorts, Tevas, and a T-shirt. He puts his hands on his hips and arches backward then does a slow twist, at which point he sees Lewis and flinches in surprise but quickly recovers, his face lighting up.

"There he is!" Bishop says. The T-shirt says REALITY above a check-marked box.

Lewis has his hand out to shake but Bishop won't hear of such "back East" standoffishness and envelops him in a tight Deadhead/Burning Man hug. He smells of bug repellent, Dr. Bronner's mint soap and high-grade weed.

Stepping back to look Lewis over, he smiles slyly and tugs at his own white beard. "I see I inspired a new look!"

"Oh, uh, yeah," Lewis says to humor him, touching his own beard reflexively. He remains silent to give Bishop a chance to explain his presence in a tent in the yard but Bishop just grins goofily, his head cocked to one side, hands open in elfin coyness.

Lewis gives in: "So what the hell are you doing out here in the yard, Bishop?"

"*Abiding near the Goddess*, of course!" Bishop declares, lifting his Tevas in a vague goat dance step.

"Who, Abby?" For there's a good chance Bishop means Gaia; there's a good chance Bishop means any number of things.

"Well, I use the term 'Goddess,'" Bishop says, making air quotes, "as a way to call forth the highest dimension of her consciousness." He waits for Lewis to indicate his comprehension.

"OK," Lewis says provisionally.

"Good!" Bishop says as if Lewis has taken the first step in a Socratic dialogue. "And I see *my being out here* and having this relation *to* her as bringing *her* to *embody* that 'Divine Feminine.' But it's also a *circuit*—between us—a symbiosis! The God in me, the Goddess in her, in a *circuit*." Bishop pauses to give this time to sink in then says, "Pretty fantastic, right?"

"It's fantastic, all right," Lewis agrees, deadpan, but if he detects the irony Bishop elects to overlook it.

"Also," Bishops says, "it's just *so clear* from various indicators that we're living on the threshold of *an enormous collective shift*. Just fucking e*nor*mous, Lewis! All the usual forms and norms are being cast off and transfigured as we speak, left and right, left and right, my man!" He makes the gestures of someone tossing flowers from a basket. "We're in the *midst* of that. And what a blessing to be incarnated as these ones at this juncture! OK, but which leaves us where on a daily basis? We're just *out here* doing what's before us to do! *That's* where it leaves us. And boy am I feeling just as joyful as hell about *that*. I mean, look around, my friend!"

Lewis glances compliantly around at the weeds and tent and Tibetan prayer flags, the hammock. He wonders whether this "we" of Bishop's includes a certain sleep-eater named Donald.

Bishop snaps his fingers. "Gave up my apartment and all the useless crap that went with it. If you don't use it at least once in three months, it should be tossed out."

Lewis strokes the side of the tent, toes one of the stakes holding down a corner. "So this is a long-haul sort of commitment?"

"Oh, yeah. Oh, absolutely." Lips pursed, Bishop surveys the terrain. "Why not? I really think I'm good year-round, though I'll probably convert to a yurt sort of structure come fall," Bishop says. "Did you know you can have a Mongolian yurt *delivered*? Here, to this very spot?" He points to the street. "A truck pulls up with a yurt tied to the flatbed with cables." He mimes a guiding-in with straight arms. "They untether the thing and convey on a forklift to the desired coordinates and *boom*." He makes a stiff-armed gesture to demonstrate the setting down of a yurt.

"How long have you been out here?" Lewis asks.

"Tomorrow will be day—" Bishop consults his wrist but has no watch. "Twenty-nine or so." He gives a thumbs-up then his smile vanishes and he says, "Well, it's not a free base, it's a salt!"

Now Lewis notices the tiny Bluetooth device clipped to Bishop's left ear.

"What do you get?" Bishop asks the air above Lewis's shoulder. "Call me *right back*, okay?"

Bishop meets Lewis's eye and shakes his head in annoyed, large-eyed wonderment. "That was Jessie." As if Lewis already knows who Jessie is but this is what it's like talking to Bishop. "The DMT the Feds sent, which arrived two days ago?" he says. "It's already decayed by thirty percent! So unless they sabotaged the stuff—" Bishop bugs out his eyes and laughs wheezily through clenched teeth. "But let's not even go there, right?"

"Right," Lewis agrees, "better not."

"Anyway," Bishop says, "this is according to Jessie, who somehow got it into his head that it's a *free base*." He lets out an annoyed bark of a laugh. "So who really knows what the fuck is going on!"

"What's DMT, Bishop?" Because it's either ask the obvious now or resign himself to simpering and nodding along in the dark.

Bishop squints at him in disbelief. "DMT? *DMT!*" As if it's the equivalent of the Beatles or Shakespeare. "N, N Dimethyltryptamine? 'Dimitri'?"

Lewis shakes his head. "Sorry."

"Well, gosh, let's see," Bishop says, casting about for suitably basic building blocks. "It's a tryptamine, like 'shrooms, only *way* more powerful." He pauses and looks at Lewis. "You *have* done 'shrooms."

Lewis nods as if of course though in fact he's never taken any psychedelic, not after seeing what happened to Seth. Reassured, Bishop says, "The Indians in the Amazon take it in snuff form for shamanic purposes. Most folks smoke it. For the study, we inject it."

"Wait, is this the toad stuff?" Lewis asks.

"Right, right—it's excreted by certain toads, sure," Bishop says with gentle condescension. "But it's also in, you know—" he gestures at the yard, "grass, lizards, peas. In *us* too, in our bloodstream, endogenously. The *human fucking brain* produces it! Basically it's the most powerful psychedelic known to man. Launches you into other universes, McKenna's whole machinic-elves realm, etc., etc."

He turns aside and raises a hand to his ear piece. "Whew!" he says, giving Lewis a thumbs-up. "That's more like it, Jessie! Later."

Bishop claps his hands and seizes Lewis happily by the biceps. "It *hasn't decayed*! He was just measuring wrong." Releasing Lewis, he spins in place, lifts his Teva'd feet in a victory dance. 'It hasn't decayed, it hasn't fucking *decayed*! You don't know how *worried* I was. Oh my God."

"What sort of study is this?" Lewis asks.

Bishop stops dancing. He looks perplexed, wounded. "Abby didn't tell you?"

Lewis shakes his head.

"Huh, that's strange," Bishop says, touching his beard. "Wonder what that's all about," he murmurs, flicking at his lip with a finger and squintingly searching Lewis's face for clues.

"You wouldn't have wanted to be in it anyway," he says finally. "*That's* why Abby didn't tell you about it. OK, that makes sense." He nods his head. "OK, yeah, what it is: we're trying to see whether a certain Big Pharma antihistamine that shall remain nameless blocks the serotonin receptor two site." Bishop grins conspiratorially at Lewis, shaking his head at the absurdity of it. "Good luck getting volunteers for *that*, right?!"

"Why?" Lewis asks.

"I mean, duh!" Bishop says with a laugh. "Receptor two is THE site for psychedelics. Who wants to be part of a study that may well LESSEN the effects of your pure DMT?"

"I see," says Lewis.

"But we've actually got a good group of folks. Of course, *Seth*'s on board," Bishop adds with a sly smile.

Lewis feels a surge of alarm. "What do you mean?"

Bishop shrugs. "Seth's betting the stuff *doesn't* work to block the effects. Which, hey, is possible, right? Assuming he passes the physical and the psych test, he's good to go. You could still be included if someone drops out, Lewis," he adds as if worried Lewis is feeling left out.

Lewis is about to say something about the recklessness of giving Seth of all people "the most powerful psychedelic known to man" but decides to take it up with Abby instead.

Bishop raises his eyebrows and spreads his arms as if to say, So that's how things stand in *his* corner of the universe. "To have the *privilege* of having to do *whatever it takes* to be near her," Bishop says, gesturing at the yard with joyous fatalism. "And *this* is what it takes right now, my friend!" He seizes Lewis by the hands as if imploring him.

Lewis smiles faintly, nods. Bishop probably has no idea about V., who must be installed at the Stonington house by now. Unless she's staying at Andrew Feeling's family summer house in Maine, which Lewis knows about through the grapevine. Bishop is clearly a nut, an eccentric. But is it just possible that Lewis gave up too easily, lacked a great lover's imagination and madness? What if he decided to go on devoting himself to V. with or without her consent and set up his own tent in the garden of the Stonington house? He can see the place for it, between the sedun and potentilla shrubs. Then he can see V.'s father, a taciturn, no-nonsense physicist on the faculty at Trinity College, and her witty, brilliant older brother, who works for a hedge fund as a quant analyst in Greenwich. They're standing in the floor-to-ceiling sliding glass door at back of the house, scowling in disbelief at Lewis and his tent. The mother, a lovely, kind woman who taught Lewis how to sail and made him feel part of the family, appears there with them now, then V. herself, hand raised to her lips. And it's like some hideous Tourette's fantasy: it would be one of the most searingly wrong, embarrassing things he could possibly do.

"AND I LOVE IT!" Bishop cries. "YES!"

A window goes up. "Bishop!" Abby hisses from within. Bishop and Lewis turn toward her voice but she's invisible behind the screen. "We're still sleeping!"

"Sorry!" Bishop calls from a crouch, hands cupped to his mouth. The window slides down with a clicking noise.

"Shit. Oh well," Bishop whispers, deflated. "Although technically I doubt she would be *telling* me she was asleep if she were actually *asleep*."

He stands thinking. "Listen, do me a favor?"

"Sure," Lewis says.

"Tell her—" he holds up a finger and drops to the ground and crawls into the tent with rapid practiced ease, like a cave-dweller or burrowing animal, then crawls backward holding a white Mac laptop and passes it up to Lewis from a kneeling position. "Tell her I finished a draft of the Grateful Gaia website?"

"Absolutely," Lewis promises. He picks up his cup of coffee from the ground and takes a sip.

Bishop looks to one side in a way Lewis now recognizes as indicative of taking a call. "I'll try that one. Later." He sighs through his nose. "The study calls for closed-eye sessions but you'd be amazed at how hard it is to find *totally opaque* eye masks. Near impossible! Anyway, there's a CVS on Oliver that supposedly has the good ones, according to Jesse."

He goes to the moped and slips the Army-surplus helmet from the handlebars and puts it on, looking like a character from a B movie comedy. "Could I have a hit of your coffee?"

Lewis passes the cup and Bishop takes two greedy gulps. "All she has to do is refresh the page and she'll see it." He takes the Mac from Lewis, bends at the waist and kisses the top then hands it back. "What a woman!"

Bishop walks the moped along the pathway beaten into the weeds, through the gate, which is missing the door, and out to the street, where Bishop bounces it over the curb, kick starts it and turns to give a thumbs-up. He rides wobblingly at first then steadies up, a wisp of bluish smoke from the exhaust hanging in the air like a § symbol.

9

L ewis walks around to the back of the house. The weeds are bowed in a rising wind. He sets the laptop down on the stoop and tugs on one of the tall tobacco-like plants. The roots release their hold on the soil with abrupt, satisfying ease. He pulls up another, cleaves his way out to the middle of yard and stands wondering whether he should start in clearing the rest.

He'd better ask Abby first. She may be letting the yard return to some pristine prairie-like state, out of an anti-lawn/pro-water-saving sentiment. If that's consistent with driving an Escalade. He can hear her quoting Whitman: "Do you I contradict myself? Very well then, I contradict myself."

His dutiful-son impulse brings to mind Virgil and Uncle Bruno divvying up lawn work and minor house repairs during the annual summer visits to Cambridge, their competitive, theatrical sighs of exertion and sweat-flickings, the pallor of their chunky calf muscles flaring in the bright sunlight.

The grandchildren were exempt from these labors but expected to be pursuing high-minded hobbies. Lewis's project last summer was learning how to identify trees. Pretty banal. Sleek androgynous Izzy—like her brother, she inherited Bruno's dark hair but their mother's narrow, collie-like features—spent her time engrossed in an online whodunit game that involved literary maps of Beijing and Vienna. That was more like it. Meanwhile Eckhart offhandedly memorized Hungarian irregular verbs using a software program he'd helped design (occasionally sneaking off to porn sites when he thought no one was watching).

"Grandma" and "Grandpa," the twins call Gerty and Cyrus. Because he barely saw them between the time of the divorce, when he was eight, and when he moved to New York to finish high school, Lewis has never been comfortable following suit, which the twins quickly noted and made a game of exposing: "Lewis, would you tell Grandpa dinner is ready?" Lewis padded down the hall and tapped on the door to Cyrus's study, the lair of the Genius. "Dinner's ready!" he called in a modulated voice.

"Very good, Lewis," Cyrus said from within.

"Lewis, that's not right!" Izzy whispered. There was a twin, demon-like at each ear. Eckhart said, "You should say,"—calling it out over Lewis's shoulder—"*Grandpa*, dinner's ready!'"

There was a stir in the office and Cyrus said irritably, "I *heard* you, Lewis!"

He sought to be like them in the beginning, even thought— why not?—to surpass them. But there came a moment early on when he saw it was futile. It was in a café near the Goethe-Institut Berlin, where he'd been sent *at considerable expense* as part of a European tour-cum-language-acquisition catch-up in the summer before his freshman year at Columbia. He was reviewing the German second subjunctive with an American girl named Alissa. They had drunken, tension-relieving sex a few times, once in a park standing against a tree. She was a freshman at Haverford but hoping to transfer to Princeton or Dartmouth, hence the hasty, apple-polishing addition of German. She had a manner Lewis was familiar with by then, that of an average-looking but neither rich nor brilliant girl who reacted to her elite private school by adopting an expression of anticipatory affront. With Alissa periodically scanning the horizon for foes, they reviewed. For Lewis, this was a bit of a joke: the second subjunctive—along with the first—was a faint strand in a swirl of modal auxiliaries, separable and inseparable prefixes, compound tenses, vocabulary. He didn't have what it took to "pick up" a language in two or three months. He could philosophize, but his memory was average; he read Hegel but not in the original. There would be no catching up to the twins, not to speak of surpassing them. They were being groomed to accomplish rare feats of comparative-linguistic scholarship, while Lewis was mainly being worried over as a potential embarrassment, a threat to the family brand.

The one thing the grandchildren had to do, on these summer visits to Cambridge, was meet with Gerty for career counseling, ideally in the guise of helping tend her tomatoes. As with other family traditions, Lewis was expected to behave as though he'd always known it, because if he'd been callously excluded all those years from the annual visits to Cambridge and Christmas gatherings and edifying spring-break trips to Europe, then the Chopiks would be at fault, which would be a rude and ungrateful way for Lewis to make them feel.

In the tomato patch, Lewis always thought of the scene from *The Godfather*, with Gerty, stolid and gray and slow-moving, played by a cross-dressing Brando. It was the kind of thing he'd learned to keep to himself: far too irreverent, above all, and pop-culture references were considered outré: the grandparents might not get them and, well, it was vulgar. A straw basket over one arm, Gerty would draw out news about grades and honors and aspirations, most of which she already knew in detail, kick the tires of research topics, propose strategies for getting this or that fellowship. When it was Lewis's turn last summer, Gerty asked what he intended to write about for his senior thesis. Gray's "Elegy Written in a Country Church-Yard," he told her and she frowned and worried aloud that the Elegy was banal, a high-school poem, like Frost's "Stopping by Woods on a Snowy Evening." What about John Clare and the textural variants? Lewis was bored with it. Boredom was no reason to abandon a project! Lewis said that part of what interested him about the Elegy was its "dual citizenship" (his advisor's phrase) in the high-school and university curricula, that the history of its uses within the school system was inseparable from its meaning. This seemed to placate or at least befuddle Gerty enough to silence objections. He told her about the "stone-cutter" and *Ignotus* theories that he was planning to dust off in order to demonstrate his mastery of the critical tradition but ultimately to make a larger deconstructive point that the "Thee" of the poem is unknowable, a cipher or blank standing for the disenfranchised political subject, the "mute, inglorious Milton" of the poem. Gerty found this to be an unsavory goal, smart-alecky and subversive. Would it add to the total sum of knowledge about the poem? That was the family tradition. There was no generation gap between the twins and their parents and the grandparents: an unbroken line of literary history and material philology and thematics. Lewis's interest in literary theory and dubious, show-offy types like Zizek were tolerated but viewed as worrisome.

She turned to fellowships. Both the Mellon Graduate Fellowships and the Rhodes had to be applied for during the fall of his senior year, she reminded him sternly; he would be *ineligible* thereafter. She had gotten wind of his then-tentative talk of taking time off after graduation. Time off from what— reading, study? And in order to do what, *work?* She sincerely hoped he came to his senses. Those who failed to go straight on into PhD programs, who "broke the daisy chain," were never regarded in the same light as those who went straight through, whatever Lewis may have heard to the contrary. When the laggards eventually did apply, they were given *at best* mere university fellowships, tuition plus stipend, and burdened with a great deal of teaching when they would otherwise be free to do research. She was very keen on the Rhodes, a feather the family cap lacked. (The Twins were on Mellons.) A Rhodes seemed like quite a stretch to Lewis. His football would help, Gerty replied. Lewis hadn't played football since high school, he reminded her. He'd also heard athletics no longer mattered for a Rhodes. Well, they don't, Gerty said, but only by default, because no one smart played sports anymore. He shouldn't worry about it; he should just apply. Oxford is magnificent, she said. Had he visited Oxford? He hadn't. A Rhodes would open innumerable doors. She wanted him to call *Declan Lang* in the English Department at Columbia, not right away, in September, the second week. Declan Lang was himself a Rhodes Scholar; he would be expecting Lewis's call.

That seemed to be the end of the conference. Then, as they headed for the wicket gate, she caught him off guard by asking about Seth, whose existence had been assiduously ignored until then, not without Lewis's passive complicity. Lewis said something vague and neutral, to which Gerty's response was: "It's *terribly sad.*"

"What's sad about it?" Lewis heard himself say and felt her bristle.

She dropped a tomato into her basket and whispered impatiently, as if Lewis were needlessly embarrassing them both, "He's *mentally ill,* Lewis—Bipolar!"

Eckhart stood at the back door, visibly wondering what in Lewis's undistinguished life could possibly be taking up so much of Grandma's time.

"That's never really been established," Lewis said.

Gerty pursed her lips and lowered her eyelids in a dismissive expression. "Well, it must be from the maternal side, since there's none on ours."

"That you know of."

"*Adversus solem ne loquitor,*" she said in reply to this impertinence, looking up at Lewis and shielding her eyes against the sunlight with a plump hand. "How's your Latin?"

Uh, compared to that of Izzy and Eckhart, who've been at it since they were six? Not so great.

"Adversus solem ne loquitor," Gerty repeated more slowly. She taught Latin in high school once upon a time, before she married Cyrus.

"Don't talk against the sun?" Lewis tried, knowing as he said it that it was too literal and worried "solem" might mean "alone."

Gerty gave a slight, disappointed shake of the head. What were they going to do about this one? "Don't *argue* against the sun—that is, what is obvious and self-evident."

And that was that: Seth was clinically insane and, for the sake of everyone's peace of mind and concentration, should be forgotten about, disowned, disavowed, barred. And Lewis needed to work harder on his Latin.

On the other hand, Gerty urged him to apply for the Rhodes. She believed in him. It was also like she was intuiting the coming of Andrew Feeling. The world is a battlefield and this is the armor you must put on in order to prevail. But Lewis didn't listen. Lewis applied for no fellowships, went his own way, which has led him here, into the weeds.

10

T hank you!" someone calls, startling him, though a split second later he recognizes the deep voice of Oren, the preacher neighbor. He stands resting his chin on the top of the fence so that his large jowly head seems to float there. "I've been hoping someone would give it a haircut," Oren says, scanning the yard.

With the uprooted weeds held in his hand, Lewis must look like he's on the job. Oren wears his own hair in the fashion of a Born-Again football coach, parted on the side and lacquered into place. Or do the coaches mimic the ministers?

Oren nods back toward his lawn, where there's a birdbath that says along the rim, *His eye is on the sparrow and I know He watches me.* "We're catching your dandelions," he says grimly.

"Good for salad," Lewis points out.

"For *salad?*" Oren says, making a face. "That what they eat in New York City?"

"They do," Lewis says.

Oren shakes his head in amazement or simple refusal. Dropping his voice into a quieter, confiding register, he says, "I want you to know your mother is just *overjoyed* you've come back home to live."

Lewis is about to say he's just here for a visit then thinks better of it and stands smiling pleasantly while letting a silence build.

"Well," Oren says, squinting up at the sky, "I'll let you get back to it." Adding sagely, as he eases himself down from what-

ever he's standing on, a bucket, a stack of Bibles, "Be too hot
for yard work before long."

When Oren has slipped from view, Lewis drops the handful of weeds and goes moodily back to the stoop, where he
sits down and resumes drinking his coffee. It's absurd—
worse than absurd, it's primitive and superstitious—to hold
Oren responsible for Seth's first episode. Though if it hadn't
been for those packets of seeds left out in the open in Oren's
garage, Seth might not have had his condition "kindled," to
use Harry's term: stirred, roused. Or not so soon, so young,
at fourteen.

Abby found a strange residue in her coffee-bean grinder
one morning. Lewis remembers her dipping in her pinkie and
tasting it and making a face. Seth had started smoking pot, they
knew. Now what? They were like parents together, Abby and
Lewis, with a bond formed around handling Seth, their strange
child. Things were about to get stranger.

They picked up his trail on the family computer. It led to
a site called Erowid and a FAQs about morning-glory seeds
that included a recipe. Lewis read it over Abby's shoulder
and doubted aloud that Seth would have gone to the bother:
there were too many steps, ethanol, petroleum ether, shaking
it up, waiting, drying out the seed power. Then they came to
this:

Q. Why is this method of preparation superior to others?

A. The virtue of this processing methodology will become
clear if you sip a bit and hold it in your mouth before swal-
lowing. VOILA: Instant Experience!

Q. How long will the experience last?

A. The morning glory voyage is clean, pure, intense and par-

ticularly enjoyable out of doors in the daytime (drink at
dawn). It lasts the standard 8–10 hours.

Abby took the car and Lewis was sent off on foot. He tried
Stacy's house, where Seth had been attending the Bible reading group led by her Born-Again hippie parents—no one
home. Then he went down to the woods at the bottom of the
neighborhood, calling Seth's name as he went, which embarrassed him but that's what being a parent entailed, overcoming
embarrassment, panicking in public.

He walked a short distance into the grove and was turning
to go when he spotted Seth resting his forehead against a tree.
He went over and touched him on the thin shoulder. He was
just a boy. "What the fuck did you take?"

"Shall not eat of it," Seth said, his eyes closed. "Neither
shall ye touch it."

Lewis felt for his cell to call 911 but he hadn't remembered
to bring it. Seth puked on the roots of the tree and said he was
fine except when he moved. Lewis kicked dirt over the vomit
and they sat on the ground beneath another tree. The trip lasted
for hours; it may as well have been LSD. Seth was quiet for
most of it, eyes closed, smiling, muttering things, but toward
the end his eyes flew open and he sat up. "You're dead, kid."
It's what someone had told him as a threat before a recent
showdown, Lewis knew. Seth was fighting a lot in school. "You
are *so dead.*"

When he finally came down, he didn't come down: he was
convinced he had died. Many people underwent a kind of ego-
death on psychedelics, Abby explained. It was considered
standard, something experienced users knew to anticipate. She
read aloud pertinent passages from Timothy Leary and others.
But what other people experienced and said meant nothing to
Seth; what he had undergone was permanent and real: he was
essentially and truly dead. And do you know the great thing

about being dead? You're aren't *afraid* all the time, because that's what every fear is based on, the fear of death. Dead, he felt more alive than ever before. It was great to be dead!

It would clear up on its own, Abby hoped. Meanwhile it was summertime. Lewis drove out to a ranch to swim in the lake, ten dollars per car: an old man took the money and opened the cattle gate. They heard that the far end of the lake there were cliffs and a rope swing, but access to it was blocked by a gang of high-school skinheads who would appear arms folded on the footpath, their girlfriends swinging their white legs in the trees. It turned out the owner of the ranch was the grandfather of the leader and had raised the boy part-time—the mother was a meth addict, the father in Leavenworth. But being dead, Seth decided to demonstrate his fearlessness by challenging the bigger, vicious-looking skinhead leader. Which meant Lewis would have to fight too and Lewis didn't particularly enjoy fighting or give a damn about some rope swing. In addition to which this Skinhead was not just a kid with a shaved head and swastika tats; he was affiliated through his convict father with a regional white-supremacist group. Even if Seth and Lewis won the fight, they might find themselves being forced off the road on the way home by a car full of Hammerskins or Hammerheads (Lewis never got the name of the group straight or wanted to) and shanked in the bushes. But in the end they settled not on a fight but on a contest to see who would jump off the highest point on the cliff above the lake, the winner having the right to be gate-keeper to the pathetic fucking rope swing. Lewis watched Seth climb higher and higher up the cliff, until on the final, winning jump he struck the water on his side and briefly passed out from the pain and Lewis leapt in, afraid he might drown. Seth's first act as rope-swing gatekeeper was to welcome his biracial friend Marley, son of a WSU faculty couple, which touched off an end-less, moronic debate about race, worse in its way than fighting would have been, Lewis often found himself thinking.

Then Seth flew to New York for his annual one-week visit to see Virgil. The night before he left, Seth came into Lewis's room. He wondered aloud about what it was going to be like, *flying on a plane when you're dead*. Lewis studied him. The kid still believed he was dead. It was the strangest thing. He referred to it in everyone's presence. Abby was out with Rennie, "lifetime companion" du jour, and when Seth lit a one-hit pipe, Lewis had a small social puff. But it was strong and he found himself thinking harder than he had about Seth's claim: he's dead, my little brother. Lewis had always lived in dread of Seth's dying—in a car crash, drowning at the beach, cancer. Now, in this strange, Alice-in-Wonderland fashion and under his nose it had happened anyway: Seth was dead. He turned to contemplating his own death, that beast of legend. Seth was dead, ergo Lewis too was going to die, one day the hour would actually come. The beast was real. He could make it out in the farthest distance, like a grainy photo of Bigfoot. But suddenly it turned and flew across that vast space and pressed itself against him and Lewis couldn't breathe, he broke down gasping out sobs of terror. "It's OK," Seth said, soothing him. But Lewis knew he was gloating too: breaking Lewis the doubter was a victory. He would do the same with Virgil.

And the minute he got off the plane in New York he was pestering Virgil to acknowledge the astonishing and quite possibly unprecedented nature of what had occurred. Ask Lewis, Dad! Once in ten thousand lifetimes an event of this magnitude occurred! But what Abby saw as a worrisome but in the end legitimate instance of "spiritual drunkenness," Virgil decided was a psychotic break triggered by the morning-glory trip, which Seth happily told him all about. Having lured him down to a clinic run by a colleague on the pretence of measuring his surely exceptional brainwave function, Virgil had Seth subjected to a battery of tests then kept there for observation for several days against Seth's will and without informing

Abby. The test results were inconclusive but Seth was so furious at the betrayal and traumatized by the clinic discipline that he refused to speak to or visit Virgil afterward, with the estrangement lasting right up until Seth decided he wanted to become an actor and the Van Sant auditions were announced.

When he returned from New York, he spoke less and less about the morning-glory trip, less and less in general. When he did speak, it was to Abby alone. They spent a lot of time in her room, the door closed. And what he said frightened her: he wanted to finish the job; he wanted to die the rest of the way.

11

On the cutting-board island in the kitchen, breakfast has been laid out on white platters—over-easy eggs, white membrane sealing in the yolks, crisp bacon, hashed brown potatoes, bagels. Not that anyone else would go to the bother, but Lewis can tell at a glance that it was made by Abby. She could so easily run a successful restaurant or catering business. But that would be too—what? Easy? Hard? Predictable, he decides. It would bore her.

He fixes a plate, sits down at the table and opens the Mac. At the tap of a key, the screen fills with an image of a smiling Abby at the wheel of the Escalade driving through Great Plains country. The window is down, her arm is hanging over the side and a sheer white scarf trails. Below the image is text, which Lewis reads while eating.

Grateful Gaia Storm Tours

You're probably well aware of the basics: from late March to late August of each year, tornado-spawning supercells are created in the area known as "tornado alley." According to conventional meteorological accounts, it's all due to the collision of warm, moist air coming up from the Gulf of Mexico, with dry cold air blowing in from the Rockies. But what do these terms really mean? What is "air," "warm," "cold," and, above all, "collision"? Is it merely a matter of agitated atoms, as per the dominant scientific view? Hardly.

The Broken Heart of Gaia

Dissatisfied with enthusiastic but essentially (offensively?—B.) empty and wrongheaded scientistic-thinking characteristic of typical storm-chase outfits, you're ready for an advanced, spiritually evolved experience of the skies, what we call Gaia Consciousness. This is not a quest for a phototrophy of a funnel cloud or lightning strike. We do not have a "passion for severe weather," and we are not interested in helping you "achieve your chasing goals." This is a journey into the broken heart of Gaia, she who has been hubristically taken for granted, pumped with pollutants and plumped with antibiotics, scorned by agribusiness and the self-destructive actions of an out-of-control patriarchy, capitalism, petrol, the relentless desacralization of the world that has been in full swing since the Industrial Revolution a scant two hundred years ago but really began four millennia ago with what has been variously represented in human myths as the Fall. This is the grieving, violent energy that fills the skies of the Great Plains in the spring months and through the summer. If you are prepared to feel the full force of that energy, please join us.

We Are Not Luddites But

While we deploy such state-of-the-art devices as Mobile Threat Radar, cameras and video recorders are not permitted on Grateful Gaia journeys, since there is abundant and obvious evidence that such mediations prevent participants from being deeply present to the lived experience of divinity. Again, we are not interested in trophy-hunting.

Range

We will be exploring storms in, near, or within a day's drive of Wichita, Kansas. We are not going to be driving all over the Great Plains in a desperate quest for "experience."

Weather is everywhere. *Simply to be here* at this time of the yearly cycle is to know Her. We let Gaia come to us. Rather, we do not pretend to be able to do otherwise.

Rates
$165 per person per day plus food, accommodations, and a per diem. On a Grateful Gaia Tour you will be in a vehicle with at most two other guests. You will in effect be part of a Goddess-loving *family*, not just another paid-up body shoehorned into a twelve-passenger van, as with other tour companies. You will be *in* a vehicle *with* vehicles of Gaia *as* vehicles of Her.

Accommodations
One option is to reserve a room at one of the many fine and inexpensive hotels on the eastside of Wichita. We recommend the Marriot on Douglas. Another is to stay in one of the guest rooms at our home in Forest Hills. Health food breakfast prepared by Abby, massage, attunement, readings. [need more here—Bishop]

Store
Grateful Gaia does not commodify the experience of Gaia, hence there are no photos or videos or sweatshirts or coffee mugs to "add to cart." There is no cart; there is only the Earth, only Goddess: lay your head on the arms of the Earth.

Contact
Email abby@gratefulgaia.com mailto:abby@gratefulgaia.com or call at 917 668 9234

He's closing the laptop as Abby comes into the kitchen. She's wearing a semi-transparent orange floral blouse, white slacks, white flats and has the refreshed air of having just returned from a spa. She sings out "Good morning!," pours a cup of coffee and sits across from him at the round table in the breakfast nook.

He slides the laptop toward her. "Bishop asked me to give this to you."

"My website?" she says, clapping her hands. "Goody!" She taps a key and her image blooms on the screen. "I love it!" she says.

Lewis goes to the cabinet for a glass, gets ice and water. He sits back down at the table, watches Abby reading over the text.

"I'm not crazy about 'Grateful Gaia Storm-Chasers,'" she says, looking up. "That was always Bishop's thing—'Goddess,' 'Gaia': it all sounds so nineties now, doesn't it?"

Reading on, she chuckles, shakes her head. "No swag, I can understand, I *guess*. But no *photos or videos*? He's out of his mind! No one will sign up! The whole *point* is photo trophies." She hits the "delete" key, types a phrase. "When did Bishop turn into such a purist? Like he doesn't have a thousand photos from his precious Burning Man trips." She types something more, goes on reading.

Finally, wondering whether she would ever bother explaining if he never asked, he says, "So what's Bishop doing living in a *tent in the yard*?"

She looks at him like a parent about to explain something to a child who may not be old enough to understand. "Have you heard of polyamory?"

Many loves? Lewis thinks. Much luvin'? Probably too literal again. Feeling a low-grade dread, he shakes his head.

"Well, it's basically just a movement to get past monogamy," Abby says off-handedly, as if describing a software upgrade. "People have more than one partner, all very out in the open and negotiated."

"Like swinging?" he asks, screwing up his face.

"God, no, not at all!" she says, waving away the comparison. "Polyamory is just multi-partner relationships, long-term and stable for the most part. Swinging—or the 'lifestyle,' as they call it—is really just organized promiscuity."

He's maybe slightly relieved. "And *Donald's* down with this?"

"That's the agreement we have," she says letter-of-the-law-ishly. Donald strikes Lewis as the last person to get involved in polyamory. She wrinkles her forehead in imitation of the anxious expression he must be wearing. "It's just something I'm *exploring*, Lewis," she says, reaching over to pat his hand.

He nods his head slowly as if taking this in as merely a "lifestyle" choice while inwardly feeling disoriented and a bit nauseous. "And *that's* why Bishop's living in a tent in the yard?"

"Oh, Bishop just likes to shake up his life sometimes. Which is fine. He's welcome to camp out and think of me as a 'Goddess' or whatever if that does the trick. I'm flattered!"

She goes back to poring over the website text and Lewis sits in silence digesting this new information about his mother along with his heavy breakfast. He's feeling distinctly queasy. He's feeling in fact like packing his bags and getting on the next plane out. Seth was one sort of surprise; this is another.

"He may have a yurt installed out there," Abby says now, glancing up, "when it gets colder."

"He told me."

"That could be neat, actually," she says, waving over the top of the laptop at the backyard. "That house behind, which belonged to the Robertson's (they got laid off), is in foreclosure. We could buy it and extend the property . . . have a sort of yurt family compound."

She often comes back to this idea of a "family compound." Maybe it's something about the region—the Mormons, the nuts in Texas Cody comes from. Some deep distrust of the government, the state.

"The irony," she adds in a confidential tone after a moment, looking up from the screen, "is that I'd just as soon be *alone*—"

It's what she usually says when a relationship breaks up: alone at last! She often goes farther: that man was in fact *the last*, because she's really had it with partnership and the whole compulsive need for companionship as it's currently structured. She's finally, truly, deeply moved past it and is *so* looking forward to being just wonderfully *alone and autonomous*, the pleasures of celibacy and solitude, the simplicity of acting on her desires without having to consult and consider someone else, prop them up as well usually, wipe the psychic crumbs from their face. But in a matter of weeks she's met someone else and the Buddhist-nun talk is forgotten. Lewis is therefore less and less apt to take these moments of renunciation seriously; she's too much like an alcoholic swearing off booze mid-hangover. At the same time, she speaks so convincingly that he finds himself wanting to believe. Since the divorce from Virgil, Abby's had a new, usually live-in boyfriend, on average, what—every two years? How great, what a relief it would be not to have to meet and, at her tacit behest, *believe in* another "lifetime companion," not to hear about and see photos of his fucking children (the Navy Seal son, the Born-Again daughter) and ex-wives (the retired Broadway actress; a "published poet"), his hunting dogs or pottery studio, the horse farm or antique car collection.

"So why not just *be alone?*" he asks.

"Well, I can't seem to manage it—so—"she says helplessly.

"You double down?"

"Exactly!"

"So let's see," he says, beginning to count on his fingers, "There's Donald . . . Bishop . . . "

"Not at the same time," she interjects blandly, her attention drifting back to the laptop screen.

"Right, okay," Lewis says, blushing. "Anyone else?"

"Bishop has a girlfriend he sees," she says, hitting the delete key several times. "A former student who lives in the old downtown section. Speaking of trophies from Burning Man. He's sometimes over at her place for a few days."

"And this doesn't bother you—the girlfriend?"

"There are *moments* of jealously, sure, but we talk it through." She takes a sip of coffee and slaps her thigh as if remembering something, turning away from the laptop screen to face him with wide eyes. "That's actually the main draw-back—having to *negotiate* everything! It can get a little exhausting, especially with Bishop, who *loves* to talk, as you know."

"What about Donald?" Lewis asks. "Does Donald have other 'partners'?" It sounds very sex-ed class, "partners," falsely or wishfully neutral in that tradition: business partners, dance partners, *sex* partners.

"Not at the moment," she says.

Lewis gets up and goes to the sink to rinse his plate. "But you're open to it," he says.

"Openness is the whole point."

He concentrates on scouring clean a skillet, dries it, then rinses toast crumbs and a streak of egg yolk from what he suspects is a plate used by Seth, who leaves such petty tasks to fools willing to do them, like Donald and Abby. And now Lewis apparently.

His cell phone buzzes on the breakfast table where he left it, turning a half-circle like a new-fangled Ouija Board stylus. He picks it up and checks the screen: his father's office number. "It's Virgil," he says.

"Don't answer," Abby says simply, reading his pinched expression.

He flips it open. "Hello?"

"Hello, Lewis!" Lewis holds the cell away from his ear: Virgil speaks into the phone like an invention he's startled to find actually works, a manner he inherited from Cyrus, from what Lewis can tell. It's like they're dictating telegrams. "Listen, the reason I'm calling is I thought we agreed you would write Grandpa a thank-you note for his Musil book he was kind enough to send you a copy of."

"No, we didn't," Lewis says, squinting with irritation at Abby, who is all ears. He's annoyed to be pestered about this but oddly happy to be plunged into a controversy out of Miss Manners on the back of the polyamory.

"I *sent a note*," Lewis says, shaking his head at Abby with deadpan incredulity. "And I *said* 'Thank you,' at the table that night. You were there. You heard me."

"Well, be that as it may," Virgil says with quickly rising irritation, as if he's anticipated just such mulishness, "there's still a feeling that you need to officially thank your grandfather, Lewis. And since he never received the first thank-you note you say you sent—"

"*Did* send," Lewis insists. "*Did* send."

"Noted: did send," Virgil says skeptically.

"I just resent the implication—"

Virgil sighs. Lewis can see him very clearly in the small, book-lined office: the blocky desk chair reclined at a forty-five degree angle, the expression of refined irritation; the three narrow stained-glass windows with their view of the quad; the language dictionaries on the shelf beside the desk in their sacrosanct ranks (Bruno would rearrange them as a prank). Even during the worst of things with Sylvie, Virgil arrived there every morning at 9:30, kept on schedule with the book. Lewis admires it despite himself. When Lewis was a boy, before the split, Virgil worked in a spare bedroom of their small faculty house. A story Abby tells about the marriage turns on this point: she meets an older woman at a party, mentions that she and Virgil just got divorced. "How long were you married?" the woman asks. "A *long time*," Abby tells her, "eight years." "Eight years isn't so long," says the woman. "But he barely left the house!" Abby cries. "Compared to how much most couples see of each other, it was more like *twenty*-eight years!"

It was only recently that Lewis saw this story from Virgil's perspective: it was by teaching as little as possible and staying at home that he finished two books. That's how Virgil wrote his way out of UT Austin—and out of Lewis's life, and Seth's— and back to the Ivy League whence he'd come. Though whether he works at home or at his office on campus, he's having the same luck with women: they leave.

"In any case, since he *never received it*," Virgil is saying, "would it be too much trouble for you to take a moment to sit down and write *another one*?"

"Fine," Lewis says. They'll never let this go; they'll follow him to the ends of the earth with this thank-you note in their teeth. He'll die in Sumatra of encephalitis and the last thing they'll say over his grave, or rather to each other over the phone (since they wouldn't bother making the trip to Sumatra): he never did send that thank-you note to Grandpa.

"You'll do that?"

"Yes."

"*Thank you*, Lewis," he says, as if to demonstrate how the words can be squeezed out when one is feeling zero gratitude.

"But it's absurd," Lewis adds.

"You certainly seem to think so."

"I need to get off now."

"Most people just consider it good manners."

"I'm hanging up, sorry."

"A gift is given, a thank-you note sent. All so straightforward, really."

"Bye—"

"My best to Abby."

Lewis claps the cell shut as if killing something and flicks it across the table. They watch it slide to the edge and stop, hanging there over the abyss. "What was *that* all about?" Abby asks, her eyes wide.

Lewis sighs and he tells her the story, which is that during the years he was at Columbia Cyrus was at work on a study of Robert Musil, chiefly his unfinished novel *The Man Without Qualities*. What a cool title, Lewis thought when he heard about it as a freshman. Expecting a portrait of a sort of Magritte figure, like Peter Sellars in *Being There*, he borrowed the translation from Virgil, but the novel turned out to be about a murderer, the style often ponderously essayistic, and after reading maybe fifty pages Lewis lost interest and put it back on the shelf in Virgil's study. Then Cyrus's big book finally came out from Harvard UP and Lewis emailed to ask for a copy, partly in the hope that it might improve his chances of appreciating *The Man Without Qualities*, but mainly because this show of interest was expected of him. Cyrus was also contracted to write his next few books in German, so this was perhaps Lewis's last chance to read a new book by Cyrus at all. Inscribed, a bit impersonally, Lewis thought, "With grandfatherly affection," a copy of the book arrived in the mail a few days later and Lewis gave it a try but Cyrus's study proved harder to stay with than the Musil novel itself. After reading ten or fifteen pages, he set it atop a stack of books that eventually got boxed up for storage and forgot about it. Later, Cyrus gave a lecture drawn from the Musil book at NYU. The hall was filled to overflowing with graduate students and professors, which dazzled V.

"No doubt," Abby remarks. "Had she started seeing what's-his-name at that point?"

Lewis sighs and nods quickly, not really wanting to think about V., certainly not V. and Andrew. Then why bring her up?

"It's so interesting," Abby remarks, "what these rigidly moralizing types get up to in their spare time, isn't it?"

They met at a conference on Isaac Watts, father of modern hymnody, which is a key aspect of V's dissertation on Emily Dickinson: hymn structure, hymn culture, bee imagery. Yawn, Lewis is free to say now. Yawn! It's a boring-ass topic and V. is a careerist whore for hooking up with Andrew Feeling, since without someone to carry her she might well never get a job, being so plodding and unoriginal in her scholarship.

Lewis goes on with the story: after the lecture, there was a dinner at Bruno's and Lynn's faculty townhouse and Cyrus asked whether Lewis had ever received the copy of the Musil study he asked for. Cyrus is a nice enough man but he is also, for all the bookishness, commanding and square-jawed and masculine in a 1950s tweedy fashion, ready with a confident, considered pronouncement on any worthy topic that might arise. His sons, Lewis knows from Sylvie, wish he would sink quietly into retirement and put a period on an already crush-ingly successful career, his twenty-five plus books. But the opposite is happening: without any teaching or administrative duties, he's more productive than ever.

There had been a lapse in conversation at that moment and everyone heard Cyrus's question and waited to hear Lewis's reply. Yes, Lewis said, he had received a copy. Well, that's strange, Cyrus said, since Cyrus never received any acknowl-edgment of it. Lewis did his best to look baffled and insisted he'd sent a thank-you note—shortly after receiving the book. Hmm, Cyrus said, while the twins cast Lewis shrewd looks. Eckhart, who was sitting beside him, whispered, "The Man Without Gratitudes!," which Uncle Bruno overheard and passed along to Lynn, who wrinkled her nose and simpered like a miniature Collie snapping up a treat. The next day, Virgil, face diplomatically blank, suggested, since the first one had appar-ently been *lost in the mail*, that Lewis write *another* thank-you note. It will take you half a minute. Here's a stamp. But Lewis never actually *agreed* to write a "second" thank-you note and never got around to writing one, hence Virgil's call just now.

Abby sits as if stunned. "Wow," she says. Then seems to have an inspiration. "I know: just use the Dick Cheney line," she says.

"Which is what again?" Then he remembers.

"'Go fuck yourself.'" She laughs. She means it as a joke of course but when he simply stares unsmilingly she looks a little stricken. "Oh, come on, Lewis!"

There's a rapping on the sliding glass door: it's Tori in short shorts, barefoot, the nipples of her enormous tits straining at the thin cotton of her faded blue T-shirt. She grins knowingly and waves by fiddling her fingers, the nails shiny with fresh black polish. She slides open the door and says in her husky voice, "Do you have, like, a bottle of *massage oil?*"

"Hi, Tori!" Abby says casually, unsurprised—delighted, in fact—to see the woman she met for the first time last night pop up in her backyard. The more the merrier: family compound. "I'm pretty sure there's a bottle in my shower. Help yourself, honey."

"Cool!" says Tori and sashays inside, her high, muscular ass churning.

"All the way back to your right," Abby directs her. "Are you sunbathing?" Abby asks as an afterthought.

"I'm giving Bishop a rub!" Tori calls over her shoulder.

"Oh," Abby says, her voice tightening up slightly. When Tori's out of sight she says in a low voice, "Bishop can be so obvious sometimes."

"You think that was meant to make you jealous?" Lewis whispers.

She's risen from her chair and is on her way out through the sliding glass door. "Uh, duh, Professor!" she says, her face wincing with impatience.

"Hey, no need to get snippy with *me*," Lewis says, feeling slapped.

She stops halfway through the open door and lets her shoulders slump. "I'm sorry, Lewis."

"I'm just an innocent bystander here!" he says with mounting outrage.

"You're right," she says, raising a finger in distracted contrition then going out into the backyard—to find and confront Bishop, Lewis guesses.

12

L ewis finds himself striding angrily down the driveway. The mutts follow high-steppingly then halt at the edge of the property and yap as if he's mad to go farther. He probably is. It's blindingly bright and too hot to be outside, which intensifies his anger, and there's nothing and no one in sight to distract him from it, not a moving car or creature, not even a squirrel.

He walks on, turning to go down the slight declivity then out to the northern edge of the neighborhood. It's a half a mile and the only sign of human activity is the whirr of an industrial ventilator built into the side window of a garage, the dusty hinged flaps quivering.

When he reaches Oliver, he stands watching the traffic but the glare on the windshields prevents him from making out the people inside the cars and pickups, which seem driverless, propelled remotely or by ghosts.

In New York he would walk down Broadway until the passage of other faces eventually washed him clean of himself and whatever mood was oppressing him. Here there's just a bus stop across Oliver but no one waiting at it and no bus in sight.

He considers, despite the heat, walking the two or three miles to Towne East mall, which is air-conditioned at least. His first job was as a clerk in the Dalton Books there. On the other hand, it had been replaced by a Shoez, last time he checked. There's a newish Starbucks at the crest of the hill on Rock Road, he remembers. He could go there.

He hears a shout and looks up expecting to catch a glimpse of some high-school classmate or teacher or coach hailing him fondly from the open window of a passing car, but sees a juice box skid over the ground by his feet spewing dark fluid.

He stoops and picks it up and is about to fling it back but isn't sure which car it came from. And the box is too light to go far enough if he did throw it. He stands holding it lamely, squinting up the road in the direction it came from, and finally tosses it on the ground and turns away. Then thinks better of it because he hates littering and goes to pick it up but stops himself mid-stoop and leaves it on the ground because it seems weak and foolish: pelt me with trash and I turn the other cheek by cleaning it up.

He retreats into the neighborhood like a disoriented beast blundering back into the forest from a highway and takes the street that runs across the bottom of the neighborhood. It's lined by tall, old-growth trees, cottonwoods and elders. In the band of sky above, a flock of crows passes, plying the air with swimming motions of their tapered wings. The sight calms him down. When the last asshole has flung the last piece of trash from the window of the last pickup, the crows will be here.

As it sinks in, his impulse to throw the juice box surprises him. Normally he would ignore something like that, not dignify it with a reaction: what they want is a show of anger, so you deprive them of that and win, to the extent winning is possible. But normally this kind of thing doesn't happen to him. Here, anyone on foot is a loser, a target. Though maybe it's the beard too.

Abby would say it had nothing to do with his appearance, everything to do with his anger, which attracted a corresponding response from the world. Abby and her wisdom. He wonders how it's serving her with Tori the stripper and Burning Man Bishop. That's what Abby's own energy has attracted, after all. Why anyone would want to complicate life with more than one lover, he doesn't get. But if you're going to have two—Bishop and Donald—why stop there?

But she said nothing about stopping there, did she?

Something from Cyrus's NYU lecture on Musil comes back to him: Musil's mother had an affair with a much younger man. Musil's father knew about the relationship and gave it his blessing; the young man even lived with the family. Does that make Abby's polyamory more acceptable, give it a roundabout high-cultural stamp of legitimation, one that even Cyrus might acknowledge? Yes, it does. She is part of the great tradition of nonconformity. Though he can hear Cyrus adding: *but you are not Robert Musil.*

So who is he? He is Lewis in Wichita. But he could so easily be Lewis somewhere else, especially with the graduation money hidden inside the flap of *When Things Fall Apart.* All he would have to do is get himself to the airport and he could go anywhere in the world. He's never had that degree of freedom before, not even close. It's heady. If he went somewhere like India or Indonesia, he could live a very long time without having to get a job.

Abby insists the money is truly his. Lewis owed her nothing beyond the thanks he spontaneously expressed when he opened the envelope. He has incurred no debt whatsoever; she is emphatically the opposite of the Chopiks, with their joy-smothering obligations and punctilios.

But she would be hurt if he left now, without a doubt, especially if he used the graduation money to exit on. She would read it as judgment of her, an indictment of polyamory, of her having sprung Seth on him too. Which is what it would be. He has to somehow hang in here for a respectable length of time before he bails. How long is respectable? It depends on how caught up in and distracted by the dramas of her own life Abby is. A month? Six weeks? At least a month. In that sense the money is not free; he's going to earn it, at least in part, maybe in full, if the past two days are any indication. As Sylvie would say, *Il faut payer*.

Up ahead, a man—Lewis's first human!—walks slowly over his lawn as if inspecting it for flaws. He has a dark moustache and baseball cap, dark sunglasses. His hands are thrust into the front pockets of his jeans. Noticing Lewis, he stares with a mixture of curiosity and distrust. Lewis offers up a reassuring little wave. After a beat the man withdraws a hand from a pocket, waves briefly back, and shoves the hand back into his pocket.

The wall of manicured hedges in the house next door is trembling as if in a high wind but there is no wind to speak of. Maybe it's being trimmed on the far side. No, someone is squeezing through an invisible gap in it—Cody. The man with the sunglasses has turned to watch too. It's like witnessing some bizarre birth.

Having extricated himself from the hedge, Cody calls out happily "Yo!" and trots over to Lewis holding up his truncated jeans with a finger hooked through a belt loop. It lifts Lewis's mood to see him, his big stoned brown eyes with their faintly sneaky expression. It's like seeing a puppy or a clown.

"Lewis!" he says in greeting then pauses as if slightly out of breath; Lewis thinks of Cody's daily pot regime, a hit on waking, then hits throughout the day preparatory to doing anything at all, the toll it must take. There are green smears on his wife-beater T from the hedge.

"I was just coming to find you, son." Now Cody notices the man with the sunglasses and his body language changes, becomes hunched and guarded. "Yo, let's bounce," he tells Lewis out of the corner of his mouth.

When they've walked around the corner, Cody says, "That fucker—whoa, he hates my guts."

"Oh, yeah?" Lewis says. "Why?"

"Stealing them flags and shit."

"Oh, he's one of *those* guys," Lewis says, glancing back.

"They were gonna lynch my ass, Seth too." Cody stands squinting at Lewis and shaking his head. "That was the *one time* I was glad to see the cops, for real. But you know what? Fuck it. I ain't gonna let it haunt me. I create my own reality, like Abby says."

"What do you think she means by that?" Lewis asks him.

"Hey, before I forget," Cody says as if he hasn't heard. "I knew you was away at college. I'm not *that* much of a stoner. I'm talking about last night at the table with Butch and all."

"No, I know, Cody," Lewis assures him. "Don't worry about it."

"I just get confused when there's more than like two people in the room. I forget stuff. If there was enough people in a room, I'd forget my own name."

Frowning, Cody holds his chin as if trying to recall something more. He raises up a finger. "And I *don't* think it's anything weird or wrong that it took you five years to graduate. I ain't graduated *at all*, from *nothing*! Never even got my GED."

"There's plenty of time for that," Lewis says, sounding insipidly fatherly to his own ears.

Cody nods absently. "I mean, I *think* I could get it if I got serious. But truth is—I don't know. I probably never will." He shrugs dejectedly.

Lewis is struggling to come up with something encouraging but non-Polonius-like to say when the mechanical whine of Stacy's wheelchair draws their attention. She's coming along the shady side of the street. When she brings the wheelchair to a halt, she speaks to Cody. Again, Lewis can't make out a word of it but he's struck by how pretty she is in her pixieish fashion and wonders whether she and Cody or she and Seth (or all three at once, here in polyamorous Wichita) have ever had a romance, had sex. There was a period when her parents forbade her to hang out with Seth: maybe sex was the cause.

"Right, yeah," Cody says mutters, then turning to Lewis, tells him: "We need to talk about Seth."

Lewis feels a wobble of dread. "What about him?"

"We're worried he's about to—go off," Cody says wincingly gently, as if Lewis might be too delicate to handle hearing this news. Stacy nods in grave agreement. Seth seems to Lewis typically hyped and performative and oppressive, nothing more. But in the years since his dark phase began, Cody and Stacy have spent more time with him than Lewis has, have witnessed Seth's "episodes" or whatever they are.

"Because of grabbing the wheel last night?" Lewis asks.

"Nah, we all do that shit," Cody says, to Lewis's surprise. "It's sort of a inside joke."

"Oh." Huh, nearly dying in a head-on crash is a regular form of fun. Cool. Could it be dry-humping Tori in front of a hundred strangers in a bowling alley? Or the look Seth gave the manager when they were being thrown out, that was scary enough for the guy to blanch and signal for back-up from two large farm-boy types?

"Have you seen the new tat?" Cody gestures to his upper chest.

"No, why? What is it?" Lewis imagines something so floridly insane, some terrorist message about killing Bush, that it will get Seth the electric chair and infamy for the family name.

Cody glances at Stacy, who seems to shake her head. "I can't say."

"What?" Lewis says, taking a step toward him. Before Seth took him under his wing, Cody got bullied by a gang of jocks and there are moments when the jock in Lewis sees the appeal Cody presented: a moist, teasing cringe to his manner.

"I ain't seen it either!" Cody protests, raising his hands and thereby letting go of his baggy jeans, which nearly fall to his knees in a puddle. He reaches down and hitches them back up.

"He just told me about it. He coulda been bullshittin. Ask *him* about it."

"I will," Lewis says.

Stacy interjects something and Cody listens, nodding, then translates for Lewis: "Anyway, it's not so much the tattoo, it's more a feeling we have. We tried talking to your mom about it? But she—we don't know. Honestly, she seems like she's giving up or something. She's had it."

"Maybe she has had it," Lewis says. "She's been through a lot with Seth."

"I'm sorry," Cody says after a silence. Gloom falls over him like a veil. He stares at the ground. "I just don't want nothing bad to happen," he says quietly, his lips quivering. "He's all I got, really, your brother."

There's a wobbling membrane of tears in his eyes when he looks up. "He's, like, my *teacher*. He schooled me how to defend myself and shit."

Lewis knows the story all too well: nobly protective Seth teaches poor victimized Cody how to ward off the drooling jock goons.

"When I got to town," Cody says, "and them motherfuckers liked to fuck with me, for, like, *no reason?* Just fuck with me cause they're *evil?*"

The memory of it is too emotional; he stares at the street, unable to speak. Stacy takes his hand and looks up at him then at Lewis with her plaintive, pretty eyes. Lewis feels he should wrap an arm around Cody's shoulder, if only to please and impress Stacy, but settles for placing a commiserative hand on Cody's bony shoulder. Lewis thinks about the dusty Mormon compound he was kicked out of in Texas, his dozen half-siblings. Sent into exile because there were too many males, he arrives in Wichita to find himself the whipping boy for the school jocks.

Cody gets himself under control enough to say, "Seth was all, 'Dude, let me . . . let me show you . . . some *moves.*'"

He lets out a tearful, relieved laugh, his eyes brightening, his posture straightening. "And we practiced and we *practiced*. Down in *your basement*," he reminds Lewis, pointing at him, as if the basement has acquired landmark status Lewis is lucky enough to have a link to. "And then one day they come after me? And I run a bit like I always did? Then I turned around and jumped up and kicked the main fucker with both feet *straight in his chest*! Snapped his head back against the locker and cold *knocked his shit out*!" He stares from Lewis to Stacy in openmouthed amazement.

He raises his hand like a Pentecostal feeling the spirit. "Didn't I?" Lewis high-fives it, moved despite himself. "*Didn't I?*" Cody turns to Stacy, who pats his hand awkwardly back, beaming crookedly at him. "*Didn't I?*" They slap high five again.

He stands grinning and shaking his head in quiet awe at this memory of himself as action hero. "And you better goddamn believe they never fucked with Cody again!"

Then abruptly grows somber again. Are they all manic? Lewis wonders. Is it in the air? Do they cluster together in herds?

"Anyway," he says lugubriously, "I just—I'm worried, is all, about your brother. Like I say, he's *it* for me."

13

L ewis takes Bishop's footpath through the weeds, passing the tent, where a butterfly flits drunkenly at the entrance, and around to the back of the house, entering stealthily through the sliding glass doors to the den/TV room. He's hoping to slip through the house to his room and take a nap without bumping into Abby. Last night's lack of sleep has caught up with him and doesn't have the energy to deal with her or anyone else. He also wants to deprive her for a little while longer of the chance to apologize properly, as he knows she's hankering to do.

But as he rounds the corner into the hall to his room, Abby is coming out of the bathroom. She's still wearing her elegant spa clothes but appears somewhat less refreshed and relaxed now. She was probably in some endless powwow with Bishop while Lewis was out walking.

She leads him by the hand to the couch in the den and pats the cushion beside her, curling her legs beneath her. She lays out bagels but never touches bread or any other such fluffy carb herself, rice or pasta, refined sugar. Thus her trim figure. He sits farther away, with his back to the armrest.

"Lewis," she says, gazing with a chastened expression into his eyes, which he averts, "I'm sorry I was flip about the thank-you letter to Cyrus. I didn't mean to belittle what you're dealing with there. And that I snapped at you. That was inexcusable." She's always been admirably quick to apologize to him when she's in the wrong. He admires her for this and now that it's happening he's glad, it's air-clearing; at the same time he feels his hurt at the injustice well up afresh.

"I'm *not* a professor," he says sullenly. By what process did "professor" become a slur? "That's what I'm supposed to be getting *credit* for."

"And you *are*," she says, squeezing his forearm for emphasis. "I was *totally* out of line. It won't happen again."

"Really?" he says. "How can you be so sure? Things are pretty volatile around here," he adds, lifting his chin in the direction of the backyard.

Annoyed or merely surprised by the degree of difficulty he's mounting, she compresses her lips in a disappointed expression but says evenly, "Because I won't let it happen again."

He makes a skeptical face, finds himself pushing his advantage. "Because, look, if this is too fraught a moment for me to *be* here—"

She sighs hissingly through her nose and seems for a second prepared to take up the gauntlet of this veiled threat. A strong light is pouring in through the living room windows and in it the lines on her forehead and around her mouth are etched unflatteringly. She won't be able to attract men forever; one day there won't be a *poly* to her *amory*. Though what do wrinkles, what do looks, have to do with it? Knowing Abby, she'll turn out to be one of those sexually frisky nonagenarians.

"You got here *last night*," she says now, having softened or decided he needs more mollifying. "All right? It's not like this around here *every day*, I can promise you that."

Now Donald walks past with exaggerated discretion, tiptoeing like a bad actor.

Abby has slid a thick family photo album from the underneath the coffee table. She traces a crack along the spine. "I need to have the binding repaired," she says then begins paging through it. It's organized into sections devoted to photos of each of them, minus Virgil's—those were expunged years ago, though he appears in a few beside Seth or Lewis.

When she turns to Seth's section—even as a towheaded toddler he looks like trouble, at least in hindsight—Lewis says, "I ran into Cody and Stacy. They're worried about him."

"Are they?" Abby says drily.

"They think he's on the verge of an episode," Lewis says.

She chuckles. "They're like animals that can sense an earthquake, those two. If only they could *prevent* the earthquake, they could actually do something for us."

Lewis's eye falls on a photo of him and Seth, ages four and seven or so, both shirtless, sway-backed, little-boy bodies, summertime. Lewis is both showing Seth an orphaned robin and fending Seth off from grabbing the bird.

"You think they're wrong."

She turns down her mouth. "Not wrong. They may be right about the episode. I think they're wrong to worry about it."

"Why?"

"What is it, worry, when you come right down to it?"

"It's natural to worry," Lewis says. Here he goes again, taking the dull middle-of-the-road truisms, as if ventriloquized by Virgil.

"'Natural,'" Abby says. "It's natural in the same way self-dramatization and egoism are natural: look at me! I'm wringing my hands so hard they're about to fall off, that's how *deeply* maternal I am!"

She slips the album back into the rack beneath the coffee table. "Worry not only doesn't do any good, it actually contributes to the reality of the thing they're so worried about. And then everyone gets to congratulate themselves because it turns out they were *right* to worry!"

He finds he's laughing along with her but at the same time he's not quite following. "So you're not worried," he says.

"I gave up worrying in general a long time ago," she says a

little grandly, "and gave up worrying about Seth specifically last year, when I flew out to San Francisco in hysterics."

"I was ready to fly out too," Lewis reminds her. This is a half-truth: in the throes of finishing a paper when the crisis erupted, he bet Abby would decline his offer, which she did.

"I wasn't questioning that," she says calmly. "I'm talking about how Mom flies out to make son stay in ICU and finds when she gets there that he's jerked the IVs out of his arms and flown the coop! He doesn't want to follow the doctor's orders." She holds up her palms: what can one do? "Seth wants what he wants when he wants it. He's a grown man. Do we strap him to a hospital bed and force him to heal? Then force him to live out his average biological life of seventy-two. Four years or whatever it is?"

She looks at him in her level, clear-eyed way and he wishes he hadn't drawn her onto this topic. He should have just accepted her apology and left it at that. As used as he is to assuming Seth may die young and by his own hand, even cavalier and callous, especially when telling friends like Eli about the situation, he forgets how frightening it is, freshly confronted, how helpless and small and unlucky he feels.

"But I *believe* it's going to be OK," Abby says. He can believe too, she means; it's just a matter of believing, of faith. She smiles and it's convincingly serene, not a falsely brave smile. "That makes all the difference."

He goes to his room and gets undressed and climbs into bed. Closing his eyes, he begins to fall asleep and sees a view of Stonington harbor from the perspective of the small jetty down the street from V's summer house, the glassy water reflecting gray sky, the paler gray of the small floating dock with its looped handrails, a cormorant on top of a wood dock pylon. It's as if he's somehow there, standing on a boulder of the jetty, seeing it in real time. Sailboats at anchor, the distant green of shoreline. His soul has gone in search of V. but can't find her. Then he's asleep.

14

I t's late afternoon when he gets up. Looking a bit spectral—cheekbones sharper, smudges of shadow beneath his eyes—Seth is sitting on the couch in the den beside Cody, who is breaking apart a bud so pungent Lewis scented it the instant he opened the door to his room. A translucent orange prescription bottle labeled in red magic marker, "O.G. Khush/3.5 g." lies uncapped on the coffee table beside a small blue bong and lighter. Sitting down in a low sisal chair, Lewis wonders whether this medical-grade stuff is what he had a hit of last night and if so no wonder he felt duct-taped to the car seat. The pot high for him is nearly always at least a little unpleasant. Why does he keep thinking it will be otherwise? It's the fragrance, the cultish enthusiasm of others, some stubborn hope that it will turn out as advertised and he'll be converted.

Seth has been smoking daily since he was fourteen, in secret at first, then more and more openly and ultimately, once the futility of opposing it became obvious, in the house with Abby's consent. It was in no small part because he lost the battle over this issue that Rennie, Abby's most conservative live-in boyfriend, moved out. And woe betide the man who would take up arms now. Still, the sight of pot so brazenly out in the open sets off faint, vestigial alarms for Lewis.

Meanwhile, as if in an unwitting nod to Seth's victory, Donald casts a gingerly glance in at the proceedings on his way past the doorway, calling, "Hi there!" which Lewis makes a point of replying to, guessing neither Seth nor Cody will bother. They don't.

Having packed its bowl, Cody passes the blue bong with two hands to Seth, who lights up, inhales and goes in a humorous Groucho Marxian crouch to blow the stream of smoke out through the screen of the open sliding glass door—Abby's one lonely little rule, obeyed intermittently. Smoke leaking from his nostrils, he offers the bong to Lewis, who declines with gusto, then to Cody, who accepts gratefully, passing the long flexible flame of the lighter back and forth over the bowl.

Lewis has been expecting some sign from Cody to do with their talk about Seth but so far it's as if Cody forgot about it, or rather *is forgetting* in the ritual details and haze of this blaze-up with Seth. But it may be that he's simply afraid to risk it. Seth being unusually alert to such things.

When first making the case for his right to smoke, Seth referred to pot as his "ally," a term from Castañeda, one of the household authors Seth and Cody discovered once Abby began homeschooling them. A psychedelic like peyote can be a shaman's "ally" or helper in the performance of wizardly deeds. Given Abby's weakness for this sort of thing, Lewis had to admire the shrewdness of the approach. But what an enormous phony Castañeda turned out to be, at least according to the same anthro course in which Lewis learned about Ponzi schemes.

In the early, idealistic days, Abby provided a syllabus and books recommended by a national homeschooling organization—Steinbeck, Harper Lee. Seth and Cody boycotted math and science completely but plucked down from the shelves in the house whatever, in addition to Castañeda (drawn by the admittedly great cover art), struck their fancy: New Age adventure tales like *Journeys Out of the Body*, *The Autobiography of a Yogi*, the Whitley Strieber accounts of abduction by UFO's, and *Seth Speaks*, by a medium named Jane Roberts, whose gaunt face in the cover photo used to frighten Lewis as a boy and to whom Seth naturally felt a special link. Abby also ordered from Amazon anything they asked for—histories of Punk like *Please Kill Me*, Kurt Cobain's *Notebooks*, "street knowledge" memoirs by gangsters and pimps. There was a Gnostic Gospels phase that led to a fiery exchange of emails between Cody and his "plyg" father back in Arizona, which Abby forwarded to Lewis because she found Cody's stand so eloquently expressed and evidence of homeschooled empowerment.

"Wake 'n Bake 'n Read" Lewis called the curriculum, in New York. He feels bad about that now. He was in fact impressed and happy that they were reading anything, stoned or sober, "classic" or New Age. In Seth's case, Lewis held out hope it would lead to college but in the end Seth never bothered any more than Cody about taking the GED exam.

Though it's not "the end," Lewis reminds himself sternly: Seth could and might still take and pass the GED, still go to college. He's *twenty years old*. He could attend Columbia himself one day, and get the faculty-brat tuition waive, just like Lewis did.

Well, O.K., not Columbia. Lewis barely got over the threshold, after attending Horace Mann for a year and half and with back-channel negotiations on the part of Gerty and Virgil a full professor on the faculty. There would be no such family push behind Seth: what was left to burn of that bridge he torched on this recent visit of his to New York. In fact, he lit that match early, when he was four and sitting between Lewis and Abby in the audience of a graduation ceremony. As Virgil and the other professors began filing into the auditorium in their bright regalia, hoods and tams and robes and gold braids, Seth stood up and shouted joyfully, "Here come the clowns!" A story Abby loves to tell, of course, and which never fails to get a laugh. Lewis thought it would amuse the Chopiks at the dinner table in Cambridge his first summer there. It did not.

An arts college, maybe. Seth showed an active interest in that route a couple of years ago, flying into New York for National Portfolio Day, typically last-minute. Lewis had two midterms the next day, in German and Astronomy, and no time to waste making sure Seth was OK under the guise of showing him around, which is what Abby asked him to do. He was deliberately late to their rendezvous at the A/C/E stop on 14th Street, expecting Seth to have forgotten the time or blown it off. But there he stood, portfolio case propped against his legs. He was heavier due to a new drug regime and his jeans looked too tight but otherwise he seemed fine, functional. Having verified as much, Lewis was about to slip back down into the stairwell and blow it off himself when Seth saw him and, as if intuiting everything, raised his hand in heartbreakingly tentative greeting. Whereupon Lewis felt as shittily cold-hearted as he'd ever felt: he was going to become his cousins if he wasn't careful.

They wandered downtown through the West Village, with Lewis pointing out the occasional landmark but wishing they were in almost any other neighborhood: the West Village was so theme-parkishily genteel, not the New York he wanted to expose Seth to, having warmed to the idea of being Seth's tour guide. He thought of searing things he'd glimpsed when he first arrived: the young couple, robbed of everything, emerging like exiled Adam and Eve from Central Park with their hands over their crotches; the refined yet street-smart face of a young man framed by the upturned collar of his elegant coat in Union Square at dusk; the pair of teenaged black boys seen from a bus as they swaggered along 125th Street in the rain, bumping into people as they moved along the street with hoodies up and skull-and-crossbones in their eyes.

But Seth seemed perfectly awe-stricken with this tamer New York. After walking east on Bleeker for a while they sat on the stoop of a multi-million dollar brownstone and looked through his portfolio: posters he had made for his band, IED's, shows at places like Glenville Baptist Church talent show; ornate skate-punk scenes in black or blue ballpoint, so densely worked over that the paper seemed almost wet and heavy with ink, a few reworked to the point of abstraction. Would this impress the folks at Parsons and Pratt? Lewis had no idea. For something to say, he asked about the title of one of the abstractions, "Terminal B."

"We're condemned to be," Seth said as if it were obvious, "to exist: terminal B." They walked east on Bleeker, talked about Virgil and Abby, caught up like any other two brothers. Seth was behaving so socially appropriately that Lewis began to believe it might be possible for him follow through with this plan. This was also before the facial tat. His appearance was weird but acceptably, familiarly weird. Art schools in New York were full of guys like Seth, arriving from Oregon and Louisiana and Vermont with their skateboards and prescription bottles. Lewis allowed himself to imagine them as students together in the city, taking walks like this whenever they felt like it.

They paused in front of a small CD shop. A toddler boy, passing behind them, announced proudly to someone, "I made it—it's beautiful!"

Turning, Seth smiled at this. "He's got the right idea. He's taking radical responsibility."

It had the ring of one of Abby's catch phrases. "That's what I'm trying to do," Seth said. "Not blame the world for my experience of it, you know?" he asked, looking earnestly at Lewis, who said, "Sure, of course."

"I made the world," Seth said, gesturing at the street. "The world is me writ large."

"You made the world," Lewis said with what he hoped was gentle skepticism.

"In the sense of its subjective qualities," Seth said, "its *meaning*, yes."

"What about, I don't know," Lewis asked, "gravity? You made gravity?"

"What gravity *means to me*, yes," Seth insisted. He held up a hand, squinting into a band of sunlight that had suddenly appeared in the west. "See, what else matters besides what it *means?*"

"Hmm, I don't know," Lewis said lightly, braced now for a resurgence of the true Seth: prophet, guru, monster.

To his relief, Seth shrugged. "Me neither, really," he said. "It's just sort of a theory."

Lewis remembered that if they kept going to the end of Bleeker they would come to the Bowery and CBGB's, a punk landmark that would thrill Seth. He waited until they were within sight of it then turned Seth by the shoulders and pointed to it and watched his face light up. When they arrived in front of the humped awning, a bespectacled man was addressing a small group of what looked to Lewis like Euro tourists.

"Founded by Hilly Kristal in 1973," the tour guide was saying, "C-B-G-B—does anyone know what these letters stand for?"

"Country, Blue Grass and Blues," someone said in maybe a Dutch accent.

"You are correct!" said the guide. "OMFUG anyone?" That was what it said on the bottom half of the awning: OMFUG. If Seth were ever to know trivia, this was it. But Seth had stalked off down the street.

"What's up?" Lewis asked when he caught up to him. He was walking fast with his head down, as if in flight from a crime. "Seth, *what's up?*"

"I don't know," he said finally, glancing back up the Bowery. "The guy, the whole—" he waved his hand and strode on.

Lewis grabbed his arm and stopped him. "Talk to me."

"I just need to eat," Seth muttered, pulling away. Lewis led him into a narrow falafel joint and they ordered standing at the glass counter, Lewis watching Seth in the mirror behind the counter. Taking a bite of his sandwich when it was served up in a plastic basket, he seemed to recover himself. He sipped from a plastic cup of water, blinked, looked over at Lewis as if seeing him clearly again. How was school going, he asked. Lewis mentioned the midterms.

"Are you ready?" It was more than he'd ever asked Lewis about college.

"Not really," Lewis admitted.

Seth frowned. "So wait—shouldn't you be at the library or whatever?"

Lewis considered telling a white lie but then said, "Probably." If he left for the subway now he might be able to cram enough, staying up most of the night, to do okay.

Behind them, a man got up from a table and, going past, bumped hard into Seth. Lewis glared after the man and Seth touched his mouth and looked at his fingers as if checking for blood then followed the man out, holding the falafel in one hand like a stone. "Hey!" he called.

"Seth!" Lewis said quietly, catching up to him on the street. Bent forward in a leather jacket, the man walked quickly away. He either didn't hear or thought better of stopping. Seth trotted up the avenue after him, reared back as if to hurl the sandwich then turned and flung it into a wire mesh trashcan.

Lewis stood next to him. What happened to Seth's radical responsibility, not blaming the world? Or was throwing the sandwich into the trash the extent of it? The wind snatched at the wax wrapping paper and Seth, staring at it and shaking his head in a continuous, palsied way, finally plucked it out and let the wind blow it away down the street.

A month later he was in San Francisco with Candy.

So maybe it is too late for Seth. He'll never go to college, of any kind or caliber. Maybe it's always been too late. Is that so tragic? The main thing is he's alive, safe at home with his weed and his stoner disciple. For the moment, all is basically well. That's a lot. That's maybe everything.

Passing through matchstick blinds, sunlight prints lozenges of wavering striated gold on the floor. It's been holding Lewis's attention for a catatonically long beat. He seems to have gotten high just sitting here breathing the air, no big surprise there.

Now Donald goes by holding a cellphone to one ear and in a loud voice says, "Representative!"

Seth and Cody look at each other with expressions of painfully suppressed hilarity. Donald, down the hall now, can be heard saying, "Member!" which sends them over the edge. Watching them flop around on the couch, Lewis finds it contemptible rather than cause for relief and gratitude. They'll live at home; they'll never leave Wichita.

He goes to the kitchen and makes a cup of Earl Grey tea. Assuming Seth doesn't, in fact, explode or implode or whatever it is Stacy and Cody fear, Lewis will just have to get through a certain number of days like this one. He needs to snap out of his blues about V. and do something, get a job, study German. It eats at him that he was never able to read it comfortably. There's an essentials grammar in his book bag. He should go back to his room and open that to page one, begin again.

Abby comes in, shoulders her purse, searching around the kitchen and breakfast nook for her keys until she finds them in the purse. "I'm going out for groceries. Any requests?"

"More beer, I guess," he says. "And a bottle of Dewar's?" He'd like to have the option of going on a bender if in fact he can't snap out of the post-V. blues.

"Okay," Abby says blithely, jotting it on a Post-It. He could ask her to pick up an eight ball of cocaine and, assuming she had a source for it and the money, she probably wouldn't blink. People should be able to pursue whatever it is they want to explore.

"Oh, I just got off the phone with Astrid," she says. "You remember Astrid."

He does: yoga instructor, plain verging on homely but with a memorable, lithe body.

"When I told her you were back in town, she asked whether you would mind coming along to the Celebration we're having tonight—did I tell you about that?"

He searches his brain carefully lest he appear absent-minded and shakes his head.

"It came together rather quickly, which is what I love: how these things just *move into being*."

"Aren't they women-only?" he asks. "What's my role?"

"Well, they are, technically. Astrid's just having a little ex-boyfriend trouble."

Ex-Boyfriend Trouble: sounds like a band. "Meaning what?" he asks.

"It's just Astrid's feeling a little worried he'll show up and make a scene. He won't, of course. Really. You would just sit nearby, or at the bar, for her sake. Dinner on us. It's the best place in town."

"So I'd be, like, security?"

"I can ask Donald if you're uncomfortable with it."

"Right," he says, scoffing lightly, though he's not sure why: Donald's big enough for the gig. Assuming he's well-rested enough to be vigilant, given the sleep-eating. Does Abby know about that? He doesn't feel like getting into it.

"Fine," he says. "Sure." And feels a surge of sexual antici-pation: Astrid in his chivalric debt.

Abby thanks him warmly and heads out to go shopping.

Lewis drinks his tea looking out at the backyard. He forgot

to ask about her position on the weeds. At how many houses is that necessary? But they look for the moment, swaying in the wind, right and good.

15

On his way to his room and the green German grammar, Lewis looks in on Seth and Cody. Seth is fast-forwarding through the opening credits of a TIVO'd National Geographic Channel documentary about tornados. Beckoning to Lewis, he presses "play" at the appearance of an enormous soot-gray twister turning in slow-motion, chunks of black debris wheeling past in the foreground, then images of corn and wheat fields shot from above. "June 23rd, 1998," intones the fateful voice of the narrator. "The heart of the American Heartland."

"God's talking about *us*!" Seth calls, elbowing Cody along the couch. "Sit! Check this out!"

Lewis hesitates then sits down between them on the couch. Reenactment shots of a man in plaid shirt going about his rural chores.

"7:02 in the evening," says the narrator. "Farmer Arlen Wilke notices a dark cloud taking shape a few miles south of his farm."

Seth leans forward. "Yo, hurry the fuck up, Farmer Willie!" Lewis gets the impression they've watched this more than a few times.

"This guy's *dead*," Cody says, rubbing his hands together.

The farmer's voice says, "The sky didn't look right."

Cody and Seth cackle. "It didn't look right *because there was a fucking tornado about to touch down!*"

Wilke says, "And then we watched the tail come down and a tornado start. Someone suggested we grab a video camera."

"Uh, that would be Satan," Seth says and again the footage of the enormous soot-gray funnel cloud turning, two telephone poles and a small white house in the foreground.

"Growing in size and charging across nearby fields," the narrator says in his sonorous voice, "it seems to be heading for Wilke's home. He's lived in the area all his life and knows the dangers of Tornado Alley well. 'Please don't hit my place!'"

Snickering Cody and Seth, lean forward intently. Shot of Wilke beside cornfield. "You could really start to hear it roar. And it really got to be spinnin' faster and it really, really built in size. It just got huge."

"Some kind of *size queen*, this guy," Seth remarks and Cody titters, shifting around on the couch with embarrassment. Seth pats his inner thigh. "Yo, I got your huge tornado right down here, Farmer *Willie*."

Seth fast-forwards as if looking for something specific and there flashes a stuttering sequence of witnesses and survivors shot from the waist up then funnel clouds, whirling debris, aftermaths of ruin and destruction, over and over, like a kind of insanity.

"We ARE in Kansas anymore!" Seth says, switching off the TV, which goes black with a static-electric sigh. "This IS fucking Kansas."

He looks from Cody to Lewis. "Are you with me?"

"No," Lewis replies.

"God is right out there," Seth says, waving vaguely at the front door, the roof of the house. He stands up. "On your feet!"

Lewis stays pointedly put but Cody follows Seth through the living room. Then, rather than actually begin reviewing German, Lewis brings up the rear, curious to see what Seth will get up to.

The air outside is humid and close. Seth is standing in the front yard, which is shielded from the street by scraggly evergreen hedges, looking up, arms spread in a V. The sky over-head is clear but there are darkish clouds approaching from the southwest.

Backing out of his driveway, Oren brakes to stare frown-ingly, going on when Seth waves him over eagerly.

He then draws Lewis and Cody into a football huddle. "Close your eyes." He squeezes Lewis's neck with his arm. "Do it!" Lewis closes his eyes.

"I want you to *feel* a twister." He's silent for a beat. "Feel *cyclonic*." He squeezes Lewis's neck. "There's a doubter in our midst. Do you know who I mean, Cody?"

"It ain't me," Cody says.

Seth holds them in the huddle. The stench from Cody's mouth-breathing and blown-out Nike high-tops is only partly diffused by a breeze. Seth releases them, spreading his arms wide again.

"Now look up!" Overhead, blue sky. Seth watches for a moment then shrugs, undeterred. "I'll do a twister dance."

He begins whirling in place on one foot with his arms out then begins striding in widening circles bent at the waist, a mosh-pit step. "I have Indian blood!"

Cody looks for confirmation at Lewis, who shakes his head.

"Course I do," Seth says, beginning to sweat. He pauses to hawk up phlegm, which he spits into the hedges then resumes mosh dancing. "*I have Indian blood.* I do, you do, Cody does. I mean, please: *we are all Indians*, tribal, big dicks, war paint."

"Sounds good," Lewis says blandly.

"You just *forgot*," Seth says, flashing that volatile street-fighting light. "Forgot who you are. Forgot who your *shaman leader is*." Nodding, he jabs a thumb at his own chest.

"You, Lewis, *left the tribe!*" He points into distance. "Went *out there* and *believed* what the sick white cousins said about self and world. 'Is that so bad, really? That's just an education, isn't it?' Well, let's look at the evidence: you came back *weak* and *thin* and *white* as a cave salamander and your *bitch*—well, I'm not even going *there*."

He pauses as if to give Lewis a chance to react and Lewis reacts by showing no reaction and Seth resumes the mosh-pit dance. "Killing in the name of!" he sings. Rage Against the Machine. Their juvenile anthem. Cody plays the three hard licks on air guitar: DOOH-dooh-dooh!

"Now you do what they *told* you!" Seth wags his finger at Lewis as he goes around and seems more like a harmless prankster again. Cody plays the licks: DOOH-dooh-dooh! "Now you do what they *told* you!"

Seth points out storm clouds beginning to reach fingers across the sky over head. "Have to go down to the *base*ment in a minute!" Seth predicts in a sing-song told-ya-so voice.

They all sit on the stoop to watch the sky. Cody points to something on Seth's right hand. "What's that?" he asks as if both miffed and remiss for not knowing every mole and mark on Seth's body. He bends down and reads. "D - D - P."

"Dominicans Don't Play," Seth says, looking at it. "My homeboys gave me that. When we got popped they thought I was headed to Riker's too. I was sort of in their gang."

"Dude, did you get jumped in?" Cody asks with big eyes.

Seth pauses as if contemplating concocting a story for Cody's entertainment then says simply, "Nah, one of them just gave me the tat. Big Biz."

Cody squints at him. "Weren't you afraid of getting ass-raped in there?"

Seth makes a nonchalant moue. "Nah."

"Damn, I woulda been!"

"Ass-raped?" Seth says, looking with concern at Cody. "Repeatedly?"

"No, *afraid*!"

"Butt-raped until you *screamed with ecstasy*?"

"Fuck you, Seth!" Cody says, raising his fist. Seth rolls his eyes at this and Cody settles back as if he's defended his honor adequately. "Seriously, dude."

"What about your *new* tat?" Lewis says and Seth looks at Cody, who shakes his head emphatically: I didn't tell him anything!

"It's not ready to be revealed yet," Seth says.

"Sounds momentous," Lewis says.

"Tornado *Ally*," Seth says, snapping his fingers. "That's what Mom should call the company."

"Won't people just think it's a typo for 'alley'?" Lewis says.

"Just fag-ass English majors."

"Castañeda!" Cody says approvingly, catching the allusion. They high-five each other.

"You know, don't you," Lewis tells Cody, "Castañeda made all that stuff up, right?"

"Bullshit!" Cody cries but looks at Seth, who hesitates then nods and shrugs as if to say, Yes, but so what?

"It's fiction," Lewis says.

Cody sits frowningly digesting this information while Seth shakes his head disappointedly at Lewis for, in effect, ruining Christmas for Cody

"Well, it don't really matter," Cody concludes finally. "It's still some rad shit you can apply. Like the *stalking technique*? That's punk as fuck!"

"Of course it matters!" Lewis says. "The whole claim of those books is that there are actual wizards doing actual supernatural things. That's the basis for all the excitement. Otherwise, it's just fantasy, Dungeons and Dragons, and no one cares."

"Hey, a *lot* of people care about Dungeons and Dragons," Seth says. "More people care about Dungeons and Dragons and Castañeda than will *ever* care about Virgil or John Clarence the pig-fucking farm poet from the 17th Century. Now why is that?"

Lewis concentrates on Cody. "It's like: did Jesus really and truly rise from the dead or not?"

Seth holds up a hand. "I'll handle this, Cody."

"He totally did!" Cody says, eyes huge with outrage and belief.

"Cody, what did I just say?" Seth says, shaking his head, and is about to reply to Lewis when a volley of shouting male voices can be heard through the ajar front door. Seth gets up and dashes inside, in the direction of the kitchen.

16

I t's a strange scene. Donald is shakily spooning coffee from a filter in the Braun coffee maker back into a clear molded plastic container. Bishop is seated in a chair at the table in the breakfast nook, shaking his head, eyelids at half-mast, as if disappointed by a child's misbehavior.

Seth has taken up a wide martial-arts stance in the middle of the floor, looking from Donald to Bishop with an open-mouthed smile. "Yo, what the hell is *going on in here?*"

Donald goes on grimly spooning ground coffee back into the plastic container as if baling water.

On the floor between Bishop's legs is a large shopping bag filled with eye masks in cellophane sheathes. Bishop has a pair on, Lewis sees now, pushed back on his head like riding goggles. "I Don't Do Mornings" is printed in white script across it.

"Hey, someone tell me *some*thing!" Seth says, shoving Donald lightly.

"I simply came in to make a cup of coffee—" Bishop begins.

Wheeling around, Donald shouts, "You make yours OUT-SIDE!"

Seth slides over to block Donald's view of Bishop. "Whoa, whoa, *whoa!*"

Donald stands glaring past him at Bishop, face red, shoulders rising and falling with big breaths.

Seth pinches a sleeve of Donald's T-shirt and gives it a provocative tug. "You keep your voice *down* in my house, mister!"

Cody glances at Lewis: this is gonna be good!

To Donald Seth says, "Hear me? You keep it down in my house or I'll kick your ass to the curb. You're homeless. You're living in a Hefty bag, fat man."

"Oh, Donald's all right, Seth," Bishop says soothingly. "Right, Donald? Donald's just having some issues around territory today."

Donald has faced away from Seth, toward the counter again. He's picked up the spoon as if to resume ladling.

"I'm asking *do you hear me?*" Seth says, tapping the words out on Donald's back.

To prevent it all from blowing up into a brawl, Lewis grabs Seth by the biceps and drags him backwards but Seth hooks a foot around one of Lewis's ankles and they reel across the kitchen floor and crash through the swinging doors on the pantry, boxes and broom handles clattering down as Seth elbows Lewis hard in the chest and scrambles back out.

Donald is storming across the kitchen like a rampaging bear when Lewis emerges. He gives Seth a wide berth but forces Cody to jump aside to clear a path, going out through the door to the garage and flicking the door so that it slams shut then bounces back open, vibrating on its hinges.

Seth looks around. "Yo, was he *growling?*" He slaps his knee, wheezes out a laugh. "He was fucking *growling!*"

"Dude, I was almost roadkill!" Cody says. He opens the door after a moment and peers out into the garage, pulls the door closed, locks it.

As if on second thought, Cody unlocks the door, opens it and trots out into the garage and on into the driveway, the low-slung jeans forcing him to scuttle like the man fleeing the exploded outhouse. Turning up toward the street, he disappears from view.

"Bishop!" Seth says. "What the hell—"

Bishop plucks a pair of eye masks from the bag and fiddles with the strap. "We can work this out," he says.

"Yeah?" Seth says, delightedly unconvinced.

"We do have an agreement," Bishop says with less assurance.

Cody scuttles back inside and closes the door behind him. "Think he went to get a gun?" he asks Seth, who rolls his eyes.

"There's stuff he could use right there in the damn garage," Cody tells Lewis. "There's a ax and some gnarly *prunin' shears* and big-ass framin' hammer."

Seth says, "The man seems pretty upset by your very *existence*, dude."

"Word, Bishop!" Cody chimes in. "Your, like, whole *right to exist* is being questioned, son!"

Bishop closes his eyes, composing himself. He sighs, giggles with embarrassment, looks at the floor, shakes his head. I'm sixty years old, Lewis hears him thinking. What am I doing? "God."

Lewis has been warily waiting for Seth to take some sort of shot, verbal or physical, for his interference in the disciplining of Donald. But with an air of having lost interest in the whole affair, Seth opens the refrigerator and fishes out a loaf of banana bread. He unwraps the cellophane, breaks off a hunk and tosses it to Cody, who catches it like a seal clapping and jams it into his mouth.

"So hey, Seth," Bishop says, tidying up his sack of eye masks. Bishop's hands are shaking, Lewis notices. He would like to move on, pretend what's just happened is already behind him but hasn't recovered from it yet. "We need to get you into the clinic for your *physical*."

Seth sniffs the banana bread and stares in a hooded, unreadable way at Bishop, who smiles his mischievous eyebrow-waggling psychonaut smile, scrubs at his white beard excitedly with one hand. "I talked to Jesse about maybe *leaving out the blocker* for one session? Pure DMT for Seth!"

The door to the garage flies open, banging against the wall and startling everyone, even Seth, who flinches.

But it's not raging-bull Donald, it's Abby, struggling in with grocery bags in each hand, her face lighting up with pleasure at the sight of so many of "her boys" gathered in the kitchen. "Hello!" she greets them.

"Gosh, you think this might be *the one*?" Seth says to Bishop, ignoring her. "The *ultimate ride* in the amusement park?"

Bishop squints in bemusement at the scorn, smiles as if Seth is surely pulling his leg, ceases smiling. Unpacking one of the bags, Abby is following the exchange with a serious expression.

"May*be*," Bishop says, adding, almost pleadingly, "I mean, my God, it's the most powerful psychedelic known to man—"

"Nah," Seth says, to Lewis's surprise, shaking his head decisively. "Count me out."

Bishop's face falls. "You don't want to participate?" It's as if the whole worth of the project were riding on his being able to give Seth this supernal drug experience, to hear Seth's report, to debrief him.

Seth drops his half-eaten hunk of banana bread through the hinged white plastic lid of the tall trash can. "Right, I *don't want to do the study*, Bishop."

"May I ask why not?" Bishop asks.

"Bishop!" Abby says. "You know I was never overjoyed about it."

Overjoyed? Lewis thinks. Why didn't she forbid it? Then he remembers that you don't forbid Seth things. You either kick him out or lock him up.

Holding up his palms to signal reasonableness, Bishop says, "I just wanted to hear Seth's thoughts on the matter."

"Sounded to me like arm-twisting," Abby says, resuming her unpacking of the grocery bag.

"My thoughts?" Seth says. "I've seen enough." He lets that sink in. He shrugs, turns down the corners of his mouth. He can't think of a better word: "*Enough*," he says again.

Bishop inclines his head, nodding respectfully as if to say, "Okay, that's acceptable. I've felt that way myself from time to time; many psychonauts have. It's a place we all come to."

At some point, Stacy has driven her wheelchair up the ramp to the threshold of the kitchen and is listening to Seth with an alert, fawn-like expression.

"Been down enough rabbit holes," Seth says, taking backwards steps toward the dining room. "Had enough 'visions' and 'experiences,'" he says, hooking his fingers into quotes. He pauses to look around the room as if including everyone there under the category: they are inextricably part of this pathetic, substandard realm or reality he has had the misfortune to find himself marooned in.

With that, he turns and walks out of the kitchen, followed by Cody, looking in his low-slung jeans like some royal dwarf out of Velazquez.

Stacy rolls forward into the house then stops and hits a switch and reverses nimbly down the ramp and leaves without a word.

Lewis and Abby and Bishop look each at a different part of the kitchen in silence. Now the sound of the stereo in Seth's room comes on, the undertones of the music reaching across the house in jagged strokes, like the needle of an EKG.

17

T heir heads bowed and close together, Abby and Bishop
walk slowly back into the rear of the house with an air
of high moral purpose. "I'm sorry, but I don't see what
that has to do with running out of coffee filters," Abby says.

"You're skipping a step," Bishop replies, his voice fading as
they move away. "The extension cord I use . . . "

Left alone in the kitchen, Lewis lets out his breath and sits
at the table for a while.

Then he gets up and washes his face and hands at the
kitchen sink. Throwing out the paper towel, he sees the trash
is full. He ties off the bag and hauls it out through the garage
to the plastic containers in the stall just inside the gate of the
fence to the backyard.

As he's pushing the full bag down on top of another, the
dying light in the gateway is eclipsed and he looks up to find
Donald standing there, breathing hard. His T-shirt is soaked
with sweat at the armpits and neckline and he exudes unpleasant, pheromonal heat and cologne-tinged funk.

"Hi!" Lewis says with forced, casual cheerfulness.
Influenced by Cody's catalogue of possible weaponry, he's
relieved that Donald doesn't seem to have, say, a hatchet pur-
chased at the local hardware store. Still, he's like a psychiatrist
greeting an inmate who's reappeared at the asylum gates after
running away: handle with care.

Looking on the verge of heatstroke, Donald holds up a finger to signal that he needs to catch his breath. Lewis wonders

what to do in case of heart attack: go in and call 911. Waiting for Donald to speak or keel over, Lewis pushes down unnecessarily on the trash bag to give himself something to do,

Having recovered enough to speak, he says, "I want to apologize for my behavior earlier," Donald says finally.

"Oh, that's OK," Lewis says, pushing down unnecessarily on the bag of trash to give himself something to do.

"No," Donald says with a quick, obstinate shake of his massive head, reversing the power dynamic: *Lewis* won't be let off the hook so easily.

"I was out of line," he insists with an Eagle Scout sort of dutifulness.

"Fine," Lewis says, smiling. "Apology accepted."

He's turning to go when Donald says, "Took a long walk." He purses his lips and nods like a man in a life-insurance commercial who's come to some sage, silvery conclusion.

Halting out of politeness to hear the rest, Lewis thinks again about how much better Abby could do. Why the attraction to these primitives? And how many more of them, with their quirks and colognes and bathrobes, their pedestrian "insights" and "breakthroughs," must Lewis get to know?

"Walking helps when I need to get some 'inner alignment,' as your mother calls it." He folds his thick, repellently furry arms across his chest and nods back toward the street. "Down Linden, I think it is," he says. Like Lewis gives a shit which street it was; Lewis is keeping a journal in which he details Donald's movements, his setbacks and revelations.

"When I was coming back up the hill there on the third or fourth go round, my right knee started acting up. Doctor says I'll need surgery eventually, maybe even a replacement, but I'm going to try some non-Western approaches first."

If Lewis had a watch on he would glance at it right now.

Donald pauses, shakes his head. "Truth is I barely noticed," he says quietly, "*I was just so damn angry!*" He bites his lower lip and holds up a finger again. "I said I was trying to get 'aligned.' Once I got what I *thought of* as aligned, I went on an inner 'fact-finding mission.' Do you want to know what I found out?"

Lewis actually shakes his head: not at all, no interest, zero.

"Fact," Donald says, either oblivious to Lewis's shake of the head or too needy of an audience to acknowledge it. "I live with your mother most of the week; that doesn't necessarily make me the man of the house, but I *resent* your little brother trying to tell me I'm NOT the man of the house. He *put his hands on me*, your brother did, and I don't tolerate that! I want you to tell him that."

"No, no way," Lewis says firmly. "If you have something to say to Seth, *tell him yourself*, Donald." And good luck with that.

"Okay, fine," Donald says, holding up his large fleshy hands. "Fair enough. But here are a few more facts for your consideration."

Lewis takes a step backward, toward the rear of the house. He'll take refuge in the weeds. "Donald, you know what—"

"*Fact*: your mother has decided to let Bishop live in a tent in the yard and have a 'polyamorous' relationship with her. *Fact*: I don't like it. *Fact*: I'm going to try to *deal* with it because I was dumb enough to give it my *blessing*."

He reaches out a hand to make sure Lewis doesn't slip away before he's had a chance to explain. "The *reason* I gave my blessing—I'm so embarrassed about this now I can barely bring myself to say it. Okay, the reason I gave my blessing is we all took Ecstasy one night and I got so damn lovey-dovey on that crap that I *agreed* to it!"

He looks at Lewis through squinty eyes, nodding shrewdly as if to say, *Now* I've got your attention. "He made the stuff we took that night, Bishop did. Calls himself an 'alchemist,' the arrogant SOB Pardon my French abbreviation. Thing is, I was stupid enough to take it, some drug he cooked up wherever he does it. I'd had a few glasses of wine, like I say. Bishop comes out with this little jeweled box. Turns out it was a great experience, don't get me wrong. Fantastic experience. But you just can't live up to what you feel on that stuff. Well, maybe your mother and Bishop can, but *I* can't." He laughs bitterly. "'The Goddess,' he calls her. How the hell do you compete with *that?*"

Suddenly they're standing in the midst of a blizzard: fibrous white puffs drift through the air.

"You know, we ran into each other last night," Lewis says. "In the kitchen. Do you remember that?"

Donald frowns. "What?"

"You were making microwave popcorn."

"This is a dream you had?"

"We were really there. Seth too."

"No," Donald says decisively, as if Lewis must have confused him with someone else. "I can't eat popcorn," Donald says. "It doesn't agree with me."

The fibrous fuzz blizzard intensifies.

"Are you taking some kind of medication maybe? I've heard Ambien can cause people to sleep-eat."

"Cottonwood fuzz," Donald says, waving a hand in front of his face. They stand there dazed by the soothing motion. Gradually the air clears.

Donald stoops and turns on the spigot and picks up the hose and runs water over his forearms, cooling himself down, rinsing away stray spores.

"I could screw him with one phone call," he says musingly, reaching up to remove a tuft from Lewis's beard in a tender, simian gesture. "One damn phone call."

18

Gar, the restaurant chosen for the Birthday Party celebration, is in a new mall on the far west side of town.
Standing on line out front with Abby, Lewis gingerly
prods his breastbone, which is bruised where Seth elbowed
him in the pantry. It's 8:30 but the setting sun burns at the
ruled-edge bottom of a cloudless sky, flares on the stems of
sunglasses and the clunky rearview mirrors of the SUV's
parked in the unshaded lot: feeding hour on an incandescent
planet.

"They specialize in lake fish from Minnesota," Abby says.
"It's flash-frozen and flown in daily to preserve the original
blandness," she adds then laughs at Lewis's taken-aback
expression. The middle-aged man ahead of them in the longish
line, his cheeks waxily closely shaven in the Middle Western
manner, turns partially around at the remark: startled blue
eyes.

"Just wanted to make sure my son was listening," Abby tells
him with a wink, touching the man's elbow. He chuckles and
his date or wife glances back to get a look at Abby, who's wearing a silky blue wraparound vintage designer dress she bought
on Ebay and black high-heeled shoes. Possible polyamorous
addition? Lewis wonders whether Abby sees everyone that
way now.

She's in high spirits: the revised storm-chase website was no
sooner up than a group of three lesbian couples from Oregon,
all friends, booked Grateful Gaia tours for next week. She's

also looking forward to the Birthday Party celebration: fine dining as subversion of patriarchal exchange value. But for most of the drive across town to the restaurant she was on her cell to a regional polyamory person in Kansas City and now Lewis listens to her thoughts on the massage-oil incident and the confrontation between Donald and Bishop as interpreted by the polyamory "expert." Lewis says nothing about bumping into Donald in the trash-can stall and what Donald had to say, partly to keep from adding another layer to things for Abby to parse, partly out of reluctance to bandy the family's *Ecstasy use* in public. Abby turns to thinking aloud about Seth's role in today's conflict, his possible reasons for not wanting to take part in the DMT study, how annoyed she was at Bishop for suggesting it to begin with, how relieved she is Seth's decided against it. Could he have had his fill of psychedelics? Or is he depressed? Or manic? She's lowered her voice somewhat but it's still pricking up the ears of more than one stoically waiting Wichitan. Lewis tries to join her in not caring.

"So what's this guy look like?" he asks as the hostess leads them to the Birthday Party table. He scans the large dining room, the booths, the large front area, the smaller back room.

"Who, honey?" Abby asks distractedly, waving festively to her friends.

"Astrid's ex? The *reason I'm here?*"

"Oh, God. Sorry!" She wrinkles her nose apologetically. "He's actually sort of horrendously *average*—height-and weight-wise. I don't know: even features. Short brown hair."

"Great, I'll just waylay half the guys in here," Lewis says.

"He's *not even going to show*," she assures him sotto voce as they arrive at the table. The first person he sees is, to his surprise, Tori. She bats her eyes at him like a Betty Boop raptor and waves by fiddling her fingers as if she's greeting his crotch, which stirs as if responding to a faint but real signal. She and Seth must have found a way to come up with the entry fee—an extra shift at the peep show. And Abby is proving how big she is by including (and thereby probably bringing into line?) a rival.

Abby introduces Lewis with glittery-eyed pride, hands on his shoulders: this is my son Lewis, our secret-service detail tonight, who just graduated from Columbia but won't, thank God! be following in the footsteps of his academic father and father's family!

She then introduces the women: Gene and Joe, a couple, one of whom—Lewis immediately forgets which is which—wears a sling in which a barely visible infant sleeps. Gene and Joe are somewhat less than delighted to make Lewis's acquaintance (is there *no occasion* free of men or the need for men?). Then there's Louise, an older woman with thick white braids who looks like a kindly primatologist and who has, Abby tells him, just completed an apprenticeship to a Mongolian shaman or *buu*.

"Ah," Lewis says with polite appreciation but wondering about the wisdom of this trend, the invocation of spirits which, assuming they exist, could be demonic for all the well-meaning Louises of the world know.

And here's Astrid herself, gazing up under wrinkled brows as if into bright light. "You're so thin!" she cries in a concerned, possibly disappointed, voice, and gets up to hug him tightly against her arousingly firm curves, whispering, "*Thank you* for doing this for me."

This interlude causes Tori to sit up slightly in her chair as if made sexually competitive but Lewis may be imagining this. Beside each place setting is a small flattish brightly wrapped packet—the cash, no doubt, twenty-five grand in total. He wonders which of them is leaving with it.

Abby walks him to the table after some confusion and the last-second redirection of people who were about to be seated there. It's in a separate section and there's a low partition of fogged glass between the areas but once she's returned to the Birthday Party table Lewis can see she blurred blond halo of her head in his peripheral vision if he sits up straight. He also has a view of the front door and the main dining area, should Astrid's ex come striding in after all. Waving a gun. Then what? They all die.

The waitstaff uniform is blue Oxford shirts, dark slacks, kelly-green aprons with enormous deep pockets. Maybe he'll apply for a job here. An Oxford shirt being as close to Oxford as he'll ever get now. He may not need the money but the more he's out of the house and the daily dramas there, the better, that's obvious. He'll work double shifts for a month, two months, then hit the road.

From his pert, slightly snouty young waitress, who has the body of a springboard diver or gymnast, he orders a pint of Sam Adams, crab cake appetizer, trout entrée. At which point, dining alone, he would normally read something but he didn't bring a book and anyway feels duty-bound to keep a weather eye on the entrance lest Astrid's ex slip by, camouflaged in his averageness. Fantasizing vaguely about the pert waitress and the athletic things they'll do in the hot summer nights once he's on staff here, he sips his water then his beer when it arrives.

The hostess leads a group of twenty something guys wearing what must be softball jerseys to the benches of a long table. Underdressed for this restaurant, which is high-end for Wichita, but no one seems to notice or care. A cheer goes up from the Birthday Party women and a waitress hustles past in that direction bearing a bottle of champagne. Lewis's crab cake arrives scribbled with orange sauce and he orders a second Sam Adams: no reason he can't catch a beer buzz on duty.

Pitchers from the micro-brewery are served to the softball players, a couple of whom look familiar, as if they might have been on the football team with him, but it's hard to say from across the room. He finds himself envying their camaraderie while being sunk more deeply into his isolation by it. It was like this when he arrived from Austin in the tenth grade. The high school was huge but the cliques had known each other since kindergarten and no one, with the exception of a few social outcasts and the coaches, always on the lookout for fresh meat, showed any interest in Lewis. Meanwhile, skate-punk Seth was attracting all the wrong sort of attention in middle school. Seth never dug himself out of marginality, or cared to, whereas Lewis, once established on the football team, found himself welcomed into the heart of things. And if he'd finished school in Wichita instead of accepting Virgil's invitation to come to New York, if he'd gone to Kansas University with most every-one else and come back to town and gotten a job in real estate or construction management or corporate sales, he'd have a place at the softball table.

Which would be worth what? To Virgil and the Chopiks, little or nothing, less than nothing: an average life, unachieved, lived out in the service of Mammon and mediocrity. To Abby, it wouldn't, it doesn't, matter in the least where he lives, what he "does." All she wants is for Lewis to be happy. That's what she's always said and he's never for a second doubted her sin-cerity. She's certainly never pressured him to do anything—to the contrary, she failed to apply *enough* pressure when it came to school; he was under-cultivated until they got hold of him at Horace Mann. But he suspects Abby harbors a grander fantasy for him, some ideal she'd like to see him become but won't admit to for fear of annoying or alienating him—a best-selling New Age prophet like Eckhart Tolle, who makes regular appear-ances on Oprah and would install her in a sprawling "family compound" in Big Sur or Santa Barbara. That's pretty close to the mark, Lewis bets, Eckhart Tolle or Deepak Chopra, Pema Chödrön. Because if she wants him to be happy, wouldn't it be great if he were *famously happy*, able to lead millions of people to happiness (and make millions doing it)? Imagine the

Birthday Parties then! The anted-up "gifts" wouldn't be five thousand, they would be more like a hundred thousand and her circle of friends, the women around the table, would include Nicole Kidman and Shirley McClain. And they wouldn't be worried about a pesky ex-boyfriend in some forgettable restaurant in Wichita; they would celebrate in lavish private residences or if in a restaurant one they owned, and there would be bodyguards wearing Armani turtlenecks stationed discreetly throughout for their peace of mind. And they would have a patent on the organic salad dressing served there, and on and synergistically on. Bling, flash, living large. Abby has no "resistance," as she would say, to the Big Time, to wealth and fame, flashbulbs on the red carpet of celebrity.

But short of a multi-millionaire happiness guru, a New Age circuit-touring intellectual would be fine, someone like Leonard Shlain, whose *The Alphabet Versus the Goddess* was Abby's Bible for a while.

One of the softball players heads for the men's room, passing close enough to be ID'd. Sure enough, it's a former teammate. Lewis used to know his name. He was second or third-string, specialty teams. Dark hair, olive complexion, unsmiling, conservative bearing, conservative core. He wears the same Beatles bangs adopted hereabouts circa 1974. Lewis remembers his vaguely embittered air: he was, he is, somehow failing to get his due. He may have recognized Lewis too, under the beard, not that he would ever let on or stop and say hello. Lewis who was on the verge of quitting the team out of flagging interest when he was given a starting position on defense, and no sooner had the position than he transferred to Horace Mann, which no one here had heard of, Lewis included.

There was another Lewis, so they called him "Lewis de Kansas," which became "LDK" then "El Decay." Most would barely have made the JV squad in Wichita but they read Thoreau on the bus to the game against Fieldston or Hackley or Kingsley-Oxford, these preppily opaque names that shed their strangeness with surprising quickness. Clear "Eastern seaboard" skies, manicured fields lit by enormous banks of lights and jolly alum in expensive clothes to whom he was pointed out like a new stallion being led down a ramp. Which was funny to Lewis, given how many there were like him in Kansas and Texas and Colorado, back in football country. But here on this small team that was happy if it won a game now and then, his playing meant something and he took pleasure in it again: he had fun.

His trout arrives, fried. He eats half and orders another beer when the waitress takes his plate away.

Lewis goes to the men's room and stands pissing for a small beer eternity. The brand of the automatic urinal is Self-Flush. It's the sort of thing Seth might call one of his bands.

He slows his steps at the sight of Seth sitting at his table. If the softball players are underdressed, how Seth got past the hostess in his torn jeans and sneakers and sleeveless T-shirt is a mystery. He must have slipped in through some back or side door.

But given the big bleak exit from the kitchen, the Seth day seemed so definitively over. Assuming there are days and nights in Seth Land. Because Cody and Stacy are right, Lewis can sense it now too: Seth is on the verge and Abby can not worry all she likes: it's coming. At least the glower is gone. Seth is looking, for the moment anyway, merely pranksterish. And in his usual helpless way, Lewis is, despite the foreboding, glad to see him.

Detecting this, Seth, who's been draining Lewis's pint glass, launches into a caught-in-the-act pantomime: sets down the glass with wide eyes, hastily wipes his lips with the back of his hand, half rises from his chair as if to steal away.

Lewis moves the table's other chair around to the side and sits so that he can keep an eye on the entrance and Seth flags down a random passing waitress and jabs at the pint glass with forked fingers. "Yo, Miss: two more of the same here? Put it on the tab of the Birthday Party table."

"Oops!" Seth claps a hand over his mouth. "Shouldn't've of said—" he hisses in a whisper—"*Birthday Party!*"

The waitress stands there looking mystified and annoyed.

"Just put it on my bill," Lewis says. He sits up straight and tries without success to catch Abby's eye.

"Rewind and delete, Miss!" Seth calls after the waitress. "The top-secret-*illegal* part!" He turns to Lewis. "Thought you might need some back-up, boss."

"Not that the guy's even going to show up," Lewis says coolly. "According to Abby." He's going to act as if it's no big deal that Seth has popped up here. Because, from a certain angle, it's *not* a big deal. And because what's the alternative.

"Better not!" Seth says too loudly, grasping the edge of the table and glaring around the room. "Coupla crazy knuckleheads waitin' in ambush for his ass!"

"Keep it down a bit," Lewis warns him.

"But yeah," he says, sitting back now, "what it was really is I was drawn by the special radiance of the ladies and their *free money*. Are you down with *free*, Lewis?"

"No," Lewis says. "And lower your voice: I'm sitting right here."

"Cause it's *all one*, bro," Seth says in a slightly more modulated tone. "Free love, free money. One big happy *freedom*. Feel me?"

He gets up restlessly and strides in his feral, mosh-pit fashion over to the Birthday Table, where he greets everyone, taking them by surprise too, causing a stir Lewis is too far from to gauge the nature of. How long before he's kicked out? Could he even end up getting Abby and her Ponzi scheme ladies busted? Lewis watches nervously for signs of alerted authorities but sees nothing so far. It's also the peak of busyness and in the rush Seth is maybe less obvious than he would be otherwise.

Now he returns to Lewis's table and sits down as the beers are set before them by a different waitress. "I asked them if they thought I should get an iPhone?" Seth says, putting a miffed face. "Didn't know what I was *talking* about."

What *is* he talking about with that? Beyond spoofing someone he's not naming?

Seth raises a pint to drink and stops. Lewis follows his gaze: pale windbreaker, white slacks, running shoes, slight frown.

"Dude, that's him!" Seth says through his teeth, peering under his wrinkled brow. The man has crossed the main dining area and is headed toward the Birthday Party section. "You *sure?*" Lewis asks.

"I met him at the house!" Seth whispers. They both stand up.

Lewis comes up from the side and stops the man by gripping his arm just above the elbow. In a low voice he says, "Yo, can I help you?" Lewis makes a point of never saying "Yo," it just comes out.

Frowning, the man stops and half turns to face Lewis. Lewis feels the curious eyes of diners all around, a general air of forks arrested mid-arc. A busboy, actually a grown man, probably Mexican, has paused in the unfolding of a service tray to look over with nervous concern.

Either it's the ex and he was not expecting any such interference or it's not the ex and he's innocently surprised to find himself accosted. Lewis glances past him at Abby, who's frowning with wide-eyed alarm and vigorously shaking her head.

Lewis lets go of the arm. "Sorry!" he says, smiling ingratiatingly, glancing around for Seth.

But Seth has disappeared.

19

A full moon, tinted orange, hangs in the clear sky. To Lewis, slouched in the passenger seat, it seems to be drawing the Escalade forward on an invisible cord: *umbilicus lunus invisibilis*, he's pretty sure. What he is is pretty drunk.

He wound up at the Birthday Party table, where his mistaken accosting of the man in the windbreaker was hailed as heroic, even by Gene and Joe. More champagne was ordered and he forgot about having been punked or pranked by Seth. When Tori went missing, Lewis figured she must have gone home or out or slipped off to be with Seth but her tacky blue purse still hung from her chair by its gold chain.

He spotted her signaling to him by the ladies room. She led him down a hallway past a busboy station and into a large closet or changing room. He expected an offer of coke but she kicked the door shut and put her hands against the wall on either side of his head and performed a drawn-out, serpentine grind along his length of his torso, mashing her augmented boobs against him, spun slowly, bent slightly forward at the waist, and rubbed her high hard ass against his crotch, swung around to face him and flicked at his lips with her tongue. He was getting a lap dance. Victoria so strongly disapproved of strip clubs ("Look a 'Gentleman's Club!'" she sneered when they drove by a billboard advertising one) that Lewis, uxoriously renouncing them in his heart, never expected he would get one but had always been secretly curious. Now he knew: it was great. What a fabulous fuck-you to Victoria and her prudery and hypocrisy. But what about Seth? His pimpish pretensions notwithstanding, would he be OK with this? Was he going to pop out of the woodwork here too?

His qualms were no match for Tori's technique. Still, he managed to say, "What's all this?"

"I'm just feeling . . . " she unbuttoned his pants and ran her hand down into his underwear " . . . grateful."

"For what?" He barely got the words out.

"Also, the whole brother thing," she said, working away with a kind of detached expertise, "makes me hot."

She chuckled huskily at the end and left him leaning against the wall like a stored prop. When he got back to the table by way of a trip to the men's room, Tori had taken her purse and gone.

In the parking lot, Astrid gave him a long erotic hug, promising to have him over for a massage as barter payment for his "warrior services."

"The now," Lewis says, staring at the moon, playing Eckhart Tolle.

"What about it?" Abby asks, pleasantly startled.

"Just trying it on," he says. "Do you know how easily I could impersonate a wise man? Make us a lot of money."

"Right," Abby says and laughs. She had one or two glasses of champagne. She has some built-in moderating force. He's never seen her drunk, never seen her do anything to excess. Lewis, on the other hand, could become an alcoholic without much effort. He's been having blackouts more often since the breakup with V. He should go on the wagon but is if anything inclined to drink more.

"Anyway, Eckhart Tolle is a lightweight," he says. He has only a passing, secondhand acquaintance with Tolle's trip, things Abby has told him about, but so what. "His ideas are simpleminded."

"Simplicity is the key," Abby says, taking him more seriously than he deserves. "It's simple."

"*What's* simple?"

"That's the question," she says. "The answer's always changing, isn't it?" She seems to sink back into her thoughts.

"I guess," Lewis says. His mother loves him but he doesn't interest her; he's always been too easy, too deeply conventional in his essence to be compelling, like Virgil. But he's not Virgil. Strange things happen to him, have happened to him. Like what? Like Tori giving him a lap dance in the janitor's closet.

Or what about the night Sylvie came into his room?

He'd sensed something different in the air and looked around from his computer to find her there, her face distraught. He thought someone might have died. It was two in the morning. Virgil was out of town at a conference. Had Virgil died? "*What's up?*" he said.

As she came toward him, he saw the syringe in her hand, for the briefest flash convinced she was going to attack him with it, she was flipping out because she wasn't getting pregnant. No one had said anything to him but he knew about the fertility treatments: mysterious vials in the fridge, red plastic "sharps" disposal receptacle in the cabinet above the coffee.

She let out a half-stifled sob and said, "I need help." She held out the syringe and he took it: the needle was long. "Here," she said, turning around and pulling down her jeans and her blouse up. Then she took the blouse off altogether. There was a small circle drawn in black Sharpie ink in the small of her back.

She looked back over her shoulder and pinched the flesh there and said, "Push it in all the way. Then pull back on the plunger slightly. If you see blood, stop and tell me. If you see no blood, inject me."

"Wait, what?" She explained it again, turning around in her bra to show him how to hold the needle.

But he's not going to tell Abby that story. It's too personal; it would be a betrayal. More recently there was another visit to his room. He was listening to music on his computer and looked around to see her standing in the doorway. She'd moved out but kept a set of keys, dropped by to pick up books now and again, when she knew Virgil wouldn't be home. Lewis tapped the volume key to bring it down.

She said, "I'm sorry I won't be able to come to see you graduate."

"I understand," he said, smiling in a way meant to make her feel better but not to diminish the importance of her attending the ceremony.

"Yes, well," she said, rocking her head side to side in the French way. "You understand a great deal," she added.

He shrugged, not knowing what to say in reply and took an automatic sip from the glass of red wine on his desk, even though he was at this point, having been partying since early afternoon, fairly sloshed.

"You understood, above all, how to resist your father's will," Sylvie said. "That's not easy to do; he has a formidable will, Virgil." She flashed a bitter smile, her puffy upper lip pulling back to reveal a gleam of slightly crooked front teeth. Maybe she'd been drinking too; there were parties everywhere on campus, in the bars along Amsterdam and Broadway. She ran with a relatively decadent crew of Euro grad students and junior faculty, occasionally went clubbing till past dawn without Virgil, who tolerated the tradition. "But yours was more resolute even than the great Virgil's. Impressive, bravo!" She clapped her hands slowly a few times.

She said more quietly and seriously then, "He has high hopes for you even so. Don't throw away your gifts just in order to foil him. Please. Think about that."

Lewis promised he would think about it. Assuming he

remembered any of this. He was just waiting for her to go at that point so that he could fall into bed and pass out.

"I have never given you any advice of this sort, have I?" she asked.

"Nope," he said. Why start now?

"So permit me a bit of stepmotherly meddling, just as I'm casting off this status of stepmother. I'm leaving soon; you're leaving soon. We may not see each other again. I don't mean to be melodramatic. But I didn't want to say nothing, in the tradition of your dear father, to act as if it was all nothing and poof! One disappears." She made a hand-washing gesture and smiled the bitter little smile. "You are not like that."

"No," he agreed reflexively, though he had no idea how he would behave in the midst of a divorce. He was going through a minor-key divorce of his own but Sylvie had barely noticed that, not that he blamed her.

"Virgil," she said, "is able to forget, to plunge into his new project. That's obvious. I envy that. I find, now that I am being tested, that in fact I cannot 'throw myself into my work.' I suppose I'll never amount to much, I won't *produce, produce, produce* no matter what. I won't work harder *because* I'm miserable. I cannot hide from my feelings. I cannot disappear from the scene of my own life, like your father." She paused and said, "May I?" Meaning enter the room.

"Of course," Lewis said, rising from his desk chair. There was another chair but it was barely discernible under a week's worth of his dirty clothes.

"No, stay. I can sit here." She sat on the edge of his bed, looking down at the carpet. Low-cut summer dress, cleavage, lovely bare legs. She took a deep breath and let it out and looked up at him sadly, which relaxed her face and made it more attractive.

"But I don't mean to bore you with my misery." Her eyes filled with tears. "It's such a cliché, I suppose. Ah, I hate this!"

she said impatiently, swiping at her cheek. She took a moment to compose herself then said, "I actually just wanted to thank you. For your help. Can you accept my thanks?"

Lewis took another automatic sip of wine. "Sure, of course."

She looked down at the carpet. "You were always terribly—*restrained* with me, when I came to you for help with my little 'problem.' But also in other ways, in general. I mean it's obvious why, that's no mystery. It was the right thing to do, certainly. But it must have been difficult, too, maintaining this stance, wearisome. No?" She looked up at him then down at the carpet again. "I admire it, I do. Even so, in *your position*, I'm not sure *I* would have behaved so admirably. I don't think so. No, I'm sure of that. I am not so good a person."

She looked up at him again, held his gaze. "But perhaps it's not a question of good. Perhaps it's a question of the intensity of one's feelings. Perhaps the so-called 'good people' simply don't struggle against powerful currents of desire. But I don't think that's actually the case with you, that you feel less. Still, you never took advantage of my situation, my weakness. How did you do that? You don't need to answer that. That's unfair. *But all that, c'est fini, tu sais?* The situation is completely changed now. And all the effort of keeping up the wall, the wall of 'family,'" she says with a sneer. "All that effort can be abandoned now. Let go. We can be as just two people now; what a relief that is, no? Do you feel the relief I mean? Lewis?"

He looked away and in looking away, forgot the rest. They say if you can't remember it, you did it. But he woke up the next morning with his clothes on.

What he likes is that they might have. What he likes is that something so unexpected happened. It has the flavor of actual life, the life that's not supposed to happen and that therefore has the force of truth, which it lends to the rest.

"Something happened between me and Sylvie," he hears himself tell Abby. He can sense her perking up: he's interesting now. "Right before I left. I'm not sure how to, you know, feel about it."

She glances over and asks in her matter-of-fact, Kinseyian manner, "You had sex?"

He twirls a lock of his beard. "We may have."

"*May* have?" she says.

"I was sort of drunk." He's sort of drunk now, he reminds himself. Maybe he should shut up. "I blacked out part of it. I've been having blackouts when I drink."

"Which part?" Abby asks with a giggle.

"I think I need to watch the drinking," he says. Or is he fabricating a problem in order to blink more brightly on her radar screen? At this mini-confession, she makes a neutral, if-you-say-so noise. "The weird thing is I don't feel totally guilt-ridden," he says.

"About the drinking or the sex with Sylvie?"

"The sex with Sylvie." He rakes his beard forward.

"Why should you?"

"Come on." He wants her to find it at least a little dark and sinful. "She's Dad's wife."

"*Was* his wife."

"They're still married."

"From what you were saying, it's been over for a long time."

"Still," he insists.

"Look, Lewis," Abby says. "Not to take anything away from your obvious attractiveness, but Sylvie was just getting her revenge."

"For—"

"For Virgil's failing to get her pregnant," Abby says, ticking off the reasons on her hand; he's too sauced to care that she must be steering with her knees. "For not being willing to adopt; for not *making it work*."

"But if it's revenge on him," Lewis says, "is she going to tell him about it?" Tell him about what?

Abby shakes her head confidently. "Listen, an attractive young woman? An attractive young woman can have just about any man she wants to have, honey. Snap of the fingers. That's the Goddess, period."

"I still feel pretty conflicted about it." He wishes he would shut up.

"Well, don't," she says. "And if anyone's 'to blame'—and I don't believe anyone is—it's clearly Sylvie. I mean, my God! You're barely out of your teens."

"I'm twenty-three."

"Still, it's nearly child molestation."

"Gosh, thanks."

A cloud moves across the moon and the rope attached to the car is cut.

20

T hree days pass. Donald goes back to work at the hospital where he's an administrator and Bishop is off at WSU immersed in the DMT project. Abby cheerily runs errands in preparation for the arrival of the storm-chasing lesbians from Oregon: has the Escalade tuned up, buys huge orange plastic reserve gas tanks, a county map of the State, a first-aid kit. As for Seth, he's out so much, gone no one knows where, that he and Lewis never cross paths.

Lewis means to apply for a job at Gar but with peace reigning in the house there's less immediate motivation, especially since it's going to entail shaving off his beard, something he didn't think of until later. He lies in bed reading or trolls the internet for traces of V., who closed her Facebook account when they broke up though Andrew didn't. Hermione, Lewis suspected, would be "friends" with Andrew by now. Having wheedled Eli into telling him Hermione's password (with Eli resisting more on the grounds that it was masochistic of Lewis to want access to Andrew Feeling's account than morally remiss of Eli to disclose his girlfriend's password), Lewis was soon poring over a trove of labeled photos: predictably precocious-looking Andrew, carrot-topped and athletic, in boyhood, prep school (lacrosse, crew), at Princeton (ditto) then Oxford, on trips to Europe, to Asia, at his family summer house in what looks, yes, like Maine, including, joltingly, a recent one of V., shielding her eyes from the sun in an Adirondack chair.

Lewis gazes at these images for long stretches, turns away,

goes back to look again. He's expecting them to yield something, some insight, pleasure, pain, but there's something deeply, deflectingly generic about them. They give up little besides truisms about privilege and good breeding and luck. Or maybe it's not that they're generic so much as perfect, images of a perfect life, and perfection is impenetrable. Perfection is generic. All happy families are alike.

Twice he hears Seth's voice across the house but by the time he gets there Seth has left. Earlier this afternoon he thought he caught a whiff of pot smoke coming in under his bedroom door. Maybe it was leaking in through his window from Bishop in the backyard because there was no sign of Seth in the den.

It's possible Seth is avoiding Lewis, because he's angry about Tori or because he feels sheepish for having made a fool of Lewis at Gar, though on a Sethean scale that prank was so minor that it's unlikely to be a factor. There's a third possibility. Seth has an elusive, reclusive side. Nature Boy, Lewis calls this persona. Whereas Seth is typically voluble and violent, Nature Boy is peaceful and quiet; he stares into space, "lost" in the recesses of his deeper experience of reality. Oh, me? Just existing; hard to explain. Nature Boy's heyday was in Seth's mid-teens, but maybe he's made a comeback, hence the mysterious absences and silence. Or all of these or none: in an information vacuum, Lewis is left to wonder.

Now it's late. Abby and Donald are in the bathroom down the hall. He hears the spray of the shower, the whine of their electric toothbrushes. When Donald clears his throat, which he does with neurotic frequency, it sounds through the walls like the mopey roar of a lion in a zoo. Finally their bedroom door closes and the house is quiet.

Lewis studies German for half an hour, checks Andrew Feeling's Facebook page for any recent additions to the photos (none), then brushes his teeth at the sink of his half bath, undresses, gets into bed.

With the lights off, his thoughts return to V, or rather he sees that's he's been thinking about her all along. It's like lifting the lid on a tank containing a few fish, a dull freshwater species. The same brown fish are making the same clueless passes from wall to wall of the tank: V. started seeing Andrew before she'd broken off with Lewis, before she'd even let on that she was dissatisfied with Lewis, but swears she didn't have sex with Andrew until afterward. (Eli doesn't believe this; Lewis is agnostic.) What eats at Lewis is less that V. revealed herself to be a hypocritical, careerist whore, sex or no sex, than why she prefers Andrew to Lewis: because she believes Lewis lacks the drive and ambition she needs in her "mate." She didn't know this about herself in the beginning or perhaps she changed. In any case, she could not imagine "building a life" around someone as adrift as Lewis is right now. Which is, from Lewis's perspective, fine, a relief really, because he's too young to get married; he doesn't want a "mate" yet. He didn't know this about *him*self or perhaps he changed. And around again—

So he switches on the bedside lamp and rummages in his book bag pockets until he finds a prescription bottle and shakes out a number of Ambien, replacing all but one, which he bites in half and swallows dry, leaving the other half on the bedside table next to *Storm Chase: A Photographer's Journey*.

Turning off the light again, he sees the man in the windbreaker turn with that look of innocent surprise, as if reached in some blameless boyhood. Lewis touches the arm; the man stops and turns. Lewis wishes he were the man in the windbreaker; the man in the windbreaker doesn't know V. or Andrew Feeling. The man in the windbreaker knew better, knew instinctively, not to attempt to rise above his modest station and so was spared knowing what Lewis now knows. There's a tapping noise like the pulse of the seconds passing in the scene. It gets louder until he realizes it's someone at the door, which opens to reveal Seth silhouetted against the hall-way light.

"Can I talk to you?" He sounds oddly plaintive.

Lewis swings his legs out of bed and turns on the lamp. "What's up?" he asks.

"Come out with me," Seth says. He's wearing a high-col-lared sleeveless black T-shirt advertising a metal band from the looks of it: "Mastodon," a wolf-stag hybrid. The ropey veins in his biceps stand out.

"I just took an Ambien," Lewis says. He's not in the mood for some aimless drive around town at this hour, stare-downs with cowpokes at red lights. "I'm not going to be able to keep my eyes open," he adds, exaggerating the pill's power, though not by much.

Seth stares as if assessing the degree of resistance he's fac-ing then sighs and digs into a front pocket of his jeans. He goes down on one knee by Lewis as if to propose marriage, unscrews the top of a tinted glass vial and dips in a plastic spoon attached to the underside of the cap. He holds out the sizable bump with a fairly steady hand.

"I thought you quit this stuff," Lewis says, frowning but aflutter at the sight of blow. He's troubled but relieved too: coke would explain Seth's odd hours and manic energy.

Cupping Seth's hand, Lewis does the hit in his left nostril. There will be that much less for Seth to do. Seth digs out another spoonful and Lewis bumps it in the right nostril. It burns, this stuff. He paws his nose and looks up at Seth ques-tioningly.

"Rhymes with 'Seth,'" he says, widening his eyes.

Ritalin and Adderal Lewis has done—to finish papers—but never meth. He braces for a big, jagged rush, gripping imagi-nary armrests, but it's smooth and assured, like a jet rising from the tarmac.

"Now get dressed, bitch."

Following Seth out to the car, Lewis tries to gauge his mood but detects only a kind of subdued purposefulness. The wind has come up, the spiky tops of the evergreen hedges dipping and plunging, the willows in Oren's front yard lashing, sweeping the grass with their hair. Backing out of the driveway, Seth says, "We never did go out in New York."

Lewis looks over at him. For Seth, the remark verges on sentimental, a sunset-tinged regret. "You were never around," Lewis counters.

A strip of green plastic lawn divider is blown skidding across the street. "I was around that first night."

"Not a very big window of opportunity," Lewis says.

"I knocked on your door," Seth says. "You were in there."

It was a Wednesday at the end of April. There was so much sighing from Virgil about the disruption to his work schedule that Lewis finally volunteered to go alone to JFK. He thought he would impress Seth with his nonchalant navigation of the whole vortex of New York but when he spotted him among the arrivals—the hooded expression, the search-and-destroy lope that was attracting a certain leery, sidewise attention—he began to have doubts about Seth's susceptibility to being wowed, at least by the likes of Lewis. On the A train somewhere in East New York, when he should have been staring nervously out at the stark low-rise ghetto, Seth fell into conversation with a Rasta who wore large soft-looking silver rings on his fingers. Lewis couldn't hear what they were saying above the noise of the train but when the Rasta rose to get off in lower Manhattan, they exchanged cell numbers, soulful embraces.

Coming into the apartment, Lewis saw it through Seth's eyes, the framed art on the walls and the white couch and the mid-century furniture, the books and rugs and lamps, the view of the Hudson. He heard the bright insincerity of Sylvie's greeting as she emerged from the kitchen with flushed cheeks and stove mitts, felt the faltering, distracted authority of Virgil's handshake. Seth grinned and nodded, unaware that this whole scene, which he was so looking forward to putting his fist through, was a kind of after-image hanging in the air. The era of dinners *en famille* was past by then: Virgil was having Chinese or Thai delivered to his office and Sylvie seemed to be subsisting on glasses of red wine, lighting up the Export A's she'd started smoking again by the open window of her study. A tight-lipped exception was going to be made for Seth's first night.

After dinner, when they were having coffee in the living room, Sylvie alluded in passing to Sade, as in Marquis de, Lewis can't remember why or apropos of what. Seth said, "Uh, yeah, it's actually pronounced 'Shah-Day?'"

Virgil and Sylvie stared at him then turned in unison to Lewis, who couldn't tell whether it was a joke or not. They may have had no idea who the pop singer was and it was just possible that Seth had no idea who the Marquis was. Later Lewis decided Seth did know and it was a joke but at the time he'd had as much as he could take of the situation, of playing translator and go-between. He excused himself, saying he needed to work on his thesis, which he did, and Virgil watched him take his leave with an approving, envious look. His room was down the hall but the acoustics were such that leaving his door open a crack and lying on his bed with his head at the foot he could hear everything back in the living room.

"Acting is a such fickle career, of course," Sylvie said.

"Ca-*reer*," Seth said, as if gamely trying to pronounce a foreign word.

"What if this role you're auditioning for isn't offered to you?"

"Oh, the Van Sant role is *mine*," Seth said. "I'm living from the perspective of that *as a given*."

Sylvie chuckled drily at this, so typical of the kooky

American optimism the mother, Abby, has instilled. "But if by some *fantastic chance* you *don't* end up with the role, Seth, what then? What's your plan B?"

"Well, there's some new stuff you can make money at now," Seth said and Lewis could hear the trap being set but not Sylvie.

"Really?" She was half curious, half dubious. "Please tell me. Many of my friends are failing to get jobs in their fields, despite their PhD's from the supposedly prestigious Columbia." Lewis imagined her cutting a look at Virgil with this.

"I don't know about your friends there, uh, Sylvie," Seth said. "I mean if they'd be willing to do what I'm thinking of, which is three things: dancing in a strip club; doing internet porn; and mixed-martial-arts cage fighting. All three excellent moneymakers."

Virgil barked out a nervous laugh then said, with a hint of warning, "I take it you're joking, Seth!"

"I'm not joking," Seth said levelly. "*Excellent* moneymakers."

As if to show that she was no bourgeois stick-in-the-mud, Sylvie asked, "Gay or straight—the porn?"

"Oh, either way," Seth said with an audible shrug, "whatever they need, you know."

Appalled silence. Then: "Well, aside from the sheer alienation of it," Sylvie said, "what about AIDS?"

"Condoms," Seth said: problem solved.

Virgil, wisely electing not to go for the bait, said, "Well, let's hope you get the role in the *film*, Seth!"

There was a pause. Lewis pictured Seth looking from Virgil to Sylvie with a faux-naïf expression, awaiting their further reaction. Virgil must have been trying to think of a way to change the subject when Sylvie, as if suddenly out of patience, said, "But Seth, aren't you being a little selfish?"

"Selfish?" Seth said.

"Let's say you actually *do* act in some porn film and word of it gets out?"

"Ah-ha, uh, *Sylvie!*" Virgil interjected.

"No, Virgil! He must know how embarrassing it would be for the family."

"The—*family?*" Seth said.

"Oh please, Seth!" Sylvie said. "I realize you want to live your life as you see fit. Fine, great, who doesn't? But your name is not your own." Virgil must have been gratified by this stance even though tactically it was a loser.

"My name is not my own," Seth said as if reading it aloud from a blackboard. "Huh. OK. Have to give that one some *thought.*"

"I think all Sylvie means," Virgil said reluctantly, with a chastisement of her buried just beneath, "is that it would obviously upset your grandparents. Also, your Uncle Bruno, your cousins."

"Oh, *I* see," Seth said. "So I have to think about how *they* react. Gee, that's a lot of folks to keep in mind."

"Your father doesn't mean it so literally—come on, Seth!" Sylvie said.

"The thing is," Seth says, "I don't really *know* these people. I wouldn't recognize them on the street. They haven't wanted much to do with me."

"Well, that can be remedied now that you're here," Virgil said.

"Gosh, you think?" Seth said brightly. "That would be so— I don't know what to say, Dad!"

There was a wheel-spinning pause, as of a decision being made, whether to go on addressing Seth's words at face value or switch to responding to the scorn and pent-up rage underneath.

"OK good!" Virgil said finally, with an air of concluding a satisfactory phone call. Lewis felt sharply sorry for him. "Since we're obviously not going to be able to resolve all this *tonight*—!"

"No," Sylvie said, chastened, amid the clink of the cups and saucers being collected onto the serving tray.

"I need to finish something before bed," Virgil said. "Seth, your room is all set up," he added, his voice moving away but with an audible pinch conveying that Seth has incurred a debt by being here and should think about ways to repay it: "Sylvie was nice enough to give up her study for you."

"It was no sacrifice," Sylvie says as if dialogue with Virgil's undertone.

"You don't study anymore, Sylvie?" Seth said, no doubt observing the cleanup without moving a muscle to help.

"Not really, Seth," she says calmly.

"Huh."

"Some day I will tell you the boring story of my loss of interest in studying, Seth."

"We can *trade* stories, Sylvie!"

"Yes, I suppose we could."

There were more sounds of dishes being cleared, of the dishwasher being loaded and turned on, beginning the first cycle. Then Sylvie led Seth down the hall to his room. An hour later there was a knock on Lewis's door; he knew it was Seth. And he didn't open it.

21

S eth brings the Escalade to a halt at the stop sign at the bottom of the neighborhood then eases it forward as if to exit in the usual way but pulls instead onto the downward-sloping grass shoulder and shifts into park. Leaning over the steering wheel, he stares past Lewis into the stand of trees where they rode out the morning-glory trip.

Lewis turns to look too. His lips are parted and dry, his tongue lies slightly swollen and tipped against his lower teeth. He wonders whether there might be some other component to this stuff, on top of the meth. But what does he ever know about the white powder he blithely sniffs up his nose?

Elms, cottonwoods, the one whose roots Seth puked on among them, not that Lewis would be able to point it out. There's a faint braided glint from the creek where the land turns down and becomes a bank. They must have passed this place, coming and going over the years, hundreds of times. It's such a sad little holdout of a grove really: thoroughfare on one side, street on other, eaten into by housing lots on the far, uphill side. Maybe Seth has taken to pausing to pay it homage. Or it's here he's planning to say whatever it is he got Lewis out of bed for. Meanwhile, the longer Lewis looks the more intense the act of looking becomes until it reaches a steady state, hollowed-out smolder and the satiny, gray-black shadows of the grove seem to be trembling in some high-frequency labor, on the verge of giving birth to a revelation.

With a slight clunk Seth puts the car in gear and pulls away before it can happen. He drives west on Douglas through sleeping neighborhoods, the road making a mournful gutted tone under the tires. There was no cause to worry about stare-downs at red lights: the cowpokes are all in bed. Lewis is beginning to crash from the first bumps though so gradually that "crash" is a misnomer. "Slide" or "slip" or "leak" would be better. "Taper."

He asks Seth for the bottle. Passing it, Seth says, not unkindly, "Keep it, tweaker." Lewis unscrews the top and, ducking down in his seat, loads the tiny spoon. The more he does, the less there is for Seth to do. He's in this way nobly working on Seth's behalf with every bump he does. After spilling a bit in his lap, he manages to do two quick hits, one in each nostril. He screws the cap back on, pockets the bottle, sits up and looks around with renewed lofty interest. He understands now how half of rural America is addicted to this stuff: he feels like a well-rested duke on a tour of his ancestral estates, which happen to include an Arbie's, a Dave's Fitness Center and the corporate headquarters of Pizza Hut.

After an indeterminate stretch of time and road, thinking to get Seth talking, Lewis tells him about the Musil thank-you note controversy. Seth frowns slightly as if having trouble grasping this quaint, Victorian convention—the *thank-you note*—but makes no comment.

They pass a sand quarry and hulking yellow machinery playing dead in the moonlight. Corrugated sheds, chutes, hills of bulldozed dirt, half-dug foundations. Then fields stretch away on both sides of the road, stands of corn.

Seth turns off onto a dirt road then into the dusty parking lot of a squat windowless bar. A white sign says, in red move-able letters, GIRLZ TONITE. Parked at the log barrier in front are a dozen cars and pickups.

Lewis doesn't like the looks of it but Seth is grinning fondly, coming fully to life.

"So Abby claims she has some technique for getting more recruits for the Birthday Party—"

Seth has his hand on the door handle. "It's always the same with her."

"Oh, yeah? *How?*" Lewis asks as if it's very important that he understand this point though in fact he's hoping to stall Seth until he can think of a way to talk him out of going into this sinister bar.

"It's always some version of 'You create your own reality.'" Seth says.

"Right, but—"

"So how do you like it?" Seth asks, opening his arms.

"Like what?"

"Me! You created me! How do you like your creation?" He cackles and climbs out of the Escalade. Lewis does two quick hits from the bottle, which Seth pauses to watch, shaking his head indulgently by the log barrier.

"This better not be a biker joint," Lewis says as they go up the railed walkway built parallel to the side. Inside, the space is bigger than it seems from the outside and dark, lit mainly by the neon-tubing beer signs hung on the wood-paneled walls. The bar is linked to a narrow stage that divides the place in two. There are two silver stripper poles that may actually be "L'il Vixen" portable models and at one of them a topless dancer in unbuttoned cutoff shorts sways to a gangsta rap hit from the nineties. Another dancer wearing only a G-string squats at the edge of the stage, gazes back over her shoulder at groups of bikers who sit on the far side wearing sunglasses and leather. One of them videos the dancers with an upheld cell phone, the flesh of his flabby underarm swaying as he moves to the beat of the music.

"They park the choppers out back!" Seth informs Lewis gleefully, leaning toward him and half-shouting to be heard over the music. He's begun dancing goofily and without inhibition as if he's alone in his bedroom, acting out the lyrics of the gangsta rap like it's some Broadway-musical version: sawed-off shotgun (he mimes cocking a gun), hand on the pump! Sippin' on a 40 (mimes drinking), puffin' on a blunt (ditto)! These antics are attracting the baleful notice of a few dudes on this side of the bar, which is not occupied by bikers but by cowpoke types in trucker hats.

Lewis hastily finds a table with two empty chairs and gets Seth to sit in one of them. Then he goes to the bar and from the bartender, who looks like a graying offensive lineman, orders a beer for Seth and a double shot of Jack Daniels for himself. When he gets back to the table, Tori is sitting in his chair, breasts crushed together in a sequined top.

"I go on at one," she's telling Seth, erotic raptor eyes flicking at Lewis then away, ignoring him. From a pair of cowpokes Lewis begs leave to use an unoccupied chair and they ignore him too. He carries the chair back and sits down next to Seth and drinks off half the Jack. Seth has Tori in a headlock; they seem to be kissing.

"Stop!" she says, pulling free. "They don't like it."

Brooding on the meaning of this "they," Lewis watches the bartender emerge from behind the bar and head toward them. Is Tori a biker-chick sex slave? Does Lewis owe the bikers money for what she did to him at Gar? Did Seth bring Lewis here to pay for that?

The bartender walks heavily up to the table. "She your girl-friend?" he asks Seth.

"Ah-hah! Gosh!" Seth says. "That's, ah, kind of *intimate*!" It's a good Virgil imitation, albeit lost on everyone but Lewis.

"Seth!" Tori scolds. "We're just friends, Bo," she tells the bartender.

"Cause there's no boyfriends allowed in here," Bo says. He has a weathered, kindly face. He's giving Seth a chance to start over, to lie about his status for the record, if Lewis is reading him right.

"Yeah, but see, I have a little problem with *commitment?*"
Seth says as if he's in group therapy. He wrinkles his nose and
looks around for sympathy. "So asking me just, boom, like
that? Wow!" He makes a mincing face and shrugs apologetically. Bo heaves a sigh.

"We're just *friends*, Bo," Tori says. "Seth, shut the fuck up!
Damn! We're just friends, Bo."

"I guess I feel, I don't know, kinda *put on the spot?*" Seth
says. "In front of the lady and all?"

Now Bo crosses his enormous arms. He's made his decision. "Gonna have to ask you to leave," he says.

"What?" Tori says.

"You and your buddy," Bo tells Seth, who's staring at him
with a pleasant, abstracted look as though he hasn't heard over
the music. Maybe he hasn't. Lewis gulps down the rest of his
Jack, registering zero through the meth, and stands up. "Let's
go," he tells Seth, pulling on his arm.

Seth gets slowly to his feet but he's looking at Bo with
dawning recognition. Lewis wonders whether he might have
been Seth's teacher or coach. When Lewis looks over, Tori's
chair is as empty as main street before a shootout.

"Wait," Seth says, pointing at Bo. "Are *you* the guy?"

Lewis makes a dismissive, soothing face in Bo's direction.
"He's just messin' around!"

"Am I *what?*" Bo asks, more mystified than provoked.
Lewis senses the collective attention of the bar turn to them, the
cow dudes and bikers uniting in the canopy of smoke below the
ceiling. Trouble being an inevitable feature of things here, this
table simply where the trouble happens to be coalescing now.

"What did he say?" Bo asks Lewis.

"The *guy*," Seth says in a low voice, unsmiling now.

Bo says, "No, I'm not the guy, son."

"Oh, OK," Seth says with a shrug: Bo's word is good
enough for Seth. He allows Lewis to guide him to the door,

pausing on the way to bend down and say to a man in a trucker hat, jabbing his thumb at Lewis, "Summa."

When they reach the door, Bo calls, "I don't know what the hell you're talking about, boy!"

"No problem!" Seth calls back as if graciously accepting an apology. As the door swings shut behind them, someone else shouts, "Crazy faggot!" and Lewis could swear he heard the scrape of chairs as people rose to come after them.

Climbing into the Escalade, he keeps an eye on the door of the bar. He's expecting it to fly open, bikers and cowboys to pour out into the night. Seth buckles his seat belt leisurely, adjusts the rearview mirror, backs slowly out of the lot, tracing a graceful C in the dust that places them tauntingly at the entrance again.

Lewis tries to use the sideview mirror to check behind them but he can't get the right angle and finally turns around and peers over the top of the seat. When after a mile or so no posse of pickups and Harleys appears, he faces warily forward, gradually settling into his seat with delicious relief, watching the town flow past along the dead quiet side streets Seth takes, trees in full leaf, poker-faced windows of houses and office buildings in some of which the Escalade appears briefly like a scrap of dream imagery, an entity possessed by two other entities.

Seth has guided the car into a winding private road or driveway, a long macadam snake at the end of which they come to high iron gates, shut and locked with a heavy silver chain. Seth turns sharply left and noses the Escalade off the road into the grass, tucking it behind a guard booth with gray shingles that sparkle in the light from a down-curved streetlamp. The branches of a tree rasp and screech across the roof, setting Lewis's methy nerves on edge.

He peers into the dark on the other side of the fence. Headstones glow dimly. Seth turns off the engine and gets out and after sitting in the ticking interior for a moment Lewis gets out too, peering around to be sure there's not a guard crouched in the dark booth or walking the rounds.

Seizing two vertical bars of the fence, Seth wedges the toe of a sneaker into a gap between a diagonal support and hauls himself up. He throws a leg over the horizontal bar at the top, straddles it, then swings the other leg over and drops to the ground, landing in a crouch and walking away without waiting for Lewis, who gets out the bottle and does two quick hits of the meth for climbing energy. He imitates Seth's holds well enough but snags the cuff of his jeans on a fleur-de-lis finial and by the time he gets free and is on the ground Seth is disappearing over a low hummock.

The ground is spongy, the grass brushing past his shoes is long and dry and sallow. Obelisks, urns, a headless angel. Engraved homesteader names—WARD, SWEET, ALLING— announce themselves from small tombs and sarcophagi.

Cresting another low rise, Seth stands out against the sky, veers right and stops under a wind-gnarled pine. Lewis catches up.

Seth has peeled off his shirt. In the hazy moonlight, Lewis can make out the new tattoo, a wide banner across the top of his chest and collarbone that says, in ornate flowing script: *In Loving Memory of Seth Chopik*

Seth watches him take it in.

"You really are crazy," Lewis says, shaking his head. It could have been worse but this is pretty floridly insane, a very bad sign. "How are you going to get that off?"

Seth stares without a word as if expecting him to change his mind but Lewis turns and walks off. Then he's on his back.

Seth's face is a moon with blue eyes and steaming breath. "There's only one way this tat is coming off," he says. Lewis tries to move but can't, he's too firmly pinned. "That's what it's *about*, IDIOT. I thought you *knew* that. I thought you could *see through your wound* but you can't see SHIT, can you? Let me spell it out for the dunce: *everything* I *do* and everything I *say* is *connected* and *sacred* and a perfect *web*. Got it now? I'm a *soul-catcher*. Should I get an iPhone? The iPhone is the SELF. I will be NOT be getting a new iPhone means I will be passing OUT OF THIS FORM into the non-material, into the ETHERIC, in your terms."

"You're *caught* in my sacred web, you always *have* been. I let you go away because I *knew you would come back*. Because you were always in my web. I could feel you out there at the edges. I knew what you were doing. You went off to listen to con men with white hair who don't know *shit* when *the whole time* your *true teacher* was your supposedly quote unquote crazy brother. But it doesn't work where YOU GET WHAT YOU PAY FOR. It works in ways you don't expect AT ALL. Like, the very LAST person YOU expected to BE YOUR TEACHER was ME. And THEREFORE God made me your teacher! GET IT? What do God and I have to DO to get that through to you? Break you like a bitch in jail?"

At this, Lewis bucks but Seth leans his weight harder on Lewis's arms.

"You should see your face! I wish I had a mirror, I really do! Just DIE WITH ME. GET IT OVER WITH!"

"I got an idea. Let's stay here until sunrise. That will be a GIFT. You talked about about a gift given but never mentioned me. AND THAT'S SO FUCKING TYPICAL. SEE, I AM THE ONLY GIFT YOU SHOULD BE THANKFUL FOR. AND IF IT TAKES LEADING YOU BY THE DICK WITH ONE OF MY SACRED WHORES TO GET YOU TO RECOGNIZE WHO I AM THEN SO BE IT. I'LL STOOP TO THAT BECAUSE I LOVE YOU AND I FEEL NOTHING BUT COMPASSION FOR YOU IN MY HEART. BUT YOU COULD AT LEAST THANK ME! BUT YOU'RE ALL WORRIED ABOUT THANKING SOME

OLD FOOL FOR A DEAD BOOK ABOUT A DEAD MAN
WHEN HERE I AM GIVING YOU A SACRED LIVING
WHORE! I MEAN WHAT THE FUCK, RIGHT? YOU
COULD AT LEAST ACKNOWLEDGE THE BLESSING
OF YOUR TEACHER'S SACRED WHORE AND GIVE OF
YOUR MONEY AND TIME, NOT HAVE IT BE TAKEN
FROM YOU LIKE A BITCH.

"So let's wait until dawn, the NEW DAY. What does the
DAY SAY? The day says: HERE I AM AGAIN, YOU
PATHETIC SCARED SQUIRREL. And no matter HOW
MANY TIMES you claw your way around the BIG OLD
OAK TREE, I'm gonna GET YOUR ASS! RIGHT? ISN'T
THAT WHAT THE DAY SAYS? YOU KNOW I'M
RIGHT."

"Okay, I'm a squirrel, I admit that. But YOU'RE MY NUT
AND YOU'RE IN MY POCKET AND WE'RE NOT RUN-
NING ANYMORE."

22

I n the summer of Alissa and the Goethe-Institut, Lewis saw a tomb effigy of a knight, the features of the face worn smooth, one shin shorn away, both feet missing, broken off. That's how he's felt, despite two Ambiens, lying on his back in bed under the lingering effects of the meth. If meth was all it was. Eyeballs dry, hinges of his jaw sore from teeth-gnashing. Upper arms bruised where Seth kept him pinned to the ground using his knees. If he's slept at all, it was briefly, feverishly. He's been tossing from side to side.

"Demosthenes," he whispers. One of the names on the entablature of the Butler library at Columbia. Homer, Herodotus, Sophocles. Behind the columns and high windows is the reading room. Plato, Aristotle, Vergil. Long tables of dark polished wood, glowing lamps. Students and faculty pass through the ornate open gate, some leaving, some entering. Hexagonal paving stones, chevroned bricks, linden trees and cherry blossoms. Where else in the world is there for Lewis other than the reading room?

He sits up in bed and the blades of white sunlight threaten to behead him. He ducks and gropes for the cord and closes the venetian blinds. He finds his cell phone in the front pocket of his jeans, along with the tinted bottle. He holds it up: there's a little left.

He calls information and gets the number for Delta reservations and somehow dials it before he forgets. When he's put on hold he takes the bottle to the bathroom and taps it into the sink. He turns on the faucet and watches the streak of powder get swept down the drain by the clear water then rinses out the bottle for good measure and tosses it into the plastic trash can, where it lands with an accusatory clunk that tightens the band of his headache.

A Delta operator gets on the line and Lewis finds a notebook and pen in his book bag. There's a flight operated by Atlantic Southeast that leaves Wichita Mid-Continent at 10:40 tomorrow morning and arrives in Atlanta at 1:51. The connection to LaGuardia departs at 2:40 and gets into New York at 5:09.

As if psychically notified by Lewis's turn back toward New York, Virgil calls. Lewis shunts it to voicemail. Would Lewis like to reserve a seat on this flight? Yes. He can always cancel it later. He jots down the reservation number as Virgil calls again or it's the same call bouncing back. He gets off the line with the Delta operator and answers the Virgil call.

"Lewis!" It's like he's charging through a door that's been flung open at the last second. "I mean, how dare you?"

"What?" Lewis says, considering hanging up and pretending the line dropped. "What're you talking about?"

"You didn't even bother to cover your tracks," Virgil cries and Lewis feels out of breath, guilty because accused. Could this be about helping Sylvie with the fertility injections?

"You need to tell me what's going on," Lewis says.

"Lewis," Virgil says, sputtering slightly, "Dad's email box has been *flooded* with your 'thank-you' notes. Don't be coy about this."

Lewis tries to speak but Virgil talks over him. "I have to say I really see this as part of a larger pattern of ingratitude on your part. You never thanked me for the Horace Mann tuition, for instance, but you were on a *partial* scholarship because of the football. *I* had to pick up the rest of the tab! That wasn't easy to come by, that private-school money. I'm a doctor of *philosophy*, not medicine." He's been saving that one, Lewis thinks to himself mid-stream. "And not one word of thanks from you."

"Why should I have to *thank you* for paying for my schooling?" Lewis asks him. "That's what a parent *does*."

"And what does a child do," Virgil replies, "just take and take and take with no acknowledgement?"

"You pushed *me* to go to Horace Mann."

"I gave you the *option* of going."

"And for your information, I didn't write any fucking *emails to Cyrus*."

There's a pause. Lewis waits, puffed up and panting slightly with outrage.

"Well, if you didn't write them," Virgil asks finally, "who did?"

"I don't know," Lewis says. But he does. He's looking around for his laptop. It was on the desk the last time he saw it.

There's another pause on Virgil's end then: "Is Seth there, in Wichita?"

"He is," Lewis says. He's down on his knees looking under the bed.

"And does Seth know about—the Musil book and the rest?" It's as if he's a bit embarrassed by the idea of Seth's view of it.

"Yeah," Lewis says. He's pulling on a clean shirt.

"Well, if it's Seth, this is not a good sign."

"I just told you I didn't do it," Lewis snaps. "Who else could it be?"

"There are over a *hundred* of these things, Lewis. I've never *heard* Mom so upset." Lewis wonders about Gerty's life, if this is the most upsetting thing in it so far.

"I'll call you later." He hangs up and is leaving the room when something makes him stop at the bookshelf. He takes down the copy of *When Things Fall Apart*, which is sticking out a bit: the money is gone.

He drops the book on the floor and stalks down the hall, pausing to listen at the closed door of Abby's bedroom—quiet—then hunts through the rest of the painfully sun-flooded house. There's no one in the TV room, the dining room, the kitchen, Seth's room.

He goes down the stairs into the basement to check there. Not in the laundry room or the storage area, stacked high and deep with Abby's unsold multi-level marketing products. In the main room, where there used to be a Ping-Pong table, a pleather Barcalounger, a TV set, there's now a chemistry lab—two long marble work tables arranged in an L. Beakers, funnels, flasks, graduated cylinders, coils of rubber tubing, a metal shelf with labeled bottles and boxes and canisters. A large mysterious machine, maybe a microscope, attached to devices that look like units for a stereo. The small windows up near the ceiling have been covered with foil.

He bounds back up the stairs and heads to Abby's room. Passing the den again, he spies his laptop on the couch. He was moving so fast he didn't notice it the first time through. He sits down and opens it and hits a key to refresh the screen and the "Sent" page of his email account comes up, all the recipients cchopik@fas.harv . . . , the subject all variously "thanks!" and "merci!" and "you can guess," the date sent all "Today," with a minute or two at most separating each one, beginning at 3:47 A.M.

Lewis opens the first few:

From: lchopik@columbia.edu
Subject: thanks!
Date: June 26, 2007 2:47:14 AM CST
To: cchopik@fas.harvard.edu

Dear Gramps,

Thanks for that book on Moosel, it rocks!

Love,

Lewis

From: lchopik@columbia.edu
Subject: thanks!
Date: June 26, 2007 2:48:56 AM CST
To: cchopik@fas.harvard.edu

Dear Cramps,

Your book on Muscle, it's something I'll always sort of want
to keep nearby.

Lovin' ya,

Lew

From: lchopik@columbia.edu
Subject: thanks!
Date: June 26, 2007 3:47:14 AM CST
To: cchopik@fas.harvard.edu

Dear Gramps,

I can't get enuf
of this thanking stuff!

Truly,

Lew-deKriss

Folding the Mac shut, he picks it up and raps more loudly on Abby's door than he meant to.

"Come in!" he hears her call in a pleasant singsong. He opens the door and goes in, closing it behind him. The light is dim, the tones of the room greenish gold, a vaguely harem atmosphere: sleepy, sensual, subaquatic. Abby is lying on her side on the enormous "California King" Tempur-Pedic bed, which feels like the world's largest slab of cream cheese. She has a book open in the light of a lamp, the covers pulled up above her breasts. "Have you seen Seth?" Lewis asks.

She puts the open book face down on the bedspread. "What's going on, honey?" she asks, scanning his face.

Lewis has already turned to go. He stops and says, "Seth is in full flip-out."

"What?" she says, sitting up. "Lewis, what happened?"

"He held me hostage in a cemetery last night, ranting about how he's my teacher, he's already dead. Again. He has a memorial tattoo *in his own name*."

"Wait, what?" Abby has sat up straighter in bed. "What's a memorial tattoo?"

"This huge new *tattoo* of his," Lewis says, gesturing impatiently at his collarbone. "It says, 'In Loving Memory of Seth Chopik.' He needs to be locked up."

He watches her absorb this. "He needs to be locked up, Abby! He's crazy."

"I don't like this talk of locking people up," she says. "And we aren't locking him up for a weird *tattoo*. We couldn't even we wanted to."

"I walked like four miles home from the cemetery," Lewis says. "I wouldn't get back in the car with him."

She's looking at him as if anew. "Were you on something last night?"

"Yeah," Lewis admits. "He gave me some meth."

"Crystal *meth*?" She looks horrified.

"It's just speed." Isn't it?

"OK, look, Lewis, you're grieving about Victoria now. You're drinking, you're doing strong drugs. That's fine, it's to be expected. But you have take your own reactions to things with a grain of salt, no?"

Lewis takes a breath. He needs to start over. "OK, remember how I owe Cyrus a thank-you note for the Musil study?"

She nods, eyes big with suspense.

"Well, I told Seth about it too, last night. And he sent *a hundred emails* to Cyrus, *in my name*, 'thanking' him for the Musil book!" He holds up the laptop like a murder weapon and Abby covers her mouth. "It's not fucking funny!" Lewis shouts.

"No, I know," she says, and he sees she's maybe not laughing after all. "I'm sorry."

"I'm like a *pariah* now!"

"Weren't you already?" she asks coolly.

Lewis scoffs. "And he stole the money you gave me."

At this, she frowns again with concern. "Then gave it to Tori," Lewis says, "that's how she could be at the Birthday Party."

"Do you know any of that *for sure*?" she asks.

"No," he admits.

"What do you know for sure?"

"That the money's missing," Lewis admits.

"Then I think you need to take a breath," she says.

"And that Seth's fucking insane!"

The cell phone on the bedside table rings. "He held me hostage!"

She glances at the screen and raises one finger and answers it.

"*What?*" Holding the sheets to her breasts, she lifts a wood slat of the blinds covering the window and peers out into yard.

"God," she says into the phone, lifting the blinds with two fingers and continuing to peer through.

Lewis goes to the window and lifts a slat higher up on the blinds. He sees Bishop in the side yard standing in profile with his hands on his hips at the flap of the tent. Making his way through the weeds is a cop, the nose of his black-and-white cruiser, parked along the street, just visible through the missing gate from Lewis's vantage. Lewis watches Bishop mutter something, presumably into the tiny headset and Abby says, "Okay."

"Bishop says open the window a little bit so we can hear," she whispers. Lewis stoops and raises it a few inches and the sounds of the yard wash into the bedroom. Lewis lifts a blade of the blinds and looks out through the gap again.

"Hello there, officer!" Bishop hails the man, hands clasped before him as if in accordance with something he read about non-threatening body language.

Heavyset, slow-moving, the sheriff—his arm patch says "sheriff" and "State of Kansas" and "Sedgwick County"—ignores the greeting. He's quite close to the window now and it seems to Lewis that if the man simply turned his head slightly he'd spot them spying there. A horsefly lands in the light brown fur of his forearm and the sheriff shoos it away by giving his arm a rotating shake. "Got permission to have a tent out here?"

"Yes, I do, officer," Bishop says. "From the lady of the house."

The sheriff nods as if absorbing this then the horsefly returns, buzzing aggressively around his head and there ensues an undignified flurry of frantic ducking and swatting while Bishop looks frowningly on, one hand raised to his lips to hide a smile. When the horsefly is finally gone, the sheriff waits a moment, scanning the air above him warily, then says, "Had complaints from the neighbors about this camp."

"Neighbors?" Bishop says with a chuckle. He points to his left. "This house is empty, foreclosed." He turns, waves vaguely behind himself. "That one back there is empty too—up for sale." He shrugs. "And if you mean Bill Oren, he can't even see me from over there."

The sheriff has been surveying the clothesline and Tibetan prayer flags behind his sunglasses. "Did Bill Oren complain?" Bishop asks.

"Mind if I look inside the tent?" the sheriff asks.

Bishop's face falls and he shoots a glance at the window. "Yes, I *do* mind, officer! I mind very *much*!"

"Stand to one side, sir." The sheriff points to a spot in the weeds to the right.

Crossing his arms, Bishop holds his ground. "I've been polite and forthcoming, sir," Bishop says stiffly. "At this stage, you need to produce a search warrant." The sheriff and Bishop stand staring at each other.

"Shouldn't we go out there?" Lewis whispers.

"All right, sir," the sheriff says. "Stand to one side or I'm placing you under arrest."

"I don't want him coming in *here* to search!" Abby whispers back. "Have you seen the lab in the basement?"

"I just did," Lewis says. "Why are you withholding stuff like that? The tent, the lab?"

"Keep your voice down!" Abby says. "I'm not *withholding* anything!"

"Well, we should go out there," Lewis whispers. "He can't just come into the house and search it."

"He sure the hell can!" she hisses. "Wake up, Lewis! They do whatever they want—*obviously*. We live in a *police state*, or haven't you noticed?"

The sheriff and Bishop seem to have been engaged meanwhile in a stare-down. Shaking his head with a kind of fatalistic disgust, Bishop crabs reluctanctly away from the entrance flap. "Play the game, officer," he says. He makes a sarcastic flourish of welcome with one arm. "*Play the game.*"

"Over there," the sherrif says, indicating a spot in the weeds to which Bishop moves while shaking his head.

The sheriff trudges forward and plucks at the peak of the tent as if expecting the whole thing to fly away at a touch and reveal its contents.

"You know," Bishop says, "there's a document you might want to read when you get a chance."

The sheriff tugs harder at the peak of the tent.

"Little something called the *Constitution of the United States of America*?"

"I've read the Constitution," the sheriff says, drawing out his flashlight and turning it on. He crouches creakily and shines the flashlight into the tent.

"I *especially* recommend the Fourth Amendment," Bishop says. "Has to do with *illegal searches*?"

Dissatisfied with his flashlit view of the interior, the sheriff gets down on all fours and crawls inside. Bishop, his mouth working in agitation inside the white beard, looks angry enough to kick the wide, uniformed ass. The sheriff has begun throwing things backwards out of the tent now—a pair of shorts, a T-shirt, magazines, computer diskettes in clear plastic covers, a paperback, two unopened cans of Starbucks espresso-and-cream. Lewis is expecting to see a baggie of pot or a bong or other "paraphernalia" at any second. Now a sex toy hits the ground, the impact causing it to begin writhing obscenely.

"Yo!" a voice calls—Seth's, Lewis knows instantly. He's to the left somewhere, in the haze of sunlight, as if he's come around from behind the house. "I can explain everything!"

Abby says, "Oh, my God."

The sheriff scurries backward out of the tent and clambers to his feet, his heavily equipped belt clanking.

"Stop right there!" he tells Seth. His sunglasses are askew.

"Welcome!" Seth says. "First of all."

"Sir, you need to go back inside the house," the sheriff says, pointing straight at Lewis without taking his eyes off Seth.

"OK, so the meaning of this moment," Seth says, speaking slowly, "is *you're right on time.*"

"Go!" Abby hisses but Lewis is already going. He dashes out the room and through the den and out the sliding glass doors and into the mashed glare of the bright hot morning. The weeds lash his pants as he races through the yard and around the corner of the house. He hears a clacking sound then a loud crack.

By the time he reaches the tent Seth is writhing on the ground like a snake. He has no shirt on and he's pawing at his chest and moaning.

When the sheriff sees Lewis he aims the pistol at him, holding it with both hands, hollers, "Stop right there!"

Lewis halts in his tracks, raising both hands high, and the sheriff aims the gun back at Seth, who's somehow hoisted himself onto one elbow and seems to be trying to sit up.

"Stay down!" the sheriff bellows incredulously. "Down!"

Panting, Lewis feels like he's going to faint or burst into tears or have a coronary. Bishop, his face drained of blood, looks on with wide eyes.

"Under arrest!" the sheriff growls at Seth, voice phlegmy with adrenaline and rage. "Arrest!" he barks.

Still aiming at Seth, the sheriff releases the gun with one hand to fumble behind himself for something then walks toward Seth holding forth a pair of handcuffs like a symbol to be read.

Suddenly Seth sits bolt upright. Someone has been screaming for a long time now. Turning, Lewis sees Abby in her bathrobe beside him, her mouth wide.

The clacking sounds fills the air again. "I said *down!*" bellows the sheriff and he fires again.

Seth falls backward, arms flung out, and hits the ground hard, bouncing slightly, and lies still.

23

The Tibetan prayer flags snap in a rising wind. A robin lights on the top of the fence then plunges from view with its wings closed. Seth sits on the ground with his hands cuffed behind his back.

Shakily Lewis tips a bottle of water into his mouth; most of it spills down Seth's chin and throat, mingling with the blood from the slit-like wounds left by the Taser darts. One of them pierced the half-moon part of the "e" in the "Memory" of the banner tattoo. After donning latex gloves like a cafeteria worker the sheriff plucked them out, slipping each one into a breast pocket of his uniform. Waste not. The watery blood runs in rivulets into the shallow folds of Seth's stomach.

"You're down here with me now," Seth says quietly.

They watch the first sheriff confer with a second who's parked his squad car at a hasty, dramatic angle to the curb.

"This is a good place for us," Seth says. "I can teach you better down here."

Lewis is impressed by how many people have gathered in the street. There must be a neighborhood-watch listserv, a text-message alert system. Lewis recognizes the lawn-inspecting man in his baseball cap and sunglasses and moustache.

"Look at 'em," Seth says. But he has his head back now and seems to be watching a jet pass overhead. The drone of the engines drifts down to them in staggered bursts.

"All the BOYS want to be PIGS," Seth says, raising his voice, "all the BITCHES want to be RADIO DISPATCHERS."

This elicits a muttering from the crowd and the two sheriffs trudge across the yard and seize Seth under the arms and haul him roughly to his feet. The first is still wearing the cream-colored latex gloves.

Seth goes limp, head hung forward. The sheriffs grunt but don't complain, as if accustomed to it. The tips of Seth's sneakers bump and sputter over the ground as he's dragged forward.

Abby emerges from the house carrying a bag and talking on her cell, to Harry from the sound of it. The dogs follow at her heels, barking shrilly.

Halfway across the lawn to the street, Seth stands bolt upright and rigid, digging in the heels of his sneakers and resisting the forward motion of the cops, who take the opportunity to catch their breath.

"My life peaked when I was five years old," Seth says, addressing the crowd, who give rapt audience, Oren among them now, Lewis sees, gazing with his brown hangdog eyes over the top of his wife's bouffant.

The sheriffs resume pulling him toward the cruisers.

"I died when I was fourteen," Seth says. "Can I get a witness, Oren?" he calls, nodding toward Oren in the crowd. "I owe it all to Minister Oren, praise be! Without whose seeds, bro, I would've stayed alive and afraid!"

Abby drapes an unbuttoned dress shirt over his shoulders.

"After dying," Seth says, "I hung around to complete a few more sacred tasks—I fucked the Queen Bitch Candy, the love of my afterlife, and got my head bashed in with a brick. I SEE THE LIGHT THROUGH MY WOUND! Oh, yeah, and I burned as many SHITTY U.S. FLAGS as I could get my hands on!"

This causes a rumble of protest from the crowd. Seth smiles and spits into the street, causing a man to hop backwards to avoid it.

The first sheriff cups his head with a latex-covered hand to protect it from the top of the door and the crowd surges forward. Lewis, who's been walking alongside the sheriffs and Seth, is pressed up against the side of the cruiser by an obese woman cradling an asthmatic pug.

As the cruiser pulls away, Seth seeks out Lewis and says through the open window, "You're not going ANYWHERE, you're DEAD BROKE!"

24

From the double-parked Escalade, Lewis watches Abby and Harry walk slowly around the benches dividing the wide paved entrance to the Sedgwick County Detention Facility.

Watery sunlight bathes everything in an air of inconsequence and irreality, the light of a dream in which some crucial thing can't be accomplished.

The man from Lucky's Bail Bonds is late. Abby found the outfit online, a shamrock-green website playing "Folsom Prison Blues" with a flashing <u>CALL NOW to speak to a LIVE bondsman standing by!</u> The charges are obstruction of justice and resisting arrest, with bail set at five hundred dollars, the Birthday Party ante, it occurred to Lewis, though he had the tact not to mention it.

On the parched front lawn, a seatless bike is chained to the single enormous light pole with a mushroom-cap shade. The wire halyard on the flagless flagpole clanks in the gusty wind. Abby and Harry reach the curb again, where the red No Standing paint is like cracked lipstick, then turn in unison and walk back up the slight incline in the direction of the entrance.

They asked Lewis to come along in case they needed help with Seth, physical help, but to wait in the car lest he feel ganged up on. OK, but if Seth is so volatile, if he's apt to bolt or attack, why the rush to spring him from the psych pod? Why not leave him in there for a lot longer?

Harry reaches back to flick his vestigial ponytail free of his shirt collar then lights a cigarette, which he stabs out in the ash-tray under the slab-like portico, and resumes discussion with Abby. Lewis has been haunted by the feeling, watching them, that their earnest talk, however well-intentioned and sensitive and intelligent, however informed by years of interventions in Seth's crises, is profoundly pointless. In terms of having any bearing or causal relation to Seth, it may as well be wind in the trees. He's punchy from sleeping poorly or not at all but keeps being washed over by the sense that *what they hope to avert has already occurred*: it's actually over and done with, the way a building is built and eventually: there it stands. And out beyond the Sedgwick County Detention Facility, there's another struc-ture called What Actually Happens or What Will Have Happened. If you travel far enough, you'll arrive at it.

Then he has another thought: The one consolation is that because it's already happened, it won't happen in the future. Because it's already happened.

Lying on the front passenger seat is a bulging green spiral binder held shut by a wide, ink-smudged rubber band. Virgil has seventeen of this make of binder on the shelf beside his desk, one for each of the first seventeen centuries of reaction to his namesake.

Lewis picks up the binder and slips off the rubber band, glancing over to be sure Harry can't see what he's doing: break-ing an official seal of sorts. There are tabs with different names, Askins, Melissa; Buford, Greg; Chopik, Seth. Odd to see that Harry has other patients. Lewis fans through Seth's file—copies of documents, arrest records, psych-ward intake forms. At ran-dom, he reads one that has written across it in Harry's hand: "San Francisco, post-breakup with Candy Mueller"

NAME: CHOPIK, SETH

A. <u>CIRCUMSTANCES OF ADMISSION</u>

Mr. Seth Chopik is an eighteen-year-old white male charged with threats who was admitted to the Psychiatric Unit forthwith from the San Francisco Superior Court.

No medical or psychiatric information accompanied him.

B. PRESENT ILLNESS

Upon admission he said he was a street person who was too happy for this "disintegrating society." He said that he was both "God" and "Satan" and that he experienced "astral projections." He gave an inconsistent report of decreased sleep time. He denied depression, hallucinations, suicidal/homicidal ideas or memory problems.

Upon mental status examination, he was alert, cooperative, and bizarre in appearance with an odd hairstyle and extensive tattoos, notably one on his right cheek and jaw. His affect was euphoric. His speech was spontaneous, increased in production and loosely associated at times. It was normal in volume and rate. There was evidence of religiosity and grandiose delusions. His recent and remote memory was questionably impaired. He was oriented as to person, time and place. He was unable to subtract serial "sevens." Some of his interpretations of abstractions were bizarre. His insight was questionably impaired. His judgment was grossly normal.

C. PAST HISTORY

Mr. Chopik dropped out of school when he was in tenth grade for reasons not clear to me. He has used cocaine, methamphetamine, phencyclidine, marijuana, lysergic acid, and other drugs. He and his wife used fifteen thousand dollars worth of cocaine in six months, seven months ago. He has lived in the streets for an unrecalled period of time and has had short periods of depression. He claimed that he tried to gas himself several months ago. He usually feels very good and can stay awake for up to two days at a time.

D. DIAGNOSTIC IMPRESSION

Mr. Chopik was thought to have Mixed Substance Intoxication (305.9); Mixed Substance Abuse (305.9) and Possibly Bipolar Disorder, Manic Type (296.4).

E. INITIAL TREATMENT RECOMMENDATIONS

Mr. Chopik said that he suffered a recent skull fracture with no loss of consciousness and no sequelae. He has a large, sutured scar in the middle of his forehead. Medical evaluation of this will be obtained.

William D. Moskowitz, MD
Program Chief
Adult Inpatient Care Branch

From somewhere above the smear of white clouds an airliner pours down its doleful flyover song. The remark about Seth's attempt to gas himself came as news—jarring, sickening. Lewis sits staring at the signature of William D. Moskowitz, MD then closes the file and the notebook and stretches the rubber band around, resealing it.

The bondsman, wearing, as promised, a shamrock-green baseball cap, is walking up the entrance pathway. As if there were a danger of his being missed in a crowd when other than a guard taking a cigarette break there's been no one here but

Abby and Harry for the past twenty minutes. As the three of them go inside, Lewis's cell thrums in his front pocket.

He fishes it out and checks the screen: it's Virgil calling again, from his own cell. Lewis has been letting them go to voice mail but this time he picks up. Instead of hello he says, "Seth's in jail again."

"Oh my," Virgil says. "What now?"

"He attacked a cop," Lewis says, his own voice trembling, as if released of the need for self-control by the civilized constraint and pinch of his father's voice.

"Oh, Lewis. Why?"

"I don't know," Lewis says. "I mean, I have an idea but I'm not sure." He knows Virgil won't pry for details; Virgil doesn't want to know any more than necessary. He would prefer to know nothing.

As if turned aside and speaking to someone else, Virgil says, "Seth's in jail again. For attacking a police officer."

"Who's there?" Lewis asks.

"Grandma," Virgil says. "I'm in Cambridge." He pictures them in the orderly, scoured kitchen that smells faintly of brisket, the neatly folded hand towels hung just-so through the handle of the stove, polished-aluminum toaster shining like a shield. Against the chill of the central air, which is turned down to frosty levels, Gerty would be wearing a thin cardigan over her broad thick shoulders. She bars doors with those shoulders, and she opens doors.

Lewis asks to speak to his grandmother. Virgil turns away from the phone to announce this with relief and anxiety.

"Hello, Lewis," Gerty says.

"I just wanted to say," Lewis says quickly, like driving a nail in, "I'm sorry about everything, Grandma."

"Everything?" she says. Slow down there, suggests the tone: first you say nothing at all, now you want to cast some hasty blanket statement over the whole matter.

"About the emails and everything." He needs to stop saying "everything."

There's a pause on Gerty's end, a silence like a chemical solution in which Lewis's words are being assayed. "Is there anything *else* you care to apologize for?"

Lewis closes his eyes as if he could prevent himself from seeing himself. Then he opens them and notices, running parallel to the sidewalk in front of the county jail, a narrow footpath beaten into the grass like a people's history. Where it meets the entrance walkway, the bald ground broadens into an ugly irregular delta.

What's so hideous about what he's doing? He's apologizing for failing to acknowledge a gift he asked to be given. "Yes," he says, "I'm sorry I never wrote Grandpa a thank-you note for the Musil study."

She sniffs. "And *I'm* sorry it took you so long," she says. "It upset your Grandpa more than you realize, getting no acknowledgment *whatsoever* for something that took him years to complete. That was really *quite* inconsiderate, *quite* thoughtless."

There's another silence. She sighs. "But I accept your apology, Lewis. On Grandpa's behalf." It goes without saying that at this hour Cyrus is in his study, tilted back in his desk chair gazing at his computer screen or reading a book open on one of his folding oak bookstands with the pegs and holes. None of this multigenerational Sturm und Drang can reach him there, at the end of the tunnel he's dug with the pickax of his will, one sentence at a time, Gerty standing guard at the entrance.

She passes the phone back to Virgil, who asks Lewis a few more questions about Seth. But Lewis has trouble concentrating because in the background Gerty can be heard hissing, "Tell him he needs to get out of there, Virgil! It's time to decide!"

Lewis hangs up as Seth bursts through the double doors.

He drops to the sidewalk and kisses the ground out of a push-up then gets up on one knee and points at the sky like a wide receiver cheesily giving all credit to God in the end zone.

Abby and Harry come out now, scurry like owners of a big dog that has slipped its leash.

Noticing the bike chained to the lamp post, Seth acts as if he's going to climb on and ride away. Only, what's this? The seat's missing. And it seems to be chained up. Oh, well. He shrugs and turns away and comes loping toward the Escalade with a cocky hitch in his step, his bearing announcing: they have not only failed to break me, I am actually *stronger* now!

Lewis holds the door open and Seth climbs in, bringing with him a cloud of institutional soap and some volatile mystery pheromone.

Did they give him the wrong drugs? His skin has a reddish, oxygen-flushed tone and the veins in his biceps are standing out like he's just been pumping iron, which maybe he has.

"Been waiting long, Lew?" Seth asks, turning toward him with tamped-down hilarity. Before Lewis has time to reply, Seth calls, "Yo, right here, Harry!" sliding over and patting the seat beside him.

Smiling pleasantly but blinking nervously, Harry gets in and closes the door softly. Seth slings an arm over his shoulder. "You and me, Harry! You and me, baby!"

When Abby takes the wheel it's clear from her carriage, the set of her mouth, that she's at the end of her patience, of her resources. As she starts the car and pulls away, Harry shakes pills into his hand from a prescription bottle and gives them to Seth along with a bottle of water. Seth tosses the pills into his mouth like beer nuts and swallows with a gulp of water then turns to stick out his long thick tongue at Lewis: yes, I really took them!

"But Harry," he says, turning to Harry. "Did you know that drugs of the sort *I just swallowed* are really *unnecessary*? That you can control your bipolar disorder with *diet, exercise and a wellness plan?"*

He stares at Harry in openmouthed amazement then lets out a hacking burst of laughter, slaps his leg, elbows Harry in the ribs. "A *wellness plan!* Oh, sweet Jesus!" He covers his face in his hands and laughs.

Abby glances warningly, worriedly in the rearview.

"She's on the rag for having to cancel on the dykes, am I right?" Seth says in a slightly quieter voice. Abby lets it pass.

As she turns out onto the street, the ship-like side of the jail, large windows covered with what looks like gray mesh, swings into view.

Waving, Seth says, "Met a number of cool dudes in there, *num*ber of cool dudes. Yo, bye-bye, Midget! bye-bye, Tiger! Turns out *that's* where they keep all the interesting folks in town, Lewis."

"Hadn't heard of DDP though," Seth says with mock puzzlement and disappointment, glancing at his tiny hand tat.

"Which came as a *shock*," he says, turning to Harry. "Here I thought I joined a *national organization!*" He chuckles, shifts restlessly in his seat.

They pass a lawn with a sign planted in it that says This House Believes.

Seth does an exaggerated double take, twisting around in his seat. "This house *bleeds*"?

"Believes," Harry says placidly.

"If it believes, it bleeds," Seth says. "Are you with me, Harry? Am I moving too fast?"

"Hmm," says Harry.

"But also," Seth says, nodding sagely, "if it bleeds, it bel*ieves*."

"Hmm," Harry says again.

"That's simple karma, Harry," Seth says. "You don't need *me* to tell you that. That's just your 'what goes around comes around.'" He falls silent, turns in his seat to look back. "Wait, the *house* believes?"

"That's what it said," Harry confirms.

"What the hell is *that*, Harry? That's some kind of *animism* or some shit, am I right? Just *hanging out in the open* for everyone to see. Wow. A guy goes in for a little rest, leaving behind a *Christian nation*, comes *out* and there's some kind of Japanese *paganism* running rampant in the streets!" He chuckles at this unfolding scenario. "How long was I *in* there? Can someone give me some perspective on this?"

"Abby?" Seth says, leaning forward to speak in her ear. "You're my mother. At least that's what I go around *telling* everyone. Cough cough. Give it to me straight. How long was I in there?"

"Seth," Abby says, giving him a blank stern look in the rearview, "I would you like you to *chill out.*"

"The thing is, mother—" He turns to flash looks of shrugging incredulity at Lewis and Harry: what's with *her*?—"I *am* chilled out."

"Good," she says, "I'm glad to hear it."

"Just ask my companions back here," Seth calls to her. "Gentlemen, can I get a wita-ness? Harry? Chilled out, or not chilled out?"

"Fairly chilled out," Harry allows.

"Harry! My man!" Seth violently smacks Harry's reluctantly upheld palm.

"Easy," Harry mutters.

"Lewis?" Seth asks. "Chilled out?"

With a note of desperation in her voice, Abby says, "Just sit back and enjoy the ride, Seth. Would you, please?" Everyone is waiting for the drugs to kick in but they should have jabbed him in the neck with syringe of thorazine. This is not working.

"Enjoy the ride," Seth echoes, suddenly ruminative. He nods slowly, rhythmically, tapping one foot. "Works for me, works for me. Though there's the question of whether you can *will* enjoyment, Harry. The Good Book says, 'Love thy neighbor.' Same problem. Can *love* be *willed*? Don't answer right away, Harry, give it some thought."

"Interesting question," Harry says.

"I recommend a light tasing, I do!" Seth says, lunging forward to address Abby. "Counterintuitive, I know, I know. The effect is *very* stimulating, but at the same time incredibly *soothing*!"

"Seth," Abby warns again in the rearview.

"No, no, no, check it out: this is an *investment* opportunity!" He chuckles to himself, rubbing his hands together as the idea takes shape. "In the not-too-distant future, *all* your spas and yoga retreats and what-have-yous will have their own *in-house Tasers*. Be common as microwaves. Along with the *fat retired pigs* to shoot them into the clients." He imitates with eerie accuracy the clacking sound of the taser gun and pretends to zap Lewis in the ribs with stiff prodding fingers.

Abby sighs irritably, strikes the turn signal lever.

A silence ensues. Seth settles back in his seat, closes his eyes. Maybe the meds have kicked in; maybe he's worn himself down. Ahead of them in their lane is a white van with an image of a man wearing a service uniform and cap. *The man is holding a gun to his head.*

Lewis glances at Seth to see whether he's noticed it. The traffic light turns red and the van slows. It's not a gun. The man is saluting. It's some kind of advertisement for a cleaning company.

Abby's cell rings. She checks the screen. "Donald, please stop calling."

Seth lets out a loud harsh bark of a laugh, glancing at Lewis and Harry, shakes his head in bitter wonderment. "'Donald, please stop calling!'" he imitates her.

"I realize that," Abby says into the phone.

"'I realize that,'" Seth mouths.

"I'm sure you didn't. But Donald? *Donald*! It *did* go too far!" She claps the cell shut.

"It went too far, all right! Truer words have never been spaketh!" Seth sits up and leans forward. "But can I just ask everyone one last thing? Abby?"

"What, Seth?"

"One last thing?"

She hesitates, sighs then says, "Ask away."

"What the hell happened to *guns*?"

"Guns?" she asks numbly.

"That fire bullets."

"I don't know what you're talking about, Seth," she says. How deeply hard to have a child like this, Lewis thinks, pitying her, pitying himself. How he would love to open the door and get out right now, walk to the airport.

"What I mean is: how's a guy supposed to *suicide by cop* if the *cops* don't use their fucking *guns*?"

Abby slams on the breaks. The tires let out a loud, drawn-out screech and everyone flops forward. Lewis nearly bangs his nose back of the seat and the cars behind honk in alarm.

She bangs the Escalade into park, unlatches her seatbelt and wheels around to face Seth. "Do you want me to turn around and take you back to the psych pod?"

She's yanked her sunglasses off to glare at him, there are faint crow's feet at the corners of her eyes, which are clotted with mascara and shrunken in fury.

"No," Seth says, chastened and shocked.

"Because that's where they *strongly urged* me to leave you!" Behind them a car whips angrily around, followed by a line of others, the passengers glaring and gawping in as they pass.

"And I'll tell you right now, you seem pretty damn insane to me. What's insane? Insane is a *lack of gratitude for life*; insane is arrogance and recklessness and impiety. That's what makes you a 'danger to yourself and to others,' Seth. And if you don't show me, pretty damn quick, that you're at least *willing* to begin taking responsibility for *your own role* in the quality and nature of your experience, then I'll have you committed! I'll do it like that—" she snaps her fingers under his nose—"and I'll feel *zero* regret. Is that clear?"

Seth sits there blinking, temporarily stunned into non-insanity. Harry, who still has his arms braced against the back of the front seat, observes this with interest.

"It's a *new day*," Abby says. She pops the car into gear and drives on.

25

Blue and white wild flowers, bees, butterflies, crisscrossing dragonflies—the backyard is like a meadow now. It's refreshing, the green-tinted air, the rustle of the leaves in the wind. Lewis likes to sit out here on the stoop, when it's not his time to keep an eye on Seth, and read or stare into space. He, Abby, Harry, and Bishop have been rotating through shifts for the past week. The goal, the main idea, is for Seth to come down from the high of the "mood episode" but not so far down as to enter a depression. Harry, who's been in daily therapy sessions with Seth, said yesterday he thought they might be through the worst. Still, just to be safe, Harry wants to put him on Symbyax, a combination of Zyprexa and Prozac, since he may have sunk a tad low on lithium alone. And if Symbyax doesn't work? They'll try Wellbutrin. Lewis didn't want to know what they would do if the Wellbutrin failed.

One of the dogs has laid his head in his lap. Stroking the fawn ears, his fingers encounter a pellet-sized thing. He clears away the fine soft fur—a tick the color of tarnished silver.

"Hold on," he says but as he tries to get a good grip on the tick—or should he use a pair of tweezers? —the mutt squirms free and leaps from the stoop, vanishing from sight in the weeds except for a thrashing ripple it makes as it flees around the side of the house in the direction of Bishop's tent.

The tallest plants come up to Lewis's chest, his chin, dim the light in his room to the point that he has to read with a lamp on in the middle of the day. The vine beginning to snake

its way up the legs of the patio furniture when he arrived now
blankets the porch like kudzu, the heart-shaped leaves tracing
the seams of the louvered windows and sliding glass doors,
seeking entry.

He cleaves his way out to the fiberglass toolshed in the corner of the yard and peels back the tendrils of ivy sealing the
door, which rumbles like stage thunder when he slides it open.
The tendrils leave a raised chevroned residue on the fiberglass.
In the dim bluish light large leggy spiders clamber into the
upper corners.

There's a lawn mower coated in bits of dried grass, a box of
garbage bags, pruning shears, a pair of canvas gloves, and, leaning against the wall beside the door, a machete in its unopened
cardboard scabbard/package.

As he's closing the door of the shed he sees out of the corner of his eye someone's head above the fence but when he
turns it's gone. Oren.

He carries the machete, the gloves, and the box of garbage
bags back to the stoop. The gloves, which are too small and
stiff, he sets aside. On the cardboard scabbard it says, "Corona
Professional 18' machete tempered steel blade for greater
strength and long service life." He pulls the serrated tab and
unsheathes it, hefts it in his hand. When a stalk of Queen
Anne's Lace bends toward him in the breeze, he leans out and
decapitates it, the blade ringing with a clean metallic *ping*.

The scouring grind of skateboard wheels on macadam
drifts over the house. Lewis goes to the gate by the trash cans
and, nudging it open with the machete he's absently holding in
his right hand, looks through the gap.

Seth is riding toward the street on the driveway. It's close to
ninety degrees out. If he works up a sweat, he could faint or get
sick; lithium levels rise as fluids are lost. Lewis read that online,
taking a break from Google-stalking Victoria (she's a panelist
on Emily Dickinson and Hymn Culture at Amherst College

scheduled for April of next year). Be wary of hot weather and limit consumption of diuretics like coffee and alcohol.

Seth has gone off his meds, Lewis imagines, maybe wishes. He's going to skateboard out of sight, to the bus station or train yards or highway.

But he pivots by the mailbox and pushes back down the driveway. He's pale and ten pounds heavier from the meds and ten days camped out on the couch in the den watching TV with Cody.

Coasting along, he looks down at his feet, knees nearly knocking, preparatory to a kick-flip move of some sort. It's ugly, so much of street skateboarding, the sudden, scalded postures. More often than not the attempts are blown. Though Seth was once quite good, won local competitions, had sponsors. Lewis is divided between hoping he lands the move and feels a little uptick of self-respect and achievement, and hoping he falls, so that his hubris and arrogance are further torn down.

If there's any left. When Harry and Abby decided it would be best to have the memorial tattoo removed, Seth agreed. Fine. No, he didn't mind that the process would be lengthy and a bit painful, whatever. He was so zombie-like that the dermatologist spoke to Abby as if he weren't there. "Was Seth Chopik a friend of his?" he asked her. "*He's* Seth Chopik." "Pardon?" The first procedure seemed to go well enough but later tiny blisters erupted over the area. Now under his T-shirt is a bandage like the one he had on when the tat was new, the skin covered in anti-bacterial unguent.

Seth squats and leaps, bringing his knees up to his chest. The board spins in the air below but something goes wrong and it clatters to the driveway. He lands with his feet planted on either side of it, flips it over with the toe of his sneaker, and pushes back toward the head of the driveway.

The door to kitchen opens. Lewis moves over to the side door with the small window and sees Bishop, whose shift it is but that doesn't mean he hasn't forgotten about it, as he did yesterday, leaving Seth unattended for two hours while he finished cooking something up in the basement lab.

Lewis is convinced that Bishop is at all times at least a little altered on one of his designer drugs. He carries around a pocket spiral notebook in which he jots down assessments of their effects, using a rating system. Lewis found it on the kitchen table the other day and flipped through it. "Visuals lasting 15 seconds," it said on one page in Bishop's scrawl, on the next: "with 175 mg, orally: intellectually lucid but odd. 2 hrs at a ++++, but ultimately a neither-here-nor-there stuff." On another page: "Distinctly dizzy, visuals minor, need to lie down" and "2–3 mg. smoked dur: 3 hrs wholesome small-town 4th of july atmospherics / the Norman Rockwell of tryptamines."

Bishop goes to the threshold of the garage and checks on Seth, who's blown another attempt from the sound of it. Bishop is wearing an unbuttoned madras shirt, shorts that might be boxers, cheap flip-flops, like he's on his drag-ass way to the communal bathroom in a flophouse. He scratches his beard, plucks a pair of pliers from the wrack of tools and rags and screws and nails and brackets washed up there over the years. Bishop stands looking at the Masonite board, finally hanging the pliers on silver clips in an outline drawn by one of Abby's other "lifetime companions" in black Sharpie, Lewis can't remember which. Maybe Bishop is high on a single-molecule concoction that inclines one to tidy up.

Turning, he notices Lewis at the window of the door and flinches, raises a hand to his heart. Recovering, Bishop smirks under his beard and says, "Everything's *under control*, big bro," Lewis having chewed Bishop out for forgetting about Seth the other day.

Lewis gives a hearty thumbs-up, semi-sarcastic, where Bishop can see it in the frame of the window and turns away.

He slips in the earbuds of his iPod and goes to work at the edge of the yard, swinging the machete backhand then forehand, as he's seen it done on TV, "natives" clearing brush for naturalists and documentarians.

Berries clinging in green and red clusters on the underside of a certain enormous weed go flying. He rips up ivy in sections like carpet, chopping hard to sever the ropey vines, the blade hacking deep wounds into the ground.

He cuts down a spray of baby's-breath-like flowers that makes him think of Izzy's engagement party in Cambridge in two weeks. She's marrying a Harvard graduate student named Ben—blond, blue-eyed, mildest of mild manners. They met two summers ago, when Ben paid a reverential visit to the house to interview Cyrus for a dissertation on post-war Anglo-American literary criticism and Izzy answered the door. Lewis was only invited once he'd groveled his way back into Gerty's good graces. Now he's probably on her shit list again for declining so that he can be here to help out with Seth.

There's a species of tough, sinewy weed he has to seize like hair and hack away at before he can sever it. Viscous white sap oozes down the stumps and into the earth. He straightens and closes his eyes and leans backwards, stretching the muscles in his back. The white sky spins like a layer of fat on tissue. He closes his eyes and steadies himself, bends at the waist and catches hold of another head of weed hair and hacks at the base.

He's become too aware of the volumetric mass of the weeds, how like fingers and fleshy appendages and limbs they are. There's a stout-stalked, sinewy plant the color of rhubarb that crumples in his hand like a windpipe when he tries to snap it off, smears his fingers with wet fiber. Ants, beetles, crickets, spiders and insects he can't name flee as before a fire. Bits of plant gore cling to his sweat-soaked T-shirt. Pausing to catch his breath, he closes his eyes, hears himself murmur, "I'm sorry."

He comes to nettles with frilly leaves that sting his hands and forearms and his legs through his socks and jeans. Resistance and resentment emanate from the plants. They know him now. His little apology, uttered too late and half-heartedly, meant nothing. The dead and mangled ones want their bodies back. They want the yard. They want the earth. They wish him ill. They would enter the house through the windows and split it open from floor to ceiling and scream with joy as the sky and rain poured in.

When he narrowly misses cutting his foot, he can hear a faint, spiteful laughter. The heel of his hand is blistered from gripping the machete handle, which is dangerously slippery with sweat running into his eyes and down his arms. He should take a break, have a glass of water, dry off the handle with a towel, but he hacks harder and faster. He'll finish the whole job in one furious assault. As he chops he's also falling to his knees, he's holding Gerty around the legs, pleading. She places her blessing hand on his head. Get out, she says, *you're being dragged down. You must decide who's side you're on, Lewis, that of the weeds or of the tomatoes.*

I have decided, he says.

Decided what?

I want to go back, I want to begin again, Grandma.

This makes me very happy. How far back?

I'd like to be six years old.

No farther?

May I?

Yes.

Then I'd like to start over, be born again.

Very well, *I* will be your mother. Where would you like to be born?

Not Austin, not Wichita. May I be born in Cambridge?

Yes, you may. But I am too old. I will bring you to term inside a hollowed-out dictionary.

The blade strikes something hard and the machete flies out of his hand. He crouches down and clears away half-severed vines. Underneath, there's a large round pale stone, a Zen-garden remnant. He picks up the machete: there's a triangular chip in the blade.

Wiping the sweat from his face with the hem of his T-shirt, he looks over what he's done. He's cleared a little more than half the backyard. That still leaves the side, where Bishop's tent is. The cut plants are wilting fast, turning brown.

Something makes him look back toward the stoop. Abby is waving her arms slowly back and forth like someone signaling a ship from a desert island. He plucks out the earbuds and walks across the stubble.

She's smiling but something's wrong. "We need to run Seth over to the emergency room." Like it's a trip to the grocery store.

Lewis's heart sinks. "What the hell happened?"

"He hit his head skateboarding," she says. "It's not bad but it needs a few stitches."

"Fuck!" he says and flicks the machete down, driving the tip into the ground by his foot. "Where was Bishop?"

"Bishop was *right there in the garage*," she says, looking at the quivering machete with a frown of disapproval. "Calm down."

"Bishop," Lewis scoffs. "He's always fucked-up on something!"

"Bishop can't stop Seth from falling on his skateboard, Lewis."

"Why did Bishop let him skateboard to begin with?"

"Why did *you*? You saw him skateboarding too, according to Bishop."

He nods, caught out, but stands there scowling. It's still somehow Bishop's fault.

"What's gotten into you?" she says, looking him up and down with narrowed eyes. "You look like you've been in a battle."

"I couldn't read!" he says, pointing at the weeds by his room, which he has yet to cut down. He should've begun over there. Then, more calmly, "It was blocking the light out."

"Oh," she says, cautiously, humoring him now. One insanely violent son is enough for the moment.

"Where is Seth?" he asks.

"In the car." Lewis starts away but Abby stops him with a touch on his arm, saying, "Don't. He's not in the best mood."

Lewis stops in his tracks. "Jesus."

Abby glances over in the direction of the driveway and says in a lower voice, "I think it's the lithium. It throws his balance off."

She turns to go then stops. "Oh, but on a sunnier note, we have a client!"

Lewis raises his eyebrows, struggles to produce a glad face. He'd all but forgotten about Grateful Gaia or Tornado Ally, whatever they're calling it.

"He's flying out tonight—from Virginia," Abby says, walking backwards toward the driveway. "I think we'll just head out in the morning."

"What about Seth?" he asks. The Escalade horn honks impatiently.

"I think Seth should come along," she says, walking backwards. "Assuming he's up to it. Don't you think it would do him good?"

"Probably," Lewis says, "yeah."

"There's room for everyone."

"Am I going?" He's actually stir-crazy enough to want to.

"If Seth comes along, you should too. You'll be sorry you missed it, whatever we end up seeing."

"Oh, and thank you for the yard work!" she says off-hand-edly, walking away.

Lewis turns to take it in. In the farthest corner, a small flock of starlings is picking its way over the stubbly ground, like a search party moving across a field.

26

Dropping Lewis off in the driveway, Astrid gives his thigh an uncertain pat. While he searches his tired brain for something to say to her, Seth emerges from the garage as from a cave and sits desolately on the rear fender of the Escalade. The stitched-up gash is at the back of his head but the thick white bandage is wrapped all the way around, WW-I-casualty style. Astrid says, "God!"

"It's not as bad as it looks," Lewis assures her and, grateful for the distraction, gets out, gets away. He frowns at Seth to discourage any quips but Seth, oblivious and meds-blunted, gazes catatonically at the ground between his shoes. Why he's bothering to come on the chase Lewis can't understand but is glad he is, since if he stayed home, Lewis would have to watch him and Lewis got so little sleep last night that it would be torture to stay awake. Now he can safely crash in the Escalade and Abby and Bishop can keep an eye on Seth.

As Astrid drives off, the storm-chase client pulls up to the curb in a white rental, which means Lewis won't have time to shower and change clothes.

Lewis and then Seth too watch the man climb out of the car. He's wearing a khaki baseball cap and a yellow T-shirt tucked into denim shorts, running shoes, a video camera on a strap that seems to yoke forward his neck. The blue-jean shorts are belted tight. He looks to be in his mid-thirties, endearingly harmless and nerdy.

"Drew," he says, introducing himself. When he shakes

Seth's limply proffered, doubtless clammy hand he can be seen struggling over whether to ask about the head wound.

"That happened on a recent chase," Lewis says deadpan then regrets it as Drew's eyes widen in concern and fear.

"Chunk o' debris," Seth says with a shrug, his speech slurred from the meds. "Price you pay for getting close to the beast." Lewis chuckles appreciatively. It's the first joke Lewis has heard Seth make in a week and he's glad, on second thought, to have created an opening for it.

"Don't believe a word of it, Drew!" Abby says, materializing beside them. She has an orange crepe scarf tied around her hair and fashionably bulbous sunglasses. "He fell on his skateboard yesterday."

"Phew!" Drew says, honking out a relieved laugh. "You guys!" he says, shaking a finger at them. "Jerking my chain!"

"Well, now that you've met my two sons—who are," Abby says, tipping down her sunglasses to cut Lewis and Seth disapproving looks—"usually better mannered!— welcome to Tornado Ally!"

She gives Drew a quick hug, which causes him to shrink back slightly.

"The day is shaping up *really* nicely, Drew!" Abby says and Lewis is mildly appalled at her adoption of a slightly hucksterish, "expert" tone. Though maybe that's what the occasion calls for. "I just checked in with our navigator, Bishop. He tells me there's an entire *string* of storms headed our way from southern Colorado." She gestures vaguely at the sky, which is a clear blue except for a long swath of white cloud like a sandbar.

"Outstanding!" Drew says, looking up at the sky.

"So let's hit the road, guys!" Abby says.

She's backed the Escalade out of the driveway and is starting off down the street when Cody appears through a break in a hedge across the street, his specialty, waving his arm to flag them down as he scoots along in his lowrider jeans.

Abby brakes and rolls down her window. "There room for one more?" Cody asks her eagerly, peering in at the empty seats through the driver's side window.

"Ooh, I'm afraid not, Cody," she says. "We're going to pick up Bishop. And other folks," she adds, apparently remembering the other seats. The Escalade is like a small bus. She eases it forward. "We'll take lots of video!"

"It's not the same," Cody says, moving alongside. He shoots a pleading look at Seth, who sits staring numbly out the window.

"No, it's not," Abby says, patting his hand. "You can come next time," she says, speeding up. "Okay?"

"Okay!" Cody says dejectedly, releasing the window. But he trots down the street in the wake of the car, holding up his jeans with one hand and waving with the other.

They immediately hit traffic. Despite the cheerful chatter Abby keeps up, the chase seems off to an inauspicious start. There's a whiff of burning tar and ahead of them for an eternity is the slot-like rear window of a black muscle car in which a blinding granular reflection of the sun is concentrated. When they finally reach the Wichita State University campus, Bishop is standing at the curb beside his moped. He's wearing sunglasses, his Reality Check Mark T-shirt, shorts, Teva-s. He has the laptop open and is shielding the screen from the glare with his forearm.

Abby toots the horn to get his attention and he waves and reaches in to shake Drew's hand, waggling the laptop. "There's a *tasty supercell* in the area, Drew!"

"Great!" Drew says, bouncing slightly in his seat. He takes a map out of his backpack and begins unfolding it. Lewis gets out and takes a seat in the back row, looking forward to napping once they're out on the highway.

"If we can head basically out *into the Flinthills* we can intercept it," Bishop tells Abby then settles in and puts on his seatbelt. Abby sits still for a moment as if giving Bishop a chance to remember then asks, "What do you want to do about *the moped*?"

"Ah, right," Bishop says, turning to look at it where it stands on the curb, sunlight glinting off the chrome.

Abby glances deadpan into the rearview, shaking her head. "Would you have left it there if I hadn't said anything?"

"Hmm," Bishop says, considering the question objectively. "I'm not sure."

He thinks for a moment and says, "Well, I don't dare leave it there, even locked up." Turning around to address Drew, he says, "The meth addiction is really bringing this town to its knees."

"Throw it in the back!" Abby cries, popping the trunk. "But let's go!"

Lewis gets out to help. They move aside one of the orange reserve gas tanks and heave the moped into the rear compartment then wrangle it to prevent the handlebars from blocking Abby's view in the rear mirror.

When they're underway, Bishop turns to face Drew again. "So what attracted you to our outfit?" Lewis can tell he's fishing for compliments about the website. "What distinguished us from the pack?"

Drew makes an apologetic duck of the head and says, "To be honest? All the other chasers were booked."

Seth quietly snorts out a laugh into this hand at this, his first sign of life, and Bishop, visibly crestfallen, says, "Ah-ha. Well, I can *assure* you, this will be a unique experience. We're *utterly* unlike the pack," Bishop says, facing forward. "We're not part of the pack *whatsoever*."

"Well, your website is definitely, um, *unique*," Drew says, nodding eagerly. "I'll say that."

Bishop turns back to face Drew. "That's because we approach weather *as inseparable from consciousness*."

"*OK,*" Drew says, nodding gamely.

"In other words," Bishop says, "we reject the whole materialist paradigm of meteorological phenomena—"

"Sorry to interrupt," Abby says. "Which way here, Bishop?"

"To be continued!" Bishop tells Drew, consulting the GPS.

"I have to tell you guys the story of the early-morning session we had!" Bishop says to the car generally.

"Bishop is involved in a drug-research program," Abby explains to Drew with a detectable undertone of caution for Bishop's ears, unsure of whether Drew is a suitable audience for whatever Bishop is about to say. "Drew has no idea what 'session' means, Bishop. And anyway, isn't this stuff *confidential?*" Nudge, nudge.

Bishop looks at her. "I won't use the subject's real name."

"I actually need you to focus on the navigating again, Bishop," Abby says. "I think I missed the turn." She passes Bishop what looks like the large bound map of the state by counties and Bishop bends over it.

Lewis stretches out across the seats in the back row and closes his eyes, memories of the night Astrid arriving in wedges, like Dopplering noise: she wants to become a "healer," she told him as he lay on the massage table, and Lewis wondered about the appeal of this idea to New Agers, the world as a holistic triage center. They drank red wine and talked until there seemed to be nothing more to say and she looked at him as if squinting into sunlight. She wore a scoop-necked spandex top that squeezed her shoulder blades together and flattened her breasts. She's nearly Abby's age, it struck him. He lay the back of his hand against her cheek and she closed her eyes with tremulous gratitude. The hair at her temples was thinning, he noticed, and the skin of her forehead so taut and papery that the skull seemed to bulge beneath. He sat back away from her, unable to go on, and he could see the hurt in her eyes.

He wakes with a guilty start and sits up. On the side of a

highway a small oil derrick pumps away like a toy bird. A wedge of five bikers with sinister insignia written in a chalky white on the backs of their leather vests—Lewis can't make out what it says—breaks apart and swoops past like the ghosts of cattle rustlers haunting the plains. Thinking of the roadside strip club, Lewis glances at Seth for his reaction but Seth has none, seems to be noticing nothing.

Lewis lies back across the seats and sleeps and is woken up later to the muffled clunk of the Escalade doors shutting. They've pulled over on the side of a narrow two-lane road in the middle of gently rolling but essentially flat, saturated green fields.

"The Flint Hills!" Bishop announces, making a broad impresario sweep of one arm.

It's quiet—insects, a single bird singing. The sky is mostly clear blue, with small white clouds in ranks trundling past from the south. Fifty feet away, Seth stands pissing into waist-high prairie grass, the rustle of the stream faintly audible.

"I dream about tornados a lot," Drew says as they're pulling out. A tour bus—long and dull green and high-windowed, sealed off like a canister—sweeps slowly past in the distance.

"Is that right?" Abby says into the rearview mirror.

"But they're not mine," Drew says. This gives everyone pause. Even Seth stirs and shifts towards him as if curious.

"What do you mean, they're not *yours*?" Abby asks.

"The tornados I'm seeing in my dreams are based on photos and videos," Drew says. "I didn't see them firsthand."

"But they're *your dreams*!" Bishop says.

"It's not the same," Drew says with a shrug. Which begins a philosophical discussion during which Lewis nods off again and when he wakes up Abby is parking at an overlook. There's a gazebo on a ridge, a walkway leading to a railed viewing platform. Lewis goes numbly along with the others and peers out at the view of a winding deeply cut creek crowded with cottonwoods and scrub in a landscape out of Africa, a faint white haze hammocked above the treetops. Along the horizon, a tumbleweed-like procession of dark clouds. Drew snaps photos of them.

A two-lane road, green fields, the yellow dividing line sunfaded. Buzzards, strikingly big seen from so close, flap up into the bright air while, fifty yards away, a doe stands looking over her shoulder at them.

They pass through a small town, white houses in one yard of which what Lewis thinks excitedly might be Outsider Art turns out to be an upturned rotary plough; more fields, open and flat and endless, isolated oaks bent from a prevailing wind; a grain elevator, bales of wheat like cubed gold.

Lewis lies down again. He's woken by the sound of the car doors slamming and joins the others outside to stare up at an enormous, multi-tiered bank of dark-gray clouds reaching into clear sky.

"This thing is just *huge*," Bishop says, looking up at the storm and down at his laptop as if not quite believing. Along the lower flanks is a ragged, restless detachment of soot-gray clouds.

"There's *rotation*," he adds in an even more surprised voice, pointing upward while looking at the laptop screen. Peering over his shoulder, Lewis sees a spinning icon within a purple blob.

Suddenly a wire-like stab of lightning then a thick, jagged bolt. Everyone flinches.

"Whoa!" Drew says and begins filming with his camcorder.

"And we're getting a bit of outdraft here, as you can feel," Abby adds, holding up her palms. She looks tired from all the driving but happy, invigorated by the beauty of the storm, the ions in the air. Drew sweeps the area to get a shot of the grasses bent in the wind.

Then it begins to rain and everyone gets back into the Escalade. For a few minutes, Bishop studies the laptop and pages through the large paperback map of the state while the rain clatters on the roof.

"Okay," he says finally, raising his voice to be heard over what's become a downpour. "Now the thing is, we're near the leading edge of the storm. Which is great, there'll be some nice views eventually? But where we really want to be is at the *back edge*."

"Which is where tornados typically form, right?" Drew says

"Right, Drew! Drew is all over this stuff! Now there's another storm to our south. We can go after that and hope for the best." This option clearly bores Bishop: too safe. "*Or* we can try to *get to the back* of this storm here. And to get to the *back* edge we'll have to cross through this area here—"Bishop holds up the laptop—"marked in purple on the radar? This is all heavy rain and probably some hail too."

"The core," Drew says.

"Exactly!" Bishop says. "The core."

"We could 'core-punch,'" says Drew. "Right?"

"Core-punch!" Bishop says, reaching back to give Drew a high-five. "And to make things even *more* interesting, the shortest route is twenty miles of dirt road." Bishop giggles and rubs his hands together, glancing over at Abby. "There's really no other option if we want to get to the rear edge. Shall we vote? All in favor of core-punching say 'Ay!'"

With the exception of Seth, everyone says, "Ay!"

"Core-punch, it is!" Bishop says. "Buckle up!" He looks at his map of the state and says, "The turn should be right up ahead, Abby!" She's leaning forward to see through the rain, which a moment later doubles in intensity and sounds like the crackling of bacon grease amplified.

"Can she see through that?" Drew asks Lewis nervously.

"I hope so," Lewis says.

The rain turns to hail, which sounds like gravel rattling angrily down on the car with a kind of sentient hostility. Out ahead of them on the dirt road it looks like salt scattered on sidewalks in a snowstorm. The air is pearlescent. Hail pings wildly off the windshield. A robotic voice comes over the laptop: "The National Weather Service has issued a Tornado Watch number 358 effective until ten P.M."

"Whoo-hoo!" Bishop shouts. "Consider yourselves *warned*!"

They're now following in the tracks of a slow-moving car whose tail lights are faintly visible. The hail sounds like it's denting the chassis.

"It's plum-sized!" Abby calls out a bit anxiously. "My poor car!"

"Wow," Bishop says, leaning forward to see better. He rolls down his window and thrusts his arm out into the air and pulls it back immediately.

"Ouch!" he says, laughing and shaking his arm. Chunky hail rains into the front seat through the open window on Bishop's side.

He holds up a jagged hunk. "Look at that! She's right!" It goes on pouring through the open window like anti-aircraft fire.

"Close the window! Jesus, Bishop!" Abby tells him.

"Shit!" Bishop says, rolling it up and tapping the keyboard of the laptop. "It broke the screen!" Lewis leans forward to see: the screen is dark and riven by a fine crack. "I've lost the satellite link."

"What's *that* mean?" Abby asks, peering over the steering wheel to see the road ahead.

"It means we won't be able to track the storm," Bishop says grimly, tapping at keys. Then, recovering, he adds, "But that's fine."

"It's fine?" Abby says dubiously. "How is it fine?"

"We're *right on course*," Bishop says, making a chopping motion with his arm. "We just continue on to the end of this road and we'll be at the rear."

"Once we get around this, we'll have a really excellent view of it, Drew!" Abby calls.

The hail turns to rain then the rain shuts off all at once and the dirt road ends in a paved one running perpendicular to it. Abby brings the car to a stop.

"And here we *are!*" Bishop announces victoriously, twisting around to give a double thumbs-up to the back seats. The sky is clear to their left and behind them, tinged the pale color of a sunset. Directly ahead and to their right is a massive gray head of cloud shaped in a swoop or twist.

"Oh, you gorgeous mesocyclone, you!" Bishop says. "*Look* at that mother!" It makes Lewis think of the Satanic image on the cover of *Storm Chase: A Photographer's Journey*. They seem foolishly close to it.

Coming toward them around a gradual curve in the paved road is a caravan of ten or so vans and SUVs. The lead van has a white radar dish bolted to the roof.

"Keep ahead of them!" Bishop cries, pounding the dash with his fist. "Go, go, go!" Abby pulls out into the road in front of the van with the Doppler dish, which honks at them merrily.

"Good job, babe!" Bishop says, looking back. "We do *not* want to get stuck behind *them*. That's the Doppler brigade."

He rolls his window down and leans out, pointing at the storm bank. "Do you guys see what I see, at about ten o'clock? That lowering? That's a *funnel cloud!*"

Abby slows the car down and leans toward Bishop to see out. The car behind them honks.

"If that touches down, it's a tornado!" Bishop cries, bouncing in his seat like a child. "We're looking at a tornado-to-be right there! Hot *damn!*"

"This is awesome!" Drew says, leaning across Lewis to see out. He turns on his camcorder and holds it out the window. Seth seems to be asleep, his head nestled into a windbreaker wadded up against the window.

"Can we find somewhere to pull off?" Abby asks Bishop.

"Right here!" he says, banging the side of the Escalade with his fist.

"Oh, this is perfect," she says, pulling onto the soft shoulder. The sunlight from the west strikes the rear wall of the storm with strong clear light. "You are *good*, Bishop!"

Everyone piles out and moves into the field, Seth too now.

"If this thing produces," Bishop says, pointing at a vague area near the bottom of the storm, "it'll be an absolutely *elegant* twister."

The supercell is mountainous but close and clear at the same time—too close for Lewis's taste, like an amphitheater. The farthest trailing edge of the storm, a ragged soot-gray wasp's leg, is almost directly overhead. The air has turned a seasick gray-green. The caravan of other chasers has driven past them and pulled over further down the road, hazard lights flashing. Spidery silhouetted figures set up tripods, bend over viewfinders.

They all stand staring across the field except for Seth, who's sitting on the hood of the Escalade with his arms folded. Maybe a mile away behind them, visible through a stand of trees, is another tiny town, a silver water tower. From that direction a tornado siren begins to wail, floating up over the trees.

"Tornado siren!" Bishop shouts happily, cupping a hand to an ear.

The air goes suddenly still then just as suddenly a stiff breeze begins to blow. His wispy white hair raised by it, Bishop holds up the palms of his hands. "That's gen-u-ine rear-flank downdraft!" he announces, his T-shirt fluttering.

A cruiser with the roof light going but no siren swoops along the narrow dark road, slowing by the Doppler radar caravan then again by the Escalade. Lewis finds himself watching narrowly, braced against the *whisk-whisk* of the squad car transmission, Tasers, handcuffs, furry forearms.

"You guys are on your own!" the cop calls out the window. "Right-o!" Bishop calls back delightedly, giving a double thumbs-up out of a crouch. He turns back to the storm as to a huge drive-in movie screen. "That's the actionary, the updraft, we're seeing," Bishop says, pointing.

They stand waiting, watching the evil lower clouds turn slowly, mutate, configure and reconfigure in a lazy ominous motion. "There's *no place I'd rather be* right now!" Bishop says.

Then nothing except for this slow swirling, which gradually halts, fades away like a mist. Minutes pass. Arms crossed, Seth has lain back on the hood of the Escalade. A flock of crows sweeps past like leaves caught in a strong gust.

Lewis contemplates a distant farmhouse and wonders what that life is like. "What now?" he asks finally.

"Now we just wait a little longer," Bishop says, a hint of disappointment entering his voice.

Drew takes a knee in the grass. He's been speaking to someone on a cellphone and when he gets off, Bishop asks him, "Did you hear what Bush said when he flew into Greenburg?"

"Is this a joke?" Drew asks with good-humored wariness, not to be fooled twice.

"If only," Abby says.

"You know about Greenburg, right?" Bishop asks. "Little town about hundred miles southeast of Wichita? An F-5 just destroyed it."

"I saw the pictures," Drew says, nodding solemnly. "Just terrible."

"It's like an atomic *bomb* went off down there," Abby says.

"Quite a few folks are moving away," Bishop says, nodding. "Lost everything; can't imagine rebuilding after that. So anyway, Bush flies in—" Bishop starts laughing in advance, bent at the waist. "So Bush flies in," he says, beginning again, "and Bush says—through a bullhorn or something, you know how he does. 'My mission—" Bishop seizes his white-bearded jaw to keep from laughing—"'my mission is to *touch somebody's soul . . . by representing our country*!"

They all burst out laughing, Drew following suit after a beat but uncertainly, peering from face to face as if to grasp the real gist.

"Touch somebody's soul!" Bishop cries. Then, as if the intimacy of it just struck him, he adds, "Don't *touch my soul*! Keep your hands *off* my soul!"

"Don't represent our *country*," Lewis says.

"Too late," Abby says.

They turn back to the storm, which has acquired a static quality—no movement at all now.

"Well, come on!" Bishop calls. "Come *on*, you mother!"

Down the road, the Doppler brigade is packing up their cameras and tripods with military efficiency. Their silhouettes then slip into the vehicles, which are soon driving past, the headlights on in the dying light.

"What's happening?" Abby asks, watching them go. Bishop watches them too, hands on his hips, squinting. He shakes his head. "I don't know," he says in his neutral, admirably honest fashion.

"You would if your laptop worked," Abby points out.

"True," Bishop admits with an embarrassed chortle.

She sighs, shakes her head. "You and your record-sized hail. One for the local newspapers!"

Bishop squints up at the storm as if willing it to send down a face-saving twister then announces, "I guess this may not happen after all, people!"

The tornado siren has fallen silent. Lewis watches the taillights of the last minivan in the Doppler brigade disappear around a descending curve in the road. To the northeast, thin slanting curtains of rain move across a golden band of horizon at the far perimeter of the storm.

"It's still *incredibly* beautiful," Abby says, waving her arm at the massive, sterile cloud creature. The twilight falls across her suddenly weary features as if to veil them from view.

Now, in the quadrant where the caravan was headed, there's a tremendous lightning strike and everyone flinches.

"I mean look at that!" Abby cries, startled out of her melancholy.

"It's the Goddess, all right," Bishop says wistfully. "If there were *any* community, they would've stopped to give us a heads-up," he adds, staring bitterly down the road after the Doppler caravan. "Every man for himself, I guess!"

"We could follow them," Lewis suggests.

"Nah, it's too late," Bishop says. "Every fucking man for himself!"

"We don't guarantee a tornado," Abby tells Drew, "but we *absolutely* guarantee *beauty*." She makes a theatrical sweep with her arm. "This is a real glimpse of Gaia."

"It's pretty incredible, all right," Drew says but clicks off his camcorder and lets it hang limp from his neck.

"Well," Bishop says with a concluding note. As they're turning to go back to the car, there's a movement in the far corner of the field.

"What's that?" Lewis asks, catching Bishop by the wrist. Bishop pauses and looks back, squinting hard, straining his neck forward tortoise-like.

"Is it *burning*?" Lewis asks.

Wisps of smoke or is it earth are rising snakily into the air, two, three of them. Lewis thinks it must be from a lightning strike, fire in the field. Then the tendrils or snakes of smoke rise in sheets and grow larger, forming a rough circle like enormous ghosts in a ring dance, Sioux warriors risen on the prairie. Now they reach up to join tatters of clouds from the bottom of the storm, helically intertwining.

Then it's simply there, out of nowhere, this long stout elephant trunk or length of intestine.

"Oh!" Abby and Bishop shout in unison, as if orgasming. "Oh my God!"

"Wild!" Lewis yells, a funny sort of happiness flooding him.

"Seth!" Abby cries, pointing at it and jumping up and down. "Look! Look!"

Lewis turns back to see Seth is snapped out of his numb detachment, grinning and shaking his head in amazement. His teeth glow in the gloaming. He eases himself down from the hood of the Escalade and takes a few steps forward into the field. Abby goes back to meet him and circles an arm around his shoulder. Lewis joins them. He leans near Seth's ear and says, "You made a tornado happen after all—it was just a bit delayed!" Seth nods. Lewis chucks him on the shoulder and they stand together watching it. Lewis is filled with a sense of great optimism and hope, as if it's borne on the air and he's inhaling it like laughing gas.

Quickly filling itself in, the tornado is more like a water tower now, thick, bluish-white, cocked to one side, phallic. Lewis walks forward to stand next to Drew, who has set up a tripod for his camcorder and is filming away meanwhile speaking into his cell phone. "It's a dream come true!" he tells whoever's on the other end. "Literally!"

Bishop is doing a little goat dance. "A tornado on our *first chase*!" he says, holding a camcorder toward it. "What a blessing, what an amazing blessing!"

"Just *look* at that thing!" Abby tells Seth. "It's truly *a god*!" As if she never truly believed all the talk about Gaia and Goddesses. "It's neither earth nor sky, it's some *new union*!"

"It's making me hot!" Bishop says, speeding up his little goat dance.

"Listen to him!" she says, letting go of Seth to run forward and tickle Bishop in the ribs. They embrace without taking their eyes off the twister and do a giddy little two-step in the wind-bent grass. "You led us *right to it!*" she tells him. "My hero! My hunter!"

"And all those conformist Doppler fools *missed* it!" Bishop crows. The outdraft is blowing his thin white hair around like cord grass. "Don't you *love* that?"

"Is it getting bigger?" Drew asks now. He looks up from his viewfinder and then back.

"I *needed* to have my laptop broken!" Bishop tells Abby. "That was *necessary!*"

"Absolutely!" she agrees.

"It's gotten bigger," Drew says conclusively.

It has, Lewis sees. It's also turning the color of the field as it sucks the earth up into itself. Just how far off is it? He holds up a hand to shield the light and squints. It's hard to gauge. The tornado itself seems safely behind glass, sealed off by the idea of it, the concept "tornado."

Suddenly there are two huge lightning blasts in the dark, widening base, like strobic bombs detonating.

"Yeah, OK, people!" Bishop says, looking sobered up, even frightened. He's walking backwards toward the car but can't seem to take his gaze from the twister.

"Just gorgeous!" Abby says, her blouse fluttering madly, the tip of the crepe scarf flickering like the tongue of a prophetess.

Lewis thought for no good reason that the twister would stay put or head off to one side or recede, rejoin the storm. But it's broken away from the matrix of the dark clouds and is headed if not right at them then in their direction.

He moves over and shouts at Bishop. "What's happening?"

"We need to *go* is what's happening!" Bishop says. Halfway across the field, what looks like a sheet of plywood sails upward and vanishes skyward in a dusty sun-struck haze.

"Now, right now!" Bishop calls. There's dirt in the air; Lewis tastes it on his tongue, squints to see through it.

No one moves for one last look, held in place by the golden-brown beauty of the twister, which is lit gold now by the light of the setting sun.

As if aware of the rapt audience, it wobbles on its axis then lunges sideways with an alarming, savage quickness, like a boxer feinting. Then it holds still. Then it jumps halfway across the field toward them, looming upward like a skyscraper thrust up through the crust of the earth.

"Seth!" Abby is shouting. Seth has opened the rear hatch of the Escalade, which is jouncing madly in the wind, and has the moped on the ground. He hops on the seat. "We're leaving *right now!*"

"Seth!" Abby shouts. "Get in the car—we're going! Seth!"

He's started the thing up, the snarl of the motor just audible in the growing shriek of the twister. Looking neither left nor right, he rides down the road in the direction the Doppler caravan went. He's panicking, Lewis thinks, he can't wait for them.

But Seth turns out onto the field and drives straight at the tornado. Objects are flashing past, clumps of grass, a branch, a section of fence. Lewis's clothes and skin are rippling in the howling wind. He can barely see through dust in the air. He shouts at Seth to stop but Seth is leaning forward over the handlebars, the white bandage on his head glowing in the gray-green light.

"Seth!" Abby shouts and breaks into a run, flashing past Lewis, who chases her down and wraps his arms around her.

"No!" he shouts. Something strikes his leg. There's a blinding flash and they're sitting on the ground ten feet apart. There's dirt in his mouth, in his teeth. He crawls to her.

"We can't leave him!" Abby sobs. She's quaking, clawing at him.

Curtains of dirt fill the air. Seth has disappeared. Bishop helps Lewis half drag, half carry Abby to the car.

Lewis can barely get the door open then he leans backwards

with all his weight to hold it as Bishop and Drew push Abby into the back seat, climb in after her.

The roar is enormous, pitiless, *chug-chug*. Lewis finds himself crawling along the ground. He gropes up into the driver's seat but can't shut the door, can't see out. The car is rocked side to side then back and forth, then both at the same time. His ears pop as the air pressure plunges and he hits his head on the dash and blacks out, coming to as an enormous star appears on the windshield.

27

L ewis gets out of bed, steps over a tray of food, goes to the window. He listens for a moment then lifts the blinds. A man is digging a hole in the backyard. He lays down the shovel and walks out of view. In the bush outside the window, sunlight traces a filament of spiderweb strung between two leaves. A breeze lifts the web, sunlight flashes along its length then vanishes as the web falls back.

The man comes back carrying a young birch. He kneels on the ground and with a blade cuts away the twine and burlap wrapping. He brushes his hands over the root ball, loosening the soil, then lowers the tree into the hole and shovels in dirt. He goes away again.

A sparrow lights in the bush and passes its beak back and forth across a branch, one-two. Then it flicks its tail feathers and drops from sight.

The man comes back with a hose and stands watering the ground around the tree, the sound of water spattering on the earth fills the air.

***

The leaves of the bush nod in the breeze, yes, yes, yes, all the leaves he can see confirm: it happened, it happened, it happened.

***

Lewis swings his legs out of bed and sits for a long time on the edge then gets up and washes his face, brushes his teeth. He finds a pair of scissors in the drawer of his desk and cuts off his beard, clumps of rust-colored hair falling onto the porcelain and his hands, coarse, foreign. He peers at himself in the mirror and considers cutting off all the hair on his head too. He raises the scissors then lets them fall.

On the bedside table, V.'s condolence letter, the grain of the paper visible in the angled sunlight coming in through the venetian blinds. He picks it up, his eyes passing over the handwriting, cramped yet clear, like brushing the features of her face with his fingertips. "Love," it's signed. She must have weighed that. It would have been too cold without it and so it gets used because there's no middle ground, it's either life or death.

Abby is coming out of her own room with an air of trying to remember something. Her smile when she notices him there in the hallway is wan.

"Very nice," she says of his clean-shaven face. From the living room and dining room comes a hushed bustle. People are rearranging furniture, laying out food. The rich, faintly nauseating fragrance of a cake baking reaches them.

The bruise on her cheek is yellow in the center shading out to mottled green and blue and purple. Beneath the house robe, her body feels warm and boneless. He intuits her as an old woman, slow-moving, replete with incorporated days. She reaches up to but does not touch the bandage on his brow. He asks whether someone planted a tree in the yard.

"A birch," she says, nodding.

"I thought I might've dreamed it."

She produces another wan smile, shakes her head: no, he didn't dream it. "It's for a ceremony Louise is going to perform."

"A tree ceremony?" he says.

'It's done to settle spirits who have had—" she pauses as if she's momentarily forgotten the phrase, "—violent passings."

In Mongolia it's done, Lewis thinks, and in Siberia. But he works to keep this disenchanted thought from appearing in his face. Over Abby's shoulder he sees Stacy and her parents come in from the kitchen, the father, wearing a bolo tie, guiding the wheelchair. Stacy's expression is strangely washed-out and disoriented, as if she's been given a powerful sedative. Her father is the designated driver.

Bishop takes Lewis by the elbow and steers him through the house. Summer light flickers at all the windows. They pause to speak to Stacy and her parents and Lewis finds that he understands what Stacy says before it's translated.

There are women from the Birthday Party evening at Gar, Astrid among them, others he hasn't seen in years. They stop what they're doing to touch or embrace him. He listens, watching words form on their lips, but doesn't quite hear what they're saying. Or he hears but he doesn't follow it.

In the kitchen Bishop pours two glasses of whisky. Lewis finds a legal pad and a pen in the cabinet underneath the phone. They take the whiskies out through the sliding glass doors of the breakfast nook and sit on the stoop.

The leaves of the young birch sift the hot air. The smell of the new black soil spread around the trunk is sharp. Succulent-looking green weeds have sprung up everywhere in the wide swath Lewis cleared with the machete.

Bishop holds out his closed hand for Lewis to take something—two capsules, white powder on a slant inside them.

"Ex," Bishop informs him quietly. "I'm going to do mine before the ceremony."

Lewis thanks him and looks down at the pills in his hand with half a mind to pop them right now. He puts them in his pocket instead. "Is it yours?"

Bishop is pleased that Lewis thought to ask. "It's a special batch," he says, nodding. "I was in the zone."

Bishop would like to give a more detailed account, Lewis can tell, and he turns slightly away and looks down at the legal pad to discourage it. He should have begun this earlier. He remembers a line from Rilke he came across online: "You are not surprised at the force of the storm—you have seen it growing."

He jots it down, thinks about it, crosses it out. The reference to storm is too fraught. They saw it coming, all right. And Lewis *is* surprised by the nameless heaviness bearing him down.

Cars have been parking along the street, the muffled clamor of doors closing. Now friends of Seth's drift outside through the open sliding glass doors to smoke and speak quietly in small clusters: a homeless-looking man with a thin scar like a helmet strap under his jaw; someone with a mohawk; someone else wearing a gray wool cap in the heat of summer; an undersized young woman, who seems to have some sort of congenital condition. A few wave tentatively at Lewis, nod. They know he's the brother, bits of his story.

"People think synthetic drugs are lacking the spirit of organics like peyote and whatnot," Bishop says. Lewis looks at him. What's he talking about?

"But if I'm in the zone, I can *feel a spirit* enter my synthetics," Bishop says, flittering the fingers of one hand trippily in the air. "It happens toward the end, like a soul entering a fetus."

Lewis nods. "That's nice, Bishop," he says. "But I need to write something for my little whatever-we're-calling it." Eulogy?

"Oh, of course!" Bishop says, rising.

Tori and Kaylee, wearing short tight black dresses, find him on the back stoop and embrace him tearfully for so long, one on each side of him, that he's growing inappropriately turned on.

Abby comes out onto the stoop and beckons everyone inside. The air-conditioning has broken down and all the windows are open. The house is crowded and ripe-smelling with so many bodies. A sort of altar has been arranged on the marble mantle above the fireplace, lined with objects significant to Seth, guitar, skateboard. Above these, a blown-up photo of him with arms crossed. He gazes into the distance with an expression of self-mocking grandeur.

When he finds Abby, she says, "This just came in." She holds up her cell phone. There's a text message: our condolences

"I had to check the caller ID," Abby says. "It's from Gerty." Lewis stands there shaking his head. "Can you believe it?" She turns to a group of her friends and shows them. "From Seth's grandmother in Cambridge."

"You are *joking.*"

There's a stir at the door. Virgil has arrived, larger and more formal in attire than the others in his immediate vicinity. He's wearing a dark-blue linen suit Sylvie bought for him in Paris. From across the room, Lewis watches him introduce himself to Astrid, who was the one to open the door. His mouth is compressed in a stoic smile that brings out a dimple in one cheek, a somber version of the public, formal face Lewis has seen him wear for post-lecture wine and cheese receptions.

Now Abby goes to him and they embrace for a long moment then stand speaking, gripping each other's forearms. They are the parents of the dead child, Lewis thinks. Together they created the boy and now he has died and they are meeting again for the occasion of his memorial service. That two such different people were married and produced offspring is so odd and unlikely as to be either mistaken and obscene or transpersonal and destined.

They embrace once more and Abby turns away and Lewis makes his way through the sweaty crush and shakes his father's hand. Virgil looks relieved and grateful to see him, as if he expected Lewis to shun him, to leave him squirming in social isolation here in terra incognita. He asks about the people around them and listens distractedly as Lewis tells him what he knows, as if the purpose of the questions is to free Virgil of the obligation to speak himself. Abby reappears with a glass of red wine for Virgil.

Lewis's cell thrums. It's Eli calling to offer his condolences again. He's in France. He asks to speak to Abby then to Virgil then gets back on with Lewis. He's feeling guilty for not flying out for the memorial. It's because of Hermione, Eli says again, and the trip to the South of France she's had planned for them for over a year. Otherwise, Eli would be there for Lewis, without question.

"Eli, it's fine," Lewis tells him again. He didn't expect anyone other than family to make the journey. But the more he speaks to Eli and listens to him bemoaning being unable "to be there for" Lewis, the more Lewis detects Eli's relief at not having to deal with the emotional mess of the situation, and the more Lewis resents being let down by his friend, who has in fact chosen Hermione and the South of France over Lewis at a moment when Lewis should have been given priority.

When he gets off with Eli, Abby touches him on the arm and says, "Let's begin."

The house falls silent as Abby makes her way to the mantle. People sit on the floor and squeezed together on the couch, stand along the walls. More than a few must be from the Inter-Faith Homeless Shelter, administrators but the homeless or semi-homeless too, including Butch, looking dazed and shrunken. Lewis is impressed at the turnout but faintly disgusted by the pong and funk in the hot house. He's having trouble catching his breath. He fans his face with a program Abby had made up for the memorial: the photo of Seth from the mantle, lyrics from one of his songs.

She closes her eyes for a moment then opens them and,

looking serenely from face to face, smiles sadly, bravely. "Well, he really outdid himself," she says and the room erupts in laughter, quietly rueful then gradually more raucous and joyful. She has nothing written down but she is a more natural public speaker than any of the professionals on the Chopik side of the family and it all emerges in effortlessly rounded paragraphs. It is wise, a wisdom born specifically of her time with Seth; there is foreknowledge and even a kind of joy in her words, but if Lewis grasps their meaning they also pour over him like music and he retains little, as if the purpose were to forget.

Now it's Virgil's turn but Virgil shakes his head, sending Lewis forward with a pat on the shoulder: you speak for both of us. Lewis wends his way through the crush to the mantle and looks out over the people sitting shoulder to shoulder on the floor, on the couch, in chairs, peering in from the dining room, craning to see in the doorway behind Virgil. In their upturned, expectant faces he seeks out Seth or signs of Seth but sees only eyes set in faces altogether their own. He's the educated, sane brother. They expect him to say something noble and touching and pitch-perfect but nothing of the sort is occurring to him and he simply stares back over them, his attention drawn to the man with the helmet-strap scar, who is weeping into his puffy wind-burnt hands. And when Lewis finally opens his mouth to speak it's as if he's being ventriloquized by this man. All that comes out is a sob.

He struggles to get control of himself but can't do it and now someone has laced an arm around him—Bishop, smelling of Dr. Bronner's and high-grade weed and whisky. Lewis allows himself to be led away from the mantle. Passing through the crowd, he is touched by many hands—consoling, congratulatory. As if by failing so completely, he's achieved something, which angers him obscurely, like a consolation prize.

He pours another glass of whisky in the kitchen and drinks it off standing alone at the counter. He can hear someone else speaking at the mantle but the words are unclear. He thinks of taking the Ex Bishop gave him but lacks the energy or belief to fish the pills out of his pocket.

He goes back to the living room and stands beside Virgil as someone plays guitar, someone reads a poem, someone sings a song Seth wrote, all of it taking place, for Lewis, in a kind of silent, obliterative roar.

It's twilight, midsummer twilight in which the light is a veil-like substance. Having declined Abby's invitation to take part in the tree ceremony, Virgil sits looking overlarge and uncomfortable in his small rental car, knees riding up and the fabric of the suit trousers pulled taut. Lewis has walked out with him to say goodbye but now Virgil pats the passenger seat. "Sit for a second," he says.

Climbing reluctantly into the car, Lewis notices the cardboard container holding half the ashes lying on its side in the back seat. Virgil plans to have a memorial service in New York for the Chopiks.

Staring through or at the dust-streaked windshield, Virgil says, "I regret sending him to the clinic that summer."

"Abby feels bad for not sending him to *more* clinics," Lewis says.

Turning toward Lewis at the unexpected remark, Virgil gives off a whiff of cologne, something Sylvie forbade because he tends to use too much. But Sylvie is not around to intervene in Virgil's personal style. Virgil is free to wear fedoras and trench coats again, sleuth his way through the stacks. "Really?" he asks.

Lewis nods. It's not true of course but Virgil seems so miserable.

"I was caught completely off guard by the whole episode," Virgil says, sinking back into regretfulness. "But why was I cut off? I should have made a point to *know him better*. All those people who showed up today, for instance. I had no idea he had so many friends!"

They sit for a moment in silence.

"Well—" Lewis says, placing a hand on the door.

"I spoke with someone," Virgil says now, holding him in place, "a friend of Abby's. She said that that was the very first time Abby had ever gone out on one of those 'tornado chases.'"

"That's right," Lewis says, thinking this can't be news and wondering where this is headed: somewhere. Virgil is not one to think aloud; he has a thesis.

"Tornado Ally, she called the company?" Virgil asks now. "A pun on Tornado *Alley*, I take it."

Lewis sighs to show his impatience with this retreading of established ground.

"I tried to find out more on the website," Virgil says in his defense, "but it had been taken down. Understandably." Lewis glances at the house in the hope of being signaled to by someone, called inside.

"We did mushrooms once, your mom and I," Virgil says abruptly, apropos of what, Castañeda/Ally? Maybe he *is* rambling. "Did she ever tell you that?"

Lewis shakes his head quickly.

"No, well, that doesn't fit so neatly with my stodgy professor image."

He pauses, savoring Lewis's surprise. "It was in Rome, when I was at the Academy. You were, let's see, you would have been two. We left you with a sitter, went to a friends' house for the afternoon." He turns down the corners of his mouth, shrugs. "I enjoyed it. It was like—being part of a sort of pneumatic mosaic."

Lewis is trying to decide how he feels about this revelation—it's like hearing Virgil recount some sexual tryst—when Virgil turns toward him with narrowed eyes and asks in an interrogator's quick, jarring cadence, "Were there drugs involved that day, Lewis?"

"Yes," Lewis says quickly, as if jolted into confessing, "lithium."

A smile flickers over Virgil's lips and his eyelids droop in acknowledgment of the deftness of the evasion. "And Symbyax," Lewis adds. "Seth had just started on that."

"'Recreational' drugs, I mean—mushrooms, LSD. Maybe Bishop and Abby? A little trip to spice up the experience?"

"No," Lewis says, frowning: how absurd, no never. Meanwhile remembering the hits of Ex in his front pocket. And who knows, Bishop might have been *mildly* high on one of his designer concoctions.

"I know Bishop is a chemist," Virgil says. "He has quite a web presence on sites devoted to psychedelics. And Abby was always so fond of her *Castañeda*." Pronouncing the name with slight curl of the lip.

Lewis holds up his hands then drops them in his lap: what can he say?

"It just seems so *crazy*, to get that close to a tornado!" Virgil cries. He reaches suddenly towards the cut above Lewis's eye, causing Lewis to draw back. "*You* could have been killed too," he says. "You *all* could have."

Lewis considers objecting to the use of "killed" but thinks better of it.

Virgil tugs at one cuff of his white shirt with an expression of abstracted annoyance. "I just don't feel like I know the whole story," he says finally.

Nudging open the passenger door, Lewis says, "Neither do I."

28

Louise comes out through the sliding glass doors wearing a quilted robe, shiny purple and high-collared, with ivory toggles. It's printed with I-Ching-ish emblems and zodiacal figures. Her boots are upturned and elfin. Lewis is sitting on the stoop. When he asks whether she's not hot in that thing, she smiles tolerantly and pauses to lay a long-fingered hand on his shoulder, the touch passing soothingly into him as if across the barrier of his skepticism about her and this ceremony.

He watches her set up a card table next to the tree and from a National Public Radio canvas tote bag she removes various items and places them on the table—a lighter, an incense burner, an evergreen sprig, strips of white cloth, a shallow circular drum with tassels, a bundle of sage tied with white string, a wooden whisk.

Lewis hears the gate by the trash stall clank and Cody comes around the corner of the house in his low-slung jeans and tight white wife-beater T. He stands staring at Louise and the tree then, spotting Lewis, scuttles over and sits next to him on the stoop. He rubs his chin to show his approval of Lewis's clean-shaven face and offers a cigarette from a pack. Lewis takes one but refuses the light and holds it unlit in his fingers.

"Sort of weird, a *tree* thing," Cody says in a confidential voice, speaking out of the side of his mouth. When Lewis says nothing, Cody leans closer and whispers, "I mean, *ain't that*—?"

Lewis closes his eyes and sighs and says, "Yeah, it is, Cody. And yeah, I think it's weird. But it's what Abby wants—"

"Nah, I hear you," Cody says assuagingly. He drapes his arm over Lewis's shoulders. He smells of Tori's patchouli musk. Lewis wonders whether she's been giving consolatory lap dances. "I hear you, bro."

Abby comes outside with the gray hexagonal cardboard box containing her half of the ashes and a stack of ceramic bowls. She sets the bowls on the ground and distributes the ashes evenly into them.

"Ash" is actually the wrong word, Lewis thinks, touching his portion: it's coarser, oilier, with bits and spurs that must be the remnants of bone. He wishes they'd found no body, that it had been translated into the sky Old Testament-style, atomized.

No he doesn't.

Midsummer night has fallen, almost fallen. Abby has Lewis and Bishop and Cody stand with their arms around each other in a kind of huddle, a silent tuning in to Seth's spirit. Lewis feels only the familiar heaviness, along with a dull impatience to get all this over with. Then they move off into the yard in separate directions, scattering the ashes wherever they like. Lewis wanders to the toolshed, flings a bit over the fence into Oren's yard on a mischievous impulse. On the far side of the house, Bishop lets out a whoop of what Lewis imagines Bishop imagines is Seth's joy at being free of his body. Which seems tone-deaf to Lewis but who knows.

They meet back at the stoop and Abby collects the empty clay bowls and takes them inside. Now Louise comes out leading the other people who will participate in the tree ceremony. They form a circle around the birch: Abby, Lewis, Cody, Bishop, Harry, Astrid, the lesbian couple whose names Lewis will never get straight, along with their infant asleep in its sling, Stacy in her wheelchair, looking less drugged now.

Louise lights the incense on the card table then the bundle of sage. She moves around the tree waving the smoking sage then directs them to take up the strips of white cloth, one strip in the right hand, one in the left. Other than Lewis, only Bishop knows about the tattered pieces of sheet caught in the tree they found Seth in. Or Abby, if he told Abby about it. But if Bishop sees the connection, he isn't letting on. But then Bishop looks pretty smashed on his Ex.

"The *barisaa*, or prayer tree," Louise says, sounding like a solemn PBS documentary, "is an important site of worship in the Siberian–Mongolian tradition. By performing this ritual, we will be creating a *barisaa* of this beautiful young birch and it will bring peace both to the area, including the house, and to Seth's spirit."

She goes to the table and lights the evergreen sprig and walks around fanning the smoke outward. Watching her, Lewis thinks: she has my five-thousand dollars; I want my five-thousand dollars back; I want to go to Bali.

"Nature spirits of this place," she intones now, returning to her place in the circle, "*Suld* souls of the recently departed! Having forgiven what has happened in the past, be aware that you can do good for all living things, inspire people with visions of the future, bring calm and confidence, fill their hearts with peace and love. Hurai! Hurai! Hurai!" She makes a wide clockwise gesture as she says, "Hurai!"

She takes up the shallow drum and playing it with her hand leads them all slowly around the birch three times, Stacy's wheelchair whirring. Then she has them take up the strips of cloth again. Lewis stands with his eyes closed but he can sense Louise circling the tree and flinging liquids and powders, can hear the salt or sugar sprinkling over the ground. This goes on for a while, accompanied by "Hurai's," then there's what sounds like a final "Hurai!"

He opens his eyes as Louise pours out the rest of the vodka around the trunk of the tree. The smell of it makes him want to get drunk but it seems he's barred from getting drunk today. She has everyone sip from the dish of water. It's over.

Lewis follows Bishop and Cody inside for another shot of whisky. After a minute the others drift into the kitchen.

Abby approaches with an entreating expression, strokes Lewis's arm. It turns out there's yet another rite Louise would like to perform. Lewis nearly lets his head roll backwards with weariness and disgust.

"It involves calling Seth's spirit," Abby says. "I'm actually not real clear on it but it's nothing too elaborate. Louise felt it would be appropriate tonight. You're free to opt out."

"I'll just sit out back then," he tells her. "If that's OK."

"Of course it's OK!" She hugs him and goes into the dining room, followed by Louise and the others, who have been hanging back deferentially. Lewis goes out to the stoop, sits down with the bottle of whisky but feeling a sudden revulsion at the idea of another shot stands up and goes out through the gate.

He walks to the end of the driveway and looks up at the sky. The stars are out, the trees barely moving in the wind. He walks down the street, past the tight-lipped houses with their bass boats under taut, snapped-down tarps.

He walks to the bottom of the neighborhood and stands looking into the stand of trees by the creek. Cottonwoods, maples, birches. Which tree was it they sat by? He closes his eyes, expecting to feel Seth's presence here at his morning-glory spot if anywhere. He waits for a while then gives up and turns to go back to the house.

When the tornado passed, silence fell instantly and the grass of the field lay still. The last red light of the setting sun shone in through the Escalade's broken windshield, through the dirt caked on the windows, cast a warm light over the figures huddled there. Drew stayed behind with Abby, whose ankle was twisted. Calling Seth's name, Bishop and Lewis searched the field. The earth was pocked and cratered, the undersoil churned to the surface. When they found no sign of him, they followed the swath of debris, crossing a creek with steep banks thick with cottonwoods, a few sheared in two low on the trunks. They went on through a backyard strewn with mangled gutters and tin siding hanging like skin in flaps from the body of the houses. Part of the roof of a house was missing. Telephone poles leaned at hard angles and sparks spewed from the tip of a dangling power line.

There was a fire truck parked in a driveway, its light bathing the house and driveway in red. They were pointing flashlights up a tree, rags and shreds of cloth caught in the broken branches flaring in the beams. Now the beams shone steadily on something. Lewis approached in a kind of trance and stood looking up with the others, unable to speak. Two ladders were set side by side against the tree.

"That's my brother," he finally told a fireman. Everyone turned. Lewis climbed one of the ladders, someone else the other. Seth's head swung to one side and Lewis caught it with one hand and cradled it against his chest. The gauze bandage was gone from his head, the one for the blisters on the chest tat gone too, half his shirt ripped away.

They lay him on a blue plastic tarp spread on the ground. Wet leaves were stuck to his chest and shoulder.

"We found him," Bishop said into his cellphone.

Lewis peeled a leaf from the flesh of Seth's shoulder. It left a fine, detailed welt—branched veins, serrated edge.

"No," Bishop said. "No, honey, he's not."

Lewis goes into the backyard through the gate. Cody is sitting on the stoop smoking a cigarette. Lewis sits down beside him. Cody asks him whether he took the Ex. Lewis shakes his head.

"Me neither." Cody snickers in surprise at himself. "That's gotta be a first."

"Seth!" they hear faintly through the open sliding glass doors. It sounds like an invocation.

"Just didn't feel like it," Cody says quizzically.

Then, hanging his head, he says quietly, "All I keep thinking about is how I should've been with you guys."

He looks over at Lewis. "*You* heard me asking your mom. I said, 'Can I come?' There was all them empty seats!"

Lewis says nothing. Darkness has engulfed the yard but the strips of cloth hanging from the branches glow. "I would've got on that bike with him, man," Cody says now.

In the light from the kitchen, Lewis can see tears on Cody's cheeks. "Don't say that, Cody."

"I mean it," Cody insists.

"Well, don't say it," Lewis tells him. "Not to me."

"All right," Cody says after a moment. "I'm sorry."

"You can't say everything that comes into your head," Lewis says gently.

"Hurai!" they hear above a general murmur coming from the dining room.

Cody says, "But I mean, what am I supposed to do now?" He seems to expect an answer.

"I don't know," Lewis says.

"He was the only person who ever gave a shit about me. Him and your mom. What am I supposed to do now?"

Lewis puts his arm around him and Cody slumps gratefully against him, his face pressed into Lewis's chest. Lewis pats him on the back. After a bit Cody seems to gather himself. He sits up and lights a cigarette but puts it out after a single drag.

"Seth!" floats out through the sliding glass doors. "Hurai!" Lewis wishes they would give it a fucking rest now. He considers going for another walk.

Cody lets out a sigh and Lewis glances over to check on him and where Cody was, Seth is sitting.

Lewis stares, thunderstruck.

Seth simply sits there, turned slightly away. The right side of his face is clear of the tattoo.

Lewis stares. It's all he can do. It's as if he's paralyzed, might pass out. But where is Cody? Has Seth possessed him, replaced him? Has Cody given his assent to this? What has happened?

Seth says nothing. But he is here and, fighting free of amazement, Lewis reaches out and wraps him tightly in his arms. He has him now, he's holding his dead brother who is somehow not dead. The problem of Cody can be worked out later. Now he's going to haul Seth into the astonished light of the house, where everyone there will see him too and nothing, not a mote of dust, will be left unchanged.

The sink has flame-shaped lavender stains under the faucets and a cracked rubber stopper attached by a chain to a kind of pierced metal nipple. When he shuts off the tap, the pipes make a high startled moan.

On the way downstairs, he stops at the front-hall window. He thought he heard gunfire last night. He parts the stiff lace curtains. The morning is shining, sunlight falling through the bone-like limbs of London planetrees from a flawless blue sky. Maybe it was firecrackers. He's not sure what gunfire sounds like.

In the dark, faintly sour-smelling kitchen there's half a pot of coffee left by the housemates who have to be at jobs by nine. He heats a cup in the microwave and drinks it in the small garden out back. A mourning dove slips through the gap between the gate and the post and pecks at the walkway then hastens out when Lewis raises his cup to drink.

A dream he had last night comes back to him now, part of it at least. Seth was alive but wheelchair-bound. Stacy, no longer in need of her own wheelchair, pushed Seth around the house in Wichita. Why did Seth steal the graduation present money? Lewis wanted to know. You were going to leave, Seth said simply.

"I wasn't going to leave," Lewis said. The more he thought about it, the more outraged he became. "I wasn't going to leave!"

Seth shook his head. "You were going to leave."

"How did you know where it was hidden?" Lewis asked then.

Stacy was pushing the wheelchair away. Turning back, Seth said, "I know how your little pea-brain works."

He finishes his coffee and goes back inside the house. On the walls of the mudroom are framed photographs, circa 1970, of the lease-holder, a semi-retired professor of sculpture named Lewellyn Lynch. Wearing overalls and cowboy boots, he's standing alone or in comradely groups against the desert scrub of Marfa, Texas, where he lives for most the year.

Rinsing his cup at the kitchen sink, Lewis hears Lynch trudging up the basement stairs. To have another room to rent out on the floors above, he sleeps down there on a futon, bare light bulbs turned on with lengths of string, forgotten boxes of stored clothes and books left by long-gone tenants, jumbled piles of furniture. He's lived here for thirty-eight years, first with a wife, then with a series of girlfriends, many of them students, then illegal subletters like Lewis, whose rents underwrite Lynch's life in Marfa. The house belongs to the Brooklyn College of the Arts, which, instead of trying to evict Lynch, refuses to do any repairs. It's slowly falling down around their ears.

Now Lynch stands bracing himself in the basement doorway, the tips of his fingers mashed against the frame as if he's dizzy from the climb and fears falling backwards.

"Morning!" he says when he notices Lewis. He has a handsome, deeply lined face, fierce blue eyes, thick straight gray hair cut in a tapering blunt line. Having recovered from the climb, he crosses the kitchen in his black, slab-like geriatric shoes and pours a cup of coffee, stands staring into the microwave window as it heats up, then decants a stream of sugar from a spouted glass dispenser.

"First day of classes, Sculpture 101," Lynch announces in a quavering voice, staring with comical bleakness at Lewis. "It never fucking ends."

He stirs the coffee with a tiny espresso spoon, takes a sip, sets the cup down. "Well, it would end if I'd *retire*, of course, but they didn't pay me enough to retire *on!*" He barks out a laugh.

"Do you realize I'm going to draw my *last breath* standing behind some kid trying to think of something to say about his shitty sculpture?!" He laughs at the vision. "I really think that's how it will fucking happen! The kid'll be waiting for my comment." Lynch hunches his shoulders and pouts in imitation an art student. "He'll have this shitty little frown on his face: 'Hey, my parents paid *good money* for this old fucker's praise! What's taking so long?' He'll finally look around and *I'll come crashing down on top of him!*"

As if remembering his manners, he lurches across the kitchen and pours cold coffee sloshingly into the rinsed cup Lewis is absently holding then carries the pot back to its place in the coffee maker.

"What I usually do on the first day is pass out copies of 'Sculpture in the Expanded Field' and have them sit there and read that," Lynch says. "Do you know it?"

Lewis considers lying but confesses that he does not and Lynch makes a slight dip of the head to indicate that he expected as much then narrows his eyes and says, "Well, if you read only one piece of art criticism in your life, read 'Sculpture in the Expanded Field' by Miss Rosalind Krauss. And not just because she talks about the kind of work I make—or made. What did ol' Lewellyn do? I dug a hole in the ground. Earth Art. It's not architecture but it's not landscape either. That was Krauss's contribution to the conversation. It came ten years after the fact, but still. It helped people grasp our accomplishment."

He makes a hat-tipping gesture to an imaginary Rosalind Kraus and Lewis glances at his watch and shoulders his backpack.

"Off to guard the horde of the Robber Baron?" Lynch asks. Lewis smiles crookedly in answer.

"You must be willing to *give your life* for a Vuillard, Lewis!" Lewis is surprised Lynch remembers his name and what he does for money. "To *give your life!*" Lynch calls after him.

On the front stoop, he pauses to open his backpack and peeks in to be sure he remembered to pack his navy-blue guard blazer, which he's responsible for having dry-cleaned once a week. It's in there.

He sets off for the subway in the clear September morning. London-planetree leaves, tan and desiccated and curled, lie scattered on the sidewalk, the shadows beneath them black, satiny voids.

Lewis wonders what Lynch, with death so much on his mind, would say if Lewis told him about the story of Seth's return in the body of Cody, how he came back from the land of the dead to see Lewis, to be seen by Lewis. Lynch, Lewis imagines, would either unhesitatingly match it with a ghost story of his own. Or he would smile pityingly and say something grimly existential like: death'll scare you into seeing all sorts of shit!

The museum is housed in the Upper East Side mansion of a family that made its money in oil. Lewis puts on the blazer in the staff room and stashes his backpack in a locker. The whiteboard where the gallery assignments are written has him in the Paul Klee salon for the second week. He goes to the sunny room where the Klees hang and takes up his post in an upholstered chair beside an air-quality monitor that scratches out a reading on graph paper with a frail needle.

A pair of middle-aged tourists enters. The woman acknowledges Lewis's presence with an indirect fraction of a smile. He's here and he's not here. He's an animatronic statue that can be called upon to give directions to the restrooms or gift shop.

After the memorial service, Abby told Lewis he could leave

whenever he liked, she was fine. The next day she couldn't get out of bed. Her limbs felt filled with mud, she said. Lewis and Bishop and a group of her friends cooked and did the chores. One morning he was with her in the bathroom. She was trying to find the strength to put on makeup at a mirror by the window. There was a spider the size of a crumb in the bottom corner of the window frame, motionless in its little web. "If I could trade places with that perfectly still little consciousness, I would do it," she said. "There's nothing ennobling about what I'm feeling, this suffering. It hurts, period." Then she went back to bed.

For exercise, Lewis walked to the Towne East mall, walked around in it. There was a path beaten into the grass alongside the road but he never encountered anyone else on foot. Twice, out drinking at night, he drove around in search of the roadside bar where Tori worked but couldn't find it. He'll supposedly get his graduation money back two-fold once Abby has resumed the Birthday Party celebrations but she seems to have lost interest in that, or at least her enthusiasm isn't what it was, and Lewis doubts he'll ever get the money back. Not that he ever really felt it was his.

Other than Abby, he's told no one about what happened on the stoop with Cody, not even Cody himself, who remembered nothing out of the ordinary except the hug from the normally restrained Lewis. Abby's reaction was unsurprised, almost blasé. "I had a feeling something like that might happen for you," she said, adding, "Bishop did too."

Bishop. Lewis wonders whether Bishop didn't slip something into the whisky that day, one of his designer psychedelics called Apparition or Vivid Ghost or Dead Brother. Or Lewis willingly took something that then erased the memory of his having taken it. Twice, since he left, Abby has asked lightly on the phone, "Have you seen Seth lately?" No, he told her, which is the truth. But her asking places him under a slight but real pressure to offer something up, something new, as time passes and what happened, astonishing though it was, fades, loses its force. He also worries that his telling her about the experience has given her false hope, caused her to skip or compress some necessary stage of grief. Whatever a stage of grief is. And didn't Kubler-Ross repudiate all that in the end anyway?

"Ooh, goody—Paul Klee!" the tourist woman stage-whispers. She claps her hands in childlike glee and, bringing her nose to within an inch of the first canvas, beckons to the man. "See the little creatures? Come closer—see?"

The man obeys. "Oh, yeah—tiny little things," he notes flatly. "Wings. Cute."

"Do you know what I adore about Paul Klee?" The man shakes his head.

"His *whimsy*!" she says "There's not enough *whimsy* in modern art, not like this." She glances at Lewis for his agreement and approbation and Lewis smiles obligingly. Lewis liked Klee's whimsy too, until he spent two weeks with it. Now it's begun to cloy.

Eli spends half the week in Cambridge, half in New York at Mi's apartment. Lewis meets him for lunch at the French restaurant Eli and his parents have been patronizing since Eli was a toddler. They're seated in the traditional family banquette in the corner by the window but Eli has been irritably distracted by changes in the décor and staff, the menu. When they've ordered their meals and their glasses of red wine arrive and Eli sips from his and seems momentarily satisfied and settled, Lewis finds himself telling the story of Seth's appearance on the stoop.

"Phew!" Eli says, sitting back, his eyes wide. "Wow."

Then his manner undergoes a subtle change. It's as if he ages, assumes the bulkier, slightly hunched body of a much older man—that of his father, the neurologist's. A pained, apologetic expression appears on his face and he says in a low voice. "Grief is a kind of stress—"

Now he frowns at a slice of baguette he's dug this thumbs into and holds it up for Lewis's inspection. "What would you call this, fiberglass? Plastic?"

He sits back in his chair and raises his hand just off the table and a waiter appears. "Could we trouble you to bring us some bread that is *actually fresh*? As in *edible*? Thanks so much!"

He sighs through his nose and watches over interlaced hands as the basket of bread is removed. "This place—I come back out of robotic habit. I need to make a change." He follows the waiter's movement to the bread station. "What was I even saying?"

"Grief is stress," Lewis prompts him. He can see where Eli is headed. He regrets having told the story, having cheapened it by telling it, but Eli's dismissal will at least allow it to go back into the dark.

"You know?" Eli says as if relieved, as if Lewis has introduced the idea himself. "*Grief is stress*: people lose their appetite, they have heart palpitations and other physical ailments as a result."

The new bread arrives and Eli pauses to poke at it skeptically. "They even have *hallucinations*," he says gravely and quietly, nodding all the while as if to encourage Lewis's agreement.

"This was no hallucination," Lewis feels obliged to say, if listlessly.

"It didn't *seem* like one," Eli says gently. "OK? Hallucinations don't *by definition* seem like hallucinations. That's what makes them so convincing!" He watches Lewis butter a bite-sized piece of baguette. He'll always remember the lesson Sylvie's mother taught at the table.

"But you don't believe that," Eli says.

Lewis shrugs, he chews the bread, swallows.

Eli stares at him, blinking thoughtfully then sits back in his chair and opens his arms in a gesture of to-each-his-own relativism. "Hey, maybe you're right not to. You know? I mean, who the fuck knows, right?"

Rising suddenly from his chair, Eli leans across the table gives Lewis a quick awkward hug, sits back down.

"Listen, I'm *sorry about your brother*. I'm glad you—saw him, or whatever. It's—I don't know, it's great." He peers at Lewis. "OK?"

Lewis smiles. "OK." He will never speak of it again.

After work, he walks uptown through crowds coughed onto the sidewalks by revolving doors and waits for the bus at 86th Street and Lexington. On the plexiglas wall of the shelter is a large poster showing a man holding a telephone, his face pixilated into anonymity. "You Don't Have to Reveal Your Identity to Help Solve Violent Crimes. Rewards Up to $5,000. Call 1-800-577-TIPS."

Virgil wanted to hold a small memorial service for Seth at his new faculty apartment, family only. As versus what else, Lewis wondered, the coke-dealers from Amsterdam Ave, Dominicans Don't Play? But twice it's been canceled. The first time, Izzy and Eckhart couldn't make it because a visiting professor they were giving a dinner for in New Haven was only available, it turned out, that evening. On the eve of the rescheduled day, Cyrus had to fly to Berlin to meet with his new publisher. Now, at Lewis's insistence, they're going to settle for scattering the ashes in the Hudson, just the two of them, and if Virgil has to cancel then he can do whatever he likes with Seth's ashes, Lewis is done.

The crosstown bus swoops into the stop. On the side-facing bench a man sits flanked by two young girls in barrettes and frilly dresses who have his large deep-set eyes. The younger girl gazes for so long and with such somber seriousness at Lewis that he finally meets her eyes, only to have her turn away with a fearful, affronted expression and whisper to her father who, as if used to this, listens but ignores her, or at least doesn't glance at Lewis.

The bus plunges into a still-lush Central Park, dark green ailanthus fronds waving in the slipstream of passing cars as if flagging them down. At Broadway, Lewis transfers to the uptown bus and at 116th Street, he gets off and waits next to the gates of the university.

Virgil is late. Lewis might try calling his office but finds himself hoping his father won't show up at all, that he's forgotten. A white cloud enters the blue sky from the south, the fibrous upper edges curling forward and undoing themselves swiftly, as in time-lapse, until it disappears behind the cornice of a building.

He watches the familiar security guards wearing Columbia-blue shirts, the exiting students and faculty, secretaries, administrators in dry-cleaned white dress shirts, blazers folded over one arm. It seems less like a monastic refuge than a management training facility.

Giving up on Virgil, Lewis is turning to walk away when he sees Andrew Feeling hailing a cab across Broadway. He's wearing a rumpled linen suit. V. is standing beside him in a summer dress, her long hair in a bun on top of her head. They are looking up Broadway but if they turned slightly they would spot Lewis. Then a cab arrives and Andrew opens the door for V., who gets in, followed by Andrew. The door closes, the cab drives off. Lewis watches its rear window, the vague outlines of the couple within, until it vanishes in traffic.

Virgil is hastening up the sidewalk in the constrained crouch he adopts when he runs in public. Lewis observes his arrival from a dazed distance, as if wounded and unable to move or speak.

"Office hours," his father says, gasping for breath to underscore how hard he tried to be on time, which makes it less believable. "Ran late." He is indebted to Lewis for this but Lewis is unable to savor it.

"Then I forgot the box and had to run back up and grab it. It's here now," he assures Lewis, patting the side of his large stiff leather book bag with its quiver-like slots for pens and its odd salmony smell. "Shall we?"

Lewis falls into step beside him, listens as Virgil fills out the account of his lateness by complaining about an eccentric alum who haunts Virgil's Classics-department office hours: Clem. Lewis has met him many times over the years. He comes to Virgil's office hours to share the latest Latin terms he's invented for new phenomena like websites and iPhones. But Lewis is too rocked by the sighting of V. and Andrew to pay any but the barest attention. Virgil jerks him back from the path of a delivery bike.

They walk down the bulging hill that 116th Street becomes, a gust of autumnal air flushing through the chute formed by the apartment buildings of Claremont Avenue—V's street. He'd expected crossing it would be the hard part, not actually seeing V. herself, much less in Andrew Feeling's company.

In Riverside Park the land continues the fall downhill in the deep shade of old trees. They descend a wide terraced walkway divided by an iron banister and stop at the fence. A star-like sweetgum leaf is caught in the mesh.

Virgil squints distrustfully at the view. Cars flash past on the Henry Hudson Parkway, visible through the trees. Beyond the highway are a bike path and the Hudson, aglitter in the late-afternoon sun. But the highway is surrounded by a high fence and guardrails.

"That's strange," Virgil says. "I distinctly remember there being a way across to that bike path by the river."

Lewis sighs and is going to suggest scattering the ashes here in the park but Virgil sets off down another terraced walkway, which leads to the main path, wide yet crowded with dog-walkers, joggers, bikers.

After walking uncertainly uptown for a while, Virgil stops to ask the way from a gray-haired man who looks deranged to Lewis. There's a tunnel where you can cross under the highway, the man tells them. It's downtown further, at 104th St. But when Virgil stands peering in that direction, the man seems to take this as a doubt cast on the reliability of his word and rises from the bench to shoo them on with an aluminum cane.

Walking quickly away, with Virgil glancing back a few times, they pass soccer fields and a basketball court, a skate park with blue ramps and half-pipes, and finally enter a curving passage that leads to the bike path and the Hudson.

A red helicopter flies downriver, its tail tipped upward; an empty garbage scow heads upriver. There's the whoosh of rush-hour traffic on the Parkway, the clank of a wire halyard against the mast of a sailboat anchored not far from shore, the treacherous near-silent bikers flashing past just behind, dog-walkers.

Into the gray weathered wood of the railing, which comes to an end where they stand, someone has hacked "Dully."

"We can go down right there," Virgil says conspiratorially, pointing to the mica-flecked boulders where wavelets are cresting and slapping the shore. It's against the law, what they're about to do. Which Seth would love, but still. Virgil has unlatched his book bag and removed the hexagonal cardboard box. A woman wearing a self-satisfied smile slices past going very fast on a ten-speed. Then, for the moment, there's no one around, only figures on foot silhouetted against the sun to the south a few blocks away.

"Now's our chance," Virgil says and clambers cautiously down over the large dry boulders, followed by Lewis.

"After you," his father says, handing him the box. Lewis removes the lid and reaches inside and takes out a handful of ash. He watches it strike the tea-colored water and vanish. He gives the box to Virgil, who shakes out the remainder with broad, upward motions, allowing the wind to do the work of dispersal, which seems to Lewis a form of cheating or laziness.

"*Sic mors, quod non potuit vita dare, dabit*," Virgil intones quickly.

"Thus death," Lewis begins, feeling like he's been given a pop quiz. "What could . . . " He looks at Virgil for help with the rest. " . . . something."

"'Thus death shall give what life could not,'" Virgil translates. "Thomas More," he adds, glancing back with a double-take. Lewis follows his gaze.

A cop is dismounting from a mountain bike—waspish helmet, black spandex, thick brown limbs.

"Shit," Virgil mutters. She pulls a thick notebook from a satchel and beckons to them with a crooked finger. They make their way back up the rocks to the bike path, Virgil going first. In his agitated haste, he slips and catches himself awkwardly, wincing in pain as he straightens as if he might have injured his back.

"It's illegal to scatter ashes in public water ways, sir," the cop tells Virgil, beginning to write up the ticket. She has a blunt, no-nonsense face, short dark hair, a dark tan.

Virgil bends over the cop, the ticket, his arms tightly crossed. "That was my *son*," he says in a low voice. Lewis is shocked by the melodrama of the words and the tone.

"I'm sorry for your loss, sir," she says briskly, without looking up. Bikers and dog-walkers slow down to rubberneck. What crime did they commit, this pair? Lewis hears them wondering. Sex in public? Right out here on the dog walk?

"He was only *twenty*," Virgil says and there are tears in his voice and then, peering at him, Lewis sees there are tears on his face. He can't tell whether it's for the cop's benefit, as a kind of ruse to get out of the ticket, or some late-arriving grief. Or both. The cop scratches away with her ballpoint.

Virgil sighs raggedly and gazes piteously down at the half-written summons. "It was a *suicide*, officer," he says.

The cop stops writing and looks at Virgil under her brow, at the tears on his cheeks. She's hesitating now but she also seems to be assessing the veracity of the emotion.

She flips shut the ticket book. "Fine," she says with a hint of disgust. "I'm letting you off with a warning." She remounts the bike. *But don't let me catch you scattering ashes down here again* hangs unsaid in the air.

"Thank you," Virgil says quietly as she pedals away. Lewis half expects him to brush away the tears and smile in sly triumph. But when the cop is gone down the path, he stands there in a defenseless posture, head bowed, weeping.

Finally Lewis puts an arm around his shoulder and, walking slowly, attracting the occasional concerned or prurient look, they make their way to the bus stop at 104th St.

Virgil insists on waiting until a bus arrives. They stand looking up Broadway in silence.

In Brooklyn, the streets shine from rain that fell while he was underground. Acacia blossoms lie in sodden drifts on the windshields of parked cars like snow. Night has fallen and there's no one else in sight, just row after row of mute brownstones. Stickups are commonplace here and Lewis walks quickly and warily but after a block his stride relaxes into an easy lope and he has a pleasant, feral feeling of being swift and light and untouchable. Tumbling along the ground in the wind, a black plastic bag keeps pace with him for nearly a block, stopping only when it meets a high iron fence and even then almost squeezing through the bars.

Sculpture in the Expanded Field.

ACKNOWLEDGMENTS

My deep gratitude to the following people and institutions: Ryan D. Harbage for his tenacious belief in book and author, Alice Sebold for her writerly edit and Ann Patty for providing revisionary keys; Michael Reynolds, Julia Haav, and Simona Olivito at Europa; Caveh Zahedi, Amanda Field, Adam Yaffe, Rachel Shteir, Nico Israel, and J. Anderson, who took the time to read and react; the John S. Guggenheim Memorial Foundation, the Andrew W. Mellon Foundation, and the Pratt Institute, specifically, Peter Barna, Toni Oliviero and Ira Livingston. Above all am I indebted to my wife, Juliana Ellman, muse and first responder, without whom it's all inconceivable.

About the Author

Thad Ziolkowski is the author of *Our Son the Arson*, a collection of poems, and a memoir, *On a Wave*, which was a finalist for the PEN/Martha Albrand Award in 2003. In 2008, he was awarded a fellowship from the John S. Guggenheim Memorial Foundation. His essays and reviews have appeared in *The New York Times, Slate, Bookforum, Artforum, Travel & Leisure* and *Index*. He directs the Writing Program at Pratt Institute. *Wichita* is his first novel.